Countdown

33...32...31...

Rose's hands were locked to Ian's lapels, as if she would never let go. The air arced between them, almost visible, coiling and floating like warm breath in a chilled night.

New life. New love. New year. 19...18...17...

Totally entranced, Ian slid his right hand behind her neck, twining his fingers in her hair. With a soft sigh, her lips touched his before he'd even asked, before he'd even begged. The kiss was honeysuckle sweet, and tasted like a new beginning.

When the crowd jostled her closer, Ian didn't complain. His left hand, riding under her coat, found the inviting curve of her waist. Around them the world blew by—showers of confetti, bursts of cold wind and the joyous shouts of millions of overjoyed partiers. Ian ignored them all, because in the midst of these people it was only him and this woman, and forever.

Somehow he'd died and was now kissing an angel.

His hand slid lower to hold her tight. She curled into him, her thigh rocking between his....

Nope. No angel. They didn't have moves like that in heaven!

Blaze

Dear Reader,

A while back I noticed a trend in my stories. Unexpected love, unexpected places. My editor suggested a trilogy, and the Harlequin Blaze senior editor came up with a grand title for it: WHERE YOU LEAST EXPECT IT.

In the the first book, *Hot Under Pressure* (Aug 2009), the characters meet on a crazy airplane flight. For *Midnight Resolutions* I focused on New Year's Eve.

When I came up with the idea of a magical kiss on New Year's, I knew I wanted to create two characters who needed to start over. It was only a matter of figuring out the why. With Ian and Rose, I found those two people. There was Ian, who knew what he needed to do, and was already on his journey. And then there was Rose, who didn't have a clue...until she started to fall in love.

I hope you enjoy the story, and I hope your 2010 is bright, joyous and full of new beginnings.

Look for the next WHERE YOU LEAST EXPECT IT book in May. There's this lake, and this hero who wants to be left alone....

Best wishes for the New Year!

Kathleen O'Reilly

Kathleen O'Reilly

MIDNIGHT RESOLUTIONS

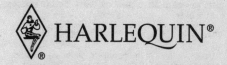

TORONTO • NEW YORK • LONDON
AMSTERDAM • PARIS • SYDNEY • HAMBURG
STOCKHOLM • ATHENS • TOKYO • MILAN • MADRID
PRAGUE • WARSAW • BUDAPEST • AUCKLAND

Recycling programs
for this product may
not exist in your area.

ISBN-13: 978-0-373-79519-2

MIDNIGHT RESOLUTIONS

Copyright © 2010 by Kathleen Panov.

www.eHarlequin.com

Printed in U.S.A.

ABOUT THE AUTHOR

First published in 2001, Kathleen O'Reilly is an award-winning author of more than twenty romances, with more books on the way. Reviewers have been lavish in their praise, applauding her "biting humor," "amazing storytelling" and "sparkling characters." She lives in New York with her husband, two children and one indestructible goldfish. Please contact the author at kathleenoreilly@earthlink.net or by mail at P.O. Box 312, Nyack, NY 10960.

Books by Kathleen O'Reilly

HARLEQUIN BLAZE

*The Red Choo Diaries
**Those Sexy O'Sullivans
***Where You Least Expect It

1

NEW YEAR'S EVE IN TIMES SQUARE. Ian Cumberland was done dwelling on last year's miseries. Tonight was about new resolutions, new hopes, new opportunities. Cheerfully he stuffed his hands in his pockets and inhaled the crisp, seventeen-degree air. It was nearly midnight, and he was primed for the winds of change to blast open new doors. The neon carnival that was Times Square had seemed the ideal location—apparently it was also the ideal place for another two million huddled masses. They were huddled because those winds of change were blowing from the north at approximately thirty-five miles per hour. And not that he wanted to complain, but okay, those winds were freaking cold.

Noisemakers and plastic horns bleated in the air, riding over the upbeat tempo of the latest and greatest boy-band—greatest, that is, until they hit puberty or got involved in the latest sex scandal, whichever came first. No—no negativity. Not tonight.

Determined to make this work, Ian gave his senses free rein, marveling at all the tiny details he'd overlooked before. Ear-blasting sounds, a kaleidoscope of brilliant colors and a melting pot of smells. He took a deep breath of New York air—a million divergent perfumes, roasted chestnuts and strangely enough, honeysuckle.

Over the past year, he'd divided his life into two distinct periods. Prelayoff and postlayoff. Prelayoff ended precisely at 4:30 p.m. on February seventeenth. Then, Ian didn't have the time to waste twelve hours standing around Times Square waiting for a giant multicolored orb to fall from the sky. Postlayoff, he still didn't have the time, but now he had the will.

New Year's at Times Square had been on his list of life to-dos since he was ten, waiting to be checked off. Prelayoff, he didn't worry much about getting to Times Square. Postlayoff, he realized that life was not cooperative and orderly, and when you got the chance to have a once-in-a-lifetime moment, you just did it.

The night's crowd was packed shoulder to shoulder. It was impossible to move, nearly impossible to breathe, and he found himself sharing the uncomfortably close personal space of a large group of awestruck foreigners who didn't understand the common English vernacular: "You're standing on my foot. Please move."

As he took in the trolling lights and squinty-eyed police and happy, perky people, Ian waited patiently for something miraculous, something life-altering, something hopeful. But all he got was a trampled foot and a deafening horn in his ear.

Still he waited, colder, sober, and now thinking that perhaps he'd been a little wiser prelayoff when he had avoided Times Square like the plague.

Hell. On what planet had he actually thought this was a good idea? It didn't matter that it was New Year's Eve, Times Square, nearly midnight. In the end, he wasn't an investment banker anymore; he was an employment counselor, and a lunatic one at that.

Beckett had told him it was stupid. Told him that nobody froze their ass off in New York in January when they could stay home and have a decent party, guzzle champagne and watch the ball drop from the confines of a well-insulated apartment. And of course, it was at that moment that Ian had looked his best friend square in the eye and launched into his winds of change spiel: new beginnings, living life—doing it right.

And there, crushed amidst two million other cockeyed optimists, he felt a killer wind shoot through him, the truth dawning with frigid clarity.

Ian was a sap. Time to pack in the New Year, accept what he had and trudge onward. Life was what it was, and nothing—not even a few mind-shattering hours in the center of the universe—was going to change it.

Feeling all sorts of foolish, he turned, starting toward the relative tranquility of the subway, because somewhere out there, his sanity and his friends were waiting. Before he managed another step, a pull at his arm knocked him off balance. Ian whirled, prepared to tell the jerkwad—foreign relations be damned—to quit touching him. But then he stopped—

Stared.

Gawked, actually.

Gorgeous.

She was honeysuckle in the flesh. She looked like it, smelled like it and damn, he wanted to know if she tasted like it, as well. His body shocked to life, filled, throbbed.

Hello, winds of change.

Watercolor-blue eyes were panicked and filled with worry. Warm, tawny hair streaked with gold spilled from her knitted cap.

"Have you seen my phone? I can't find my phone. Help me find my phone. Oh, God. I lost my phone."

Her voice was soft and tense against the noise of the crowd. She was searching for her phone. *Help her.*

"Where'd you lose it?" he asked, raising the volume, noticing the beefy tourist sizing her up with beady eyes.

"On the ground. I dropped it and I really need to find it. I shouldn't be here. It's a complete zoo. Why did I come here?"

To meet me, thought Ian, a stupid, romantic thought, right up there with his winds of change spiel. Ian grinned, a foolish, romantic grin, but he couldn't help himself. "We'll find it," he offered, and bent to the ground. She hesitated, her eyes wisely fearful, but then she bent, too, testing the restraint of millions of drunken partygoers, probably taking her life in her own hands, yet still trusting him.

At ground level it was like being underwater, swimming against the tide of directionally challenged fish. The dim light was diffused by shifting legs and restless feet and a continuous swirl of coats. Her hands grabbed for the edge of his sleeve, her eyes terrified. "You okay?" he asked, and she nodded once, but still he worried.

"We'll find it," he assured her again, keeping one hand tied to hers. With the other, he searched for what had to be the most important phone in the world.

"I can't believe I lost it," she chattered, the words tumbling out in a panic. "I can't believe I screwed up. I'm not careless. I can't be careless. I won't be careless." A clumsy set of legs bumped into her, and she jumped, flying closer to him.

"Don't get crazy. It's got to be here somewhere," he soothed, heroically gathering her closer, trying to find her phone, trying to keep her from being flattened, all the while warning himself that just because a beautiful woman stumbled into his arms, it did not mean the winds of change had finally blown his way.

Blindly he groped the rough asphalt. His hand got stomped on twice, but apparently the gods actually owed Ian something good this year and apparently Frank Capra wasn't dead in spirit—because at that moment Ian's fingers latched on to plastic. Rectangular, sturdy, magical plastic.

"Got it," he yelled, quickly pulling her upright before they were both trampled to death—which never happened in Frank Capra movies.

The flashing neon signs lit up the jittery alarm in her eyes, and he pulled her to him, instinct more than reason. "It's okay. It's here," he said, feeling the tremors run through her, absorbing them into himself. "It's a phone," he murmured, whispering against her hair. "It's only a phone. Don't cry."

"Don't like the crowd," she muttered, her face buried in his shoulder.

"You picked the wrong place to figure that out." He was relieved to hear her awkward laugh, and decided that holding a beautiful crowd-o-phobic was worth a layoff, worth being labeled a sap.

In the end, Ian had been right. New hopes. New opportunities, and they all smelled like honeysuckle.

He stroked the back of her woolen coat, feeling the slow ease of her shivering. It didn't take her long, and he knew the exact moment when she stiffened, her chin lifted and the fear had passed. "I'm not crying. I don't cry," she told him, her voice a lot firmer than before.

Then she gazed at him—her eyes dry, and more focused than before. "I'm not crying," she repeated. "Thank you. This was stupid. I'm sorry. I don't like being stupid."

Her profile seemed so fragile, so oddly out of place in the chaos of the crowd, the lights and the noise. Her face was thin, delicate, a medieval maiden out of a fairy tale. Yet there were hollow shadows in her eyes, shadows that didn't belong with such beauty. It took more than a lost phone to cast shadows like that. Gently he tracked her cheek, pretending to wipe at nonexistent tears, only wanting to touch the golden rose of her skin.

"You're not being stupid. Everything's fine now. Everything's perfect now," he said, watching as the control eased back into her face.

"Thank you for finding my phone."

He casually shrugged off her gratitude, knowing the night was young, the year was young. What was a job, anyway? What was financial security? Totally oversold. In the big scheme of life, could anything compare to that world-by-the-tail feeling of her dreamy eyes looking at him as if he was a hero—and not just any hero, but *her hero?*

"It's nothing. You're okay now?" he asked, leaning in to be heard over the crowd. Oh, yeah, right.

"Sorry. I never fall apart," she answered, her head close to his, so close he could make out the carefully concealed freckles on her nose.

"Don't apologize. I fall apart on a regular basis."

She glanced at him oddly. "I was joking," he told her, and cursed himself for being a blockhead. There was something in her face, in her moon-kissed gaze, that held him fast. Hidden behind the composure, he could see a child's curiosity peering out.

Her mouth curved up, a pink Cupid's bow that touched him somewhere near his heart.

Right then, one of the tourists jammed her into him, and she started at the movement, until he pulled her close again, fast adjusting to the heady feel of her in his arms.

"I shouldn't have come here tonight. I thought I could do this."

"I know, a bunch of idiots who think New Year's Eve is a night for new dreams. What a bunch of dorks. I should have been home guzzling champagne instead of freezing my... Never mind." Once again he felt her muffled giggle and decided he didn't mind being a blockhead, didn't mind being a fool. To hear her hesitant laugh, to fit those lush curves to his body, to have her hair brush against his face.

After a moment, she raised her head and carefully studied him. "You ever do this before?"

"Nope. You?"

"Never again," she answered firmly.

Apparently God was still watching, Frank was still filming and the winds of change were definitely on the move because suddenly, miraculously, the crowd began to count.

Thirty-three. Thirty-two. Thirty-one.

Her eyes glowed bright, the muted blue heating to liquid, trapping him there. Her hands locked to his lapel, as if she'd never let go. The air began to arc between them, almost visible, coiling and floating like warm breath in the chilled night.

New life. New love. New year.

Nineteen. Eighteen. Seventeen.

Totally entranced, Ian slid his right hand behind her neck, twining it in her hair with a lingering sigh. Her lips touched his even before he asked, even before he begged. Soft, sweet, and tasting like a new beginning.

When the crowd jostled her closer, Ian didn't complain, his left hand riding under her coat, finding the glorious skin of her back, the inviting curve of her waist. Around them, the world blew by, showers of confetti, bursts of cold wind and the joyous shouts of millions of not-quite-sober partiers. Ian ignored them all, because in the midst of these millions, it was only he and this woman, and the rest of their life.

Her generous mouth opened, her tongue merged with his, coaxing, seducing. Oh, yes, he was so seduced, no coaxing necessary. His nerves fired, pulsing with life, pulsing with ideas that were older than time. He would take her home. He would make love to her. He would marry her. It was the Frank Capra way.

Impulsive arms locked around his neck, burying her fingers in his hair. He could feel the insistent touch of her restless hands. Against his greedy mouth, she moaned. Music. Bells. Chimes. Somewhere he'd died and was kissing an angel.

His hand slipped lower, pressing her against him, soft to hard. Her hips curled into him, her thigh rocking between his. His eyes crossed. Nope. No angel. They didn't have moves like that in heaven.

An irritant vibrated against his leg—not his cock, nor his pulse, which were both buzzing in their own overjoyed condition. She broke away, her breathing heavy, then lifted the phone, the exact phone he'd found for her only moments before. Which, if he had not found, she would not be talking into. No, they would still be kissing. Man, he was such a stupid dweeb.

Next to them, one of the tourists shot him a look of male approval, but Ian ignored it, trying to restart his brain. Here was the inspiration he'd been seeking.

As she talked, her gaze scanned the length of his cashmere coat. For the first time, he could see that elusive recognition flicker in her eyes—seeing him as a man who was worthy—financially viable. Possibly insecure, but there it was. Maybe the male code had some unwritten law saying it was cowardly to trade on his past life, but did geeky Clark Kent ever want to throw open his jacket, exposing the all-powerful *S?* Hell, yeah.

The shouts of the crowd fell away. Only her words touched his ears. She was talking, trying to reconnect with her date. Date? No! Ian wanted to yell at her to hang up because this was kismet, karma, and the entire outcome of his postlayoff life rested upon this one moment—no pressure. Instead, he kept his mouth shut, a confident grin plastered on his face as if this didn't mean a damn thing.

When she looked at Ian again, the soft blue eyes were so lonely and sad. He wondered if she had sensed the pull, too. Ian had never felt it before, never met a woman who stepped out of his dreams and into his arms. It should have been fate.

"I'm over here," she said into the phone, waving a graceful hand in the air for someone other than Ian. *Other than Ian.* He wanted to stop her because she couldn't be with someone else. This was a new year. New opportunities. New loves…

"I have to go. He's my date," she apologized, dashing the final vestiges of his hope to the ground much like last year's sodden confetti.

"No surprise there," answered Ian, his voice faux cheerful. "Have a good year." *Have a nice life.*

One heartbeat later, her expression turned to the well-mannered smile given to a stranger on the street. Without another word, she politely asked her beefy neighbor to move out of the way, and then she moved out of Ian's life.

All before he'd even gotten her name.

The winds of change blew cold and heartless, and Ian stomped on Hans's foot, hard—international-incident hard—and Ian was gratified when the giant oaf muttered something in another language that probably involved mothers and copulation, not that he cared. Tourism was overrated anyway.

As he made his way home, Ian looked back at the ball that was glittering like a fallen star, making outrageous promises it wasn't going to keep.

Happy New Year.

In a crowd of two million, Ian had never felt so alone.

Damn.

2

ROSE HILDEBRANDE WANTED TO wind back the clock to last year, when Remy wasn't sipping his champagne and discussing in elaborate detail his latest performance in the operating room.

Rose wanted to return to that unforgettable instant when the stranger had been kissing her with such desperate need, as if he couldn't get enough of her. As if with one kiss, he had found something golden and fleeting inside her. Romance—that was what they called it.

The people, the crowds, the fear. Everything had been a black, paralyzing blur—except for the feel of that strong body holding her tight. Not to punish, no, it was protection.

On a normal day, Rose knew exactly when she wanted to be touched, when people expected it and how she was supposed to react. That blood-pounding, swept-away sensation should have terrified her. But it was tempered by something new. Something almost…warm.

Quickly she shook off the weakness. Control. Always in control.

Now, sitting in the lobby of the Four Seasons with New York's crème de la crème, her blood was neatly congealing back to its more reserved state. Her date for the night, world-renown pediatric cardiology surgeon Dr. Remy Sinclair, was cheerfully describing his day. The rest of the universe was planning a celebration, and Remy was slaving over the operating table, saving the lives of small children. Heroic, handsome, charming and rich. The man had zero flaws.

So, why was Rose merely nodding at suitable intervals with a polite bob of her head, while her mind clicked back to that dazzling feeling inspired by one exquisitely hard, hungry mouth? No, she thought, pushing the dazzle aside. More hocus-pocus that had no basis in anything real.

Idly, she shuttered her lashes, an indication of perhaps not actually listening, but a sincere pretense of it.

It was a look she'd perfected by the age of six, when Rose had been primped, painted, powdered and coiffed, and then ordered to skip down the charm school runway with bubbly poise and a lollipop smile. Her parents had had big dreams for her—beauty pageants, charm school, marrying well. Rose Hildebrande's heart-shaped little face was their ticket to a better life, and Rose had quickly learned to fall in line. There was no little girl better at perfection, a concrete diamond mined from the worst of hell.

The suffocating blackness filled her, but she took a long, purging breath. This was safe. This was good, and Remy was everything she had always dreamed of. He was a fourth-generation Sinclair, heir to the Sinclair fortune, in case being a heart surgeon wasn't secure enough. And there was something princely about him—a chiseled profile, the Roman nose. His dark hair was carelessly brushed back from his face. The dove-gray suit was tailored perfectly to show sculpted shoulders and a tapered torso.

Best of all, the man was on the wrong side of thirty and trolling for a wife. A beautiful blonde to hang up on his wall along with his summa cum laude diploma from Columbia, his medical license from the State of New York and the live-action photo of the impala he'd seen on his last safari in Tanzania.

"Have you thought about the auction?" she asked, shifting the conversation from surgery toward a more stomach-surviving topic. She had promised the countess she'd deliver, and it was a promise Rose intended to keep. Sylvia was her boss and her friend; Rose owed her a lot more than a charity auction.

"Yes, I've thought. The answer is no."

"Please," she asked, not blaming him for saying no, but still determined to change his mind. It was demeaning, it was embarrassing, but truly, there was no more perfect bachelor in the entire tri-state region.

"No." Those princelike eyes were firm, but Rose was undeterred.

"Think of the puppies, those little fluff balls that need a good home. You can't be that heartless."

"I'm a heart surgeon. I replace hearts on a daily basis. I don't fear heartlessness like ordinary mortals without a god complex."

They were more alike than he would ever suspect. He saw her as the ideal, the perfect woman, and she never let him see behind the flawless mask to the person that was missing both a heart and a soul. Very rarely did she dwell on that loss, except on a starry night like this one. When a sexy stranger had appeared like magic, a Prince Charming coming to sweep her away to some-place quiet and glorious and decadently warm. Oh, yeah, right, next thing you know, you're flossing your teeth with a diamond-studded tiara perched on your head. Rose lifted a hand to her hair, just to check. All clear. No, if Rose wanted her happy ending, she was going to have to work for it.

"Would you do it for me?" she asked in her best, most earnest voice. This was only their fourth date, so really it was too soon to ask things from him. Still… Their relationship was a battle plan, carefully executed, plotted, and to date, proceeding exactly on schedule, with the countess cheering on from the sideline. Very few people saw similarities between relationships and battle, but Rose had read and memorized *The Art of War.* Those similarities were all Rose had ever known.

"You're going to make me, aren't you?" he said, affectionate resignation in his voice. It was why she liked him so much. He never asked anything of her, never told her what to say or what to wear, all she had to do was sit prettily at his side and listen. Piece of cake.

"Make you? Me?" She fluttered her lashes and he laughed.

"You can say all the heartless jokes you want, but I'm on to you."

"Do you always get your way?"

"Yes. You should have figured that out by now."

She waited, fingers crossed under the table, until finally he nodded, and she remembered to breathe. "I'll do it."

Rose was so excited she nearly kissed him, except for the hot hunger that still lingered on her lips. She wanted to keep that taste there, just for a little longer.

"You're sure? I mean, if you *really* don't want to…"

"You'd let me off the hook that easily?"

"Not really, but I'm trying to show some pretense of sensitivity. Humor me, here." Because she owed him, she endured three more blow-by-blow surgical descriptions without even a visible quiver of nausea.

Before he moved to number four, he glanced down at his watch. "It's late. You look tired."

A secret peek at her watch said it was nearly one, and all Rose wanted to do was go home and fall into bed. Alone.

She'd had exactly zero lovers. When you were groomed for matrimony as a blood sport, virginity was highly prized, right up there with a clean complexion and a coming-out dress. Her parents hadn't had the money for white satin and richelieu lace, so the Hildebrandes had over-compensated with endless lectures on virtue and a lifetime supply of Neutrogena. Rose—being a bright girl and not one to rebel—had taken the hint.

Now she yawned, not exactly faked. "I'm exhausted, and with your day—honestly, I don't know how you do it."

"Good drugs," he answered with an easy laugh.

And the stamina of a camel. Mentally, she slapped herself, feeling tired, punchy, and the bubbles in her blood were starting to die down. A master of efficiency, he helped her into her coat, always the gentleman, and she took a last sweep of the patrons in the lobby. Everything was so beautiful here, the polished marble, the gleaming silver, the people with their gentle laughter and placid faces. The six years of charm school had been so similar to this. Every day, the candle-glow lights and high-gloss perfection had been a safe haven for her, a few peaceful hours away from home. There, here, Rose had survived and thrived, grown hard and strong.

Her chin lifted, perfectly parallel to the ground, and she pivoted smoothly, slow and elegant, and the entire room watched her leave.

As they made their way out the doors, her heel caught on the step and when her foot moved on the shoe stayed behind. Remy—happy, smiling, gloriously rich Remy—swooped down and brandished it with a romantic flourish. "You did this on purpose?" he asked, as if she could be that clever.

He bent down, dark hair gleaming in the light, and placed the shoe on her foot. It should have been enchanting.

"Do you believe in fairy tales, Remy?" she asked curiously. If you lived within the invulnerability of the castle walls, did the myth of ever-after seem a big con on the rest of the world?

"Do you think this night is magic?" he countered, rising to his feet, and she saw a flash of something in his eyes. Something that she'd seen when she kissed the stranger. Hope. On New Year's, everyone wanted to believe.

"I think people deserve one night of magic," she answered, almost the truth.

It was his cue, his moment, and Remy was not stupid. He leaned closer and took her mouth, and Rose was too determined to pull back. Remy was a lot more viable than a fairy tale. He was everything she'd worked for, and his kiss was every bit as accomplished as it should be. So where was the triumph? No triumph, only the persistent taste of a hot hunger that even a fourth-generation Sinclair couldn't ease.

Patiently she waited for the thrill of victory, the absoluteness of her control. Perhaps she hadn't won the war, but this battle belonged to her. So why did she feel the same as before, the same as yesterday, the same as she'd felt all her life—

Numb.

As his hand moved purposefully toward her waist, Rose realized the hot hunger wasn't going to return. It couldn't be forced, it couldn't be tricked.

Damn.

Deliberately, her hand covered his, and she raised her head, gave him her nicest smile—a pretend smile designed to make people believe she had a heart.

"I can't."

"Too quick?" he asked.

"Yes," she told him, regret in her voice. "I'm sorry, Remy."

And she was, disappointed in herself, in her trickster mind. Sometimes she saw monsters where there were none, and sometimes she felt nothing when she should be pulsing with life.

"Soon," she promised. "I'm still not there, yet."

Remy thought her heart was involved elsewhere, that Rose was pining for a man who was desperately unworthy of her affections. A failed love affair had been Sylvia's idea, but Rose had approved because it solved a lot more problems than it created.

"I can wait," he said gallantly, not wanting to imagine a woman would be stupid enough to turn him down forever. Someday, Rose wouldn't turn him down, but not tonight.

"Can I see you home?"

"I'll manage. It's not far." Another big fat lie.

He took her hand, as if she were a princess, and kissed it once. If she were being honest with herself, she'd stop playing this game and get on with the life that she had planned. Instead, she stood there watching him go, a worried smile on her face.

After Remy had left, Rose hoofed it on aching feet to the number six train, which would take her to the Bronx. The Bronx was home, but not for too much longer. Rose had big goals for her life. She was grown, a woman fully formed, and stronger than her parents had ever guessed that Little Mary Poofster could be.

Rose wouldn't live on false hopes and broken dreams. She didn't have to worry about whether fairy tales or magic truly existed because they didn't; all she had to do was foster the illusion. Rose had long ago mastered the art of the illusion. Money was security, money was real, money made you invulnerable to whatever the Fates chose to throw your way.

After she got off at her stop, she walked past the pet store boxed between the bodega and the OTB site. It was an odd place for animals, and she liked to stand outside the glass, watching the puppies from a safe distance.

The puppies always fascinated her, confined to a small pen that they didn't seem to mind. Five tiny black fur balls with twinkling brown eyes that saw only the best in the world. They always looked carefree and content and safe behind that store window. The Hildebrandes never had a pet. Not even a fish. And

Rose hadn't missed them. Dogs were smelly and loud and dirty and could rip a hole in pink satin, quick as you could say boo.

But she liked watching from behind the window, and she wondered what they thought while they played behind the pane. Sometimes she'd put her hand on the glass and leave it there, waiting to see if they'd come to her, but they never did. Animals didn't like her, knowing things that people never would.

Tonight, there were no puppies, only a big black monster dog with huge jaws, but tired eyes. He was curled up on the hay, with absolutely no faith that tonight was the start of something new. Lazily he opened an eye, squinted at her, and Rose squinted back. She placed her hand to the window, because from behind the glass, there was nothing he could do to her.

The dog growled.

Rose quivered, her hand falling to her side.

However, she did defiantly stare him down, until he realized she was no threat and shut his eyes, prepared to sleep once again.

Yup, animals knew things that people never would.

Before she climbed the steps to her building, Rose looked one last time at the lights of the skyline, the late-night partygoers making their way home, shouts of happiness ringing in the air, as if all was right with the world.

For a second, for one heart-stopping second, she had felt that way, too. Rose pressed a finger to her lips, remembering his kiss.

Somewhere he was out there. Was he alone? Was he thinking about her?

My prosperous Prince Charming.

The words whispered inside her, seductive and golden and warm. Quickly Rose shushed them away.

She turned and went inside.

It was New Year's Eve, and all she wanted to do was be alone, let down her hair and slip into a pair of cushy polka-dot socks. Bright lights and a polished world might put stars in her eyes, but it sure was hell on the feet.

3

THE HOME OF COUNT ANTON Simonov and his lovely, Brooklyn-born wife, Sylvia, was a stately twelve-room penthouse with soaring painted ceilings, a bank of windows overlooking Central Park and frame after gilt frame of stony-faced Old Masters. In the count's private offices was a set of ornate cabinets that displayed his most treasured possessions—glass shelves full of Imperial eggs, handcrafted by Fabergé.

Every morning, a truckload of fresh flowers was brought in, all in white, because Sylvia adored white. As Sylvia's personal assistant, it was Rose's job to ensure that the flowers were properly placed, dead petals properly plucked, and that there were no nasty chrysanthemum's in the bunch. According to Sylvia, "Mums look cheap, and if I wanted cheap, I'd have Anton spring for 36 double Ds and dye my hair platinum."

To Rose, Sylvia was a living, breathing, teetering, stiletto-wearing hero. Nearly thirty years ago, Sylvia had risen from the ranks, trading in on her beauty and her wildly successful fundraising abilities to snag one of New York's wealthiest bachelors—who happened to be a Russian count to boot.

Rose had been doing a fine job working at a shipping insurance office in Pittsburgh, but there were always whispers that trailed after her. What the heck was *she* doing in an insurance office? Oh, her name wasn't famous and her face wasn't one they'd seen before, but her profile was too striking, her posture too straight, her walk a little too prissy for the shipping business. The curse of expectations never met.

When she spotted the profile on Countess Sylvia Simonov, a

plan emerged. For two weeks, she had taken the 4:37 a.m. bus from Pittsburgh to Manhattan to volunteer at the Simonov food pantry. Not only was she helping feed the hungry, but in less than ten days, she had convinced Countess Sylvia Simonov that Rose was a charity organizer extraordinaire.

For the past three years, Rose had been in the Simonov employ, where the smell of peace and prosperity filled the air. It'd taken her twenty-seven years, but she had finally found a place where she fit. Here, under Sylvia's nurturing eye, she was given on-the-job training on how to belong in the upper echelon, as well as steady exposure to Manhattan's most desirable bachelors. Best of all, Sylvia and Anton were the poster people for how affluence can positively affect your life.

With Sylvia's energetic influence, Rose had watched and learned how to achieve the life she wanted.

Today, January 1 in the Simonov household, Rose's happy gaze touched on polished wood, perfumed satin and, most appealing of all, contentment. *Dorothy, you're not in Kansas anymore. Attention World: Dorothy is now arriving at the Plaza.*

A stack of engraved envelopes landed on Dorothy's desk, reminding her that Rose was actually paid to do more than daydream. Impatiently, Sylvia tapped a scarlet nail on the blotter.

"Rose. Thank-you notes for the Christmas gifts. Be a darling. Linda kept a running list with three categories: mine, Anton's, ours. Here's what I need. For mine and ours, write a personal, funny message, and let your gushing know no bounds. Sound like me if at all possible, preferably without the accent. For Anton's list, especially the blue bloods, be impersonal, cold and stodgy. They really seem to go for that."

At fifty-five, Sylvia was an odd contradiction of humility and beauty in an approachable, yet elegant package. Her dark hair never looked meticulously coiffed, but Rose knew the truth. The stylist was there every morning before Anton woke up in order to make the "high-glossed, natural softness" a fait accompli. Anton affectionately called it Sylvia's bedroom hair. Sylvia would then shoot a conspiratorial wink at Rose. Rose never winked back, but sometimes she wanted to.

Daintily Sylvia stroked a black brow back into place. "Do you know the best cure for hot flashes? Believe it or not, Cristal. Seriously. But the next morning, oh, my God, the hangover is killer. Speaking of hot flashes, how'd the date go with Dr. Sinclair? Do I need the caterers and printers on speed dial, eagerly awaiting my call?"

Four dates and Sylvia was ready to post the banns. Unfortunately, Rose moved tortoiselike to Sylvia's hare, not wanting to go too fast, not wanting to go too slow, which usually stalled things to not going anywhere at all.

"It was nice," Rose answered vaguely.

"Yessss?" prompted Sylvia, who braced her hands on the fili-greed wood, causing fingerprints aplenty. "Tell. Spill."

Spilling wasn't easy for Rose. She wasn't impulsive or im-promptu, she was meticulous and well rehearsed. Being around Sylvia, though, she had learned to relax. Sylvia was…a friend. "I froze. I shouldn't have clammed up. I should have been forth-right, open. Instead, I'm with world's most perfect man, and I find flaws. I think my standards are wonky." She ended the whine with a perky smile, which never seemed to fool Sylvia.

"You're too hard on yourself, Rose. A woman like you? Your poise, your face, those boobs. If I weren't on the Forbes list, I'd have to hate you. Lighten up. It's early yet. Give yourself a little time. Not everyone can move at light speed like moi."

And in case life affirmations were required, Sylvia waltzed to the piano, her sheer leopard print caftan billowing around her. Delicately she plucked a white magnolia from the crystal vase and inhaled, beaming at Rose with a "yes, your life could be this grand," gleam.

Then she squinted, stared.

"Why are you pale? You're missing the usual glow. And those circles. You either need another brand of concealer, or else some-thing's keeping you up."

"It's nothing," answered Rose, but Sylvia waggled a creamy white flower in her direction.

"Let me be the judge of nothing."

Carefully Rose made neat stacks of the envelopes on the

blotter, then dabbed at the smudged glass with the edge of her blazer, and finally adjusted the tiny silver desk calendar, all of which made her feel better, but did nothing to stop Sylvia's tapping foot.

Of all the topics that Rose would love to discuss with Sylvia, this wasn't one. Although, maybe if she talked about it, maybe if she put it out there, it would be no big. After all, it *was* no big, not big at all. The countess's shoe clicked on the marble like a ticking time bomb.

Frantically, Rose scanned her desk, but there was absolutely nothing else to straighten. Because she was not a coward nor intimidated by the idea of confessing meaningless minutiae, Rose crossed her legs and lifted her chin in her best "it was nothing" attitude.

"I kissed someone last night."

"Remy?"

"Another him," Rose admitted.

Now looking completely intrigued, the countess raised her eyebrows, but didn't speak. Rose was on her own. Grudgingly she owned up to the truth.

"I met someone. Times Square. It was a total fluke. I dropped my phone. He helped me out. He was... I don't know, but..."

"And you kissed this flukey someone?" the countess asked, cutting to the heart of the matter.

"Yes."

"At midnight?"

Evenly, Rose met her eyes, showing no fear at all and nodded.

"I see."

"What do you see?"

"New Year's Eve. Times Square. Midnight. Stranger. Handsome, I presume."

"Certainly, but it wasn't the handsome that bothered me."

The countess flew to the desk. "Bothered you? Grab the police sort of 'bothered you'?"

Rose shuffled the envelopes. "No. Worse."

"Are you going to make me play twenty questions, Rose?"

There was an empty pit in her stomach when she looked up. The countess was a friend, the mother Rose had always known existed, but confiding never came easy to her. This time, however, the temptation to talk was strong, to understand, to purge.

"You had a plan, you executed, you got exactly what you wanted. Along the way, did you ever get sidetracked? Did you ever think you weren't in control? That life wasn't going to cooperate with what you wanted? Or is that part of it? A test of strength to see if you can overcome getting sidetracked?"

That nefarious possibility crept up on her, making Rose nervous. When you needed your life to be plotted, planned and perfectly implemented, the idea of bigger forces being at work was a disaster.

No, the bigger force was self-will and determination. Rose had to stay focused. Think Sun Tzu, think tough. Think…*magic*.

No.

Yes.

Maybe?

All muddled inside, she looked to the countess for advice, not even concerned that she was frowning, which wasn't her best look.

"You believe in fate, an invisible nudge that is pushing you toward that perfect someone?"

"No." *Probably not.*

Sylvia tapped a finger to her head. "And that is the correct answer, young grasshopper. Never forget. As women we can't sit back and let the world whip us around, gusting this way and that, all because we're too spineless to design our own destinies. Take this place. Do you think this is destiny? Hell, no. I adore Anton, there is no other man for me, but…"

"But what if we have a soul mate?" The words were clearly audible, yet Rose's gaze flicked worriedly around the room, because there was no way that she had said that.

"Right, and there are three crones sitting around a pot, cackling like constipated hens. The hard truth is that they all live on the thirty-second floor of Central Park West, not somewhere in the wilds of a Shakespeare fable, missy."

Relieved, Rose nodded once. "You're right. When you're right, you're right."

The countess patted her hand. "Don't get caught up in the

fantasy, Rose. A kiss can linger, sticking in your brain like yesterday's chewing gum. Are you going to see him again?"

"I can't. I don't even know his name."

"Problem solved!" Sylvia popped away from the desk, and spread her arms wide.

"It's a billion to one shot I'd even run into him a second time," Rose reasoned. Manhattan was huge, it was impossible to find someone unless they, for example, wanted to be found, or put an ad in missed connections. Why, if she didn't read missed connections then she'd never know. On the face of it, the odds against her ever meeting him again were boggling.

"Not just a billion to one," the countess corrected, "a gazillion. But, let's walk down the primrose path. Let's say you do run into him. Then you let him take you home, screw his brains out and promptly get him right out of your head. Unless he's royalty. And then, dear Rose, you have my permission to marry him. But there's no screwing with royalty. At least not at first. Women must appear to be patient, passive and never, ever, eager beavers. You have to think about these things. Sex has repercussions. Consequences."

Rose didn't want to think about sex; she'd spent all last night *not* thinking about sex, and frankly, all that not thinking about sex was making her dizzy. Finally she snapped back to the present. "I'm pretty sure he's not royalty. Maybe finance."

Sylvia's mouth tightened into a disapproving moue.

"He looked like he was still doing okay," Rose added, wanting to defend him.

Still, Sylvia appeared doubtful. "I can see you've got your mind preoccupied here. It's written all over your little dreamy face."

Hearing that, Rose removed all traces of dreamy from her face, and Sylvia continued.

"If you do have a chance encounter, go ahead, work him out of your system, and then come back and we'll start in immediately on Plan B."

"The bachelor auction?"

"Of course. You're going to win the bid, you're going to bed him, and it will turn out to be the best night of your life." Sylvia strolled over to her flowers, then looked up and shot Rose a wink. "But do not forget. If there's any sex to be had with this Prince Charming, you have to share every sordid detail. And leave nothing out."

Rose held up a solemn hand. "I promise."

FOR IAN, BEING A RUTGERS men's basketball fan was a testament to his unwavering loyalty. Win, lose or pulverized, the three friends were always there. It had started during college. He, Beckett and Phoebe had hung out at the games between exams. After graduation, after all the life choices had been made, they moved from the student section into the moderately snazzy mezzanine where the alumni presided, secure in their life choices and their employment decisions.

On the first day of the New Year, Ian was no longer secure in his employment decisions, but the Rutgers team was sucking like a vacuum and the arena was empty, so hey, he kept his head high.

After grabbing a soda and springing for an order of nachos, Ian jogged up the concrete steps to his spot. There was the standard ritual of unspoken greeting. Phoebe waved a red cup, slightly rumpled in jeans and a Knights sweatshirt. Beckett merely grunted.

All social obligations aside, Ian checked the score. Down by ten already. Okay, not a good night at the RAC, but the Knights could come back, never say die.

However, by the second period, the Knights were still losing, and no one was talking. Worse, Beckett was pale, unshaven and crabby. Now, crabby wasn't that unusual—Beckett put the mud in curmudgeon—but Beckett always shaved. Precise grooming was one of those boarding school rules that Beckett conformed to without even realizing it. Since boarding school was a sensitive topic, Ian chose to keep his mouth shut. "Bad hangover?" he asked instead.

"Yeah."

"Sorry about last night. I couldn't go to your place and smile and be all friendly."

Phoebe leaned in, peering around Beckett. "Don't worry

about it, Ian. How was Times Square? Nightmare on Forty-Second Street, sardined in until you are intimately acquainted with people of questionable hygiene whom you never want to see again?"

"More or less. But I'm glad I went. You have to do it in order to say you've done it, unless you lie, and what's the satisfaction in that? Think about it. On December 31, it's the most perfect place in the world to be—and we live here. Why not take advantage? You ever stop to wonder about how many things we don't do?"

Beckett didn't look convinced; of course, Beckett never looked convinced. "There's a reason why we don't go to Times Square, Ian. You can watch it on TV."

TV. As if all life's problems could be solved on a twenty-seven-inch screen. "But you miss all the excitement," Ian pointed out, knowing it would do no good, but needing to try anyway. Life involved spontaneous kisses and meeting the woman of your dreams, having her visit you in your dreams. Of course, it would be nice if the evening ended a little better—not that he was going to think it was a sign.

"I'll live without the excitement, thank you," Beckett answered, completely unenthused.

Choosing to abandon the impossible, Ian turned his attention to Phoebe. "Sorry about Dexter." Dexter had been Phoebe's latest.

"Eh," she answered with a shrug.

"Don't worry. You'll meet somebody new."

"Yes, I could meet someone new. Possibly. Or the world could end first, destroying all male civilization as we know it, leaving me the sole survivor, and alone I must discover the path to mono-sexual reproduction without any knowledge of biology at all. I'm thinking that's the more likely scenario."

Beckett snorted. "You could do it."

Phoebe quirked a brow over her lenses. "Meet someone new?"

"The asexual reproduction thing. You're really smart."

"Bite me," she replied with very little heart, and then frowned in Ian's direction. "Why are you so happy? It sounded like last night was a bust."

For a second he considered keeping his secret, but too few

charmed things had happened to him. Right now, he needed to share the miraculousness of the kiss, cement it in his head and probably ride it out for the rest of the year.

"I kissed this woman. In Times Square. It was absolute magic, the best time of my life, topping graduation, my first bonus check, the day I bought my first place."

Phoebe looked worried. "You kissed a stranger?" she asked. "Really?"

"Like you've never done it," Beckett argued, both of them completely missing the profound significance of the moment.

"Not in Times Square. I think that's creepy."

Ian laughed, because he didn't expect the rest of the world to understand. "It wasn't creepy. It was like an old movie. She was there and then poof, she was gone. It's a sign. A bubbling glass of Dom Pérignon, a rainbow after the storm, a golden unicorn."

"I'm concerned about you, Ian. You shouldn't be talking about unicorns with a serious face."

"It's only an expression, Beckett. You know, when you feel as if all around you the world is full and bursting, and you need to soak it in."

Okay, that was laying it on too thick, but if a man couldn't have big dreams on January 1, then there was no hope for him at all.

"Missing the firm, aren't you?" Beckett asked, not fooled by Ian's never-say-die smile.

Ian met his eyes, man to man. "Hell, yeah."

Phoebe looked at them, confused. Honest to God, females had no idea the pressure that society put on men. It wasn't smart, and eventually, some poor sap could break under the strain.

Right then, a roar went up as the Scarlet Knights took the ball on a streaking run, layup, net, followed almost immediately by a steal and a three-pointer. Phoebe shot up from her seat, fist-bumped Beckett, and then sat down, adjusting her glasses. "What was her name?"

Details, details. Ian coughed. "I don't know her name. We didn't have a lot of time, and then she had to go find her date." Even to his own ears, it sounded weak.

"She kissed you, and she had a date? Ballsy," murmured Phoebe.

"She didn't like the guy," explained Ian, because he knew it wasn't ballsiness on her part, more the inescapable truth that for one perfect night, two souls were brought together, merging into one incandescent flame that was bigger than either of them…. He sighed. Maybe she'd been drinking too much. No. He wasn't going to be put off. If the Scarlet Knights could win—

The visiting team got a steal, three-points, followed by a foul. Ian buried his head in his hands.

"Why don't you try and find her?" asked Beckett. "Put an ad on missed connections. What if she's The One? You can't miss out on that."

Ian glanced over at Phoebe, noticed the way her face softened.

"You should," she told him. "Women would eat it up. Trust me, as a woman, I'm almost seduced."

"It doesn't take much, does it?" drawled Beckett, who usually didn't take this many shots at Phoebe.

"Don't be an ass," Phoebe fired back.

"I'm not. You're the one who's talking about the destruction of the entire male species."

"It was a joke, Beckett."

"I'm sorry, when it comes to you and men, sometimes it's hard to tell."

"What does that mean?"

Beckett swore and fixed his eyes on the court, and the three of them watched the game, or at least Ian pretended to watch the game. He was still dwelling on the mystery woman of last night, trying to figure out if the ideal of a dream was better than charging in, throwing the dice, only to watch the Big Bad Wolf blow down the house he'd made out of happy straw.

The doubt, the insecurity, the mixed metaphors, they were all postlayoff, because prelayoff, he would have gambled all night and not panicked about losing his house at all.

At the half, when the Scarlet Knights were down by twenty-six and all hope had left the building, Phoebe turned to him, scarfing his last nacho. "Seriously. We'll help you write the ad. Maybe she's searching for you, too."

Ian looked at the scoreboard, saw his future and worried. "So she meets me and she asks what I do for a living, then what am I supposed to say?"

In his mind, there were certain advantages to staying virtual strangers. Okay, there would be no sex, but on the bright side, he wouldn't have to explain the prelayoff, postlayoff stages of his life. In the battle between his libido and his pride, pride trumped all. Although after a few days, that might be subject to change.

"All you have to tell her is that you help people find employment. Ian, it's very noble. You should be proud of it."

Phoebe talked in that faux-sincere voice, as if being an employment counselor was on par with working with millions of dollars at an investment bank. Not even in Phoebe's noncompetitive universe were the two on the same scale. Pointedly, Ian stared at the emptying stands.

This wasn't a conversation Ian wanted to have, not now, not ever. Instead, he wanted to dwell on the happy memory of last night. On her honeysuckle lips and the burst of electricity that was still humming inside him. To have her, splayed out below him, above him, truly he wasn't picky. Just to see the warm invitation in her eyes, that ripe mouth parted and plump breasts rising, falling, tips begging to be teased...

"You should find her. Place the ad." Beckett's voice cut through his fantasies. *Thanks, dude.*

Ian weighed the options, the thought of her underneath him, surrounding him, damp thighs glistening, waiting... For him.

In the end, libido ruled. "I'll do it."

4

ROSE'S APARTMENT WAS a far cry from the Simonov decadence, but it was neat, tidy and for now it was home. Her frown was automatic when she walked in the door, her eyes critical.

It never felt right. It didn't matter if the slipcover for the sofa was hand-sewn, or that the coffee table was a steamer trunk covered in a designer print. She could hear that growling voice in her head telling her that it wasn't straight, or that it looked cheap. Automatically she pulled at the fabric until the pleats hung at a precise ninety degrees. When she noticed the stain on the sofa, she attacked it with spot remover until the light beige fabric was restored to perfection. Yes, there was a certain cathartic satisfaction in having a clean home, but she hated that it was *that* voice that was responsible. Frustrated, she threw the rag in the trash and decided to concentrate on the things that made her happy.

Her pride and joy was a darling little writing secretary that she had discovered at a thrift store on Staten Island, buried between a nonworking television set and an overgrown stuffed rabbit named Helen. The desk was a solid wood Queen Anne with lots of hidden components, delicate carved legs and a drop-front lid. After changing into her pajamas, she grabbed the thank-you cards from her bag and settled down to work.

By the time it was midnight, she wasn't tired—she was buzzing. Not caffeine. Careful excitement, the kind that almost made her squirm in her chair. Sylvia had given her the green light to proceed. Not that she was going to proceed, but…*what if?* Dangerous words. Rose rolled her eyes, told herself to get a life and picked up the pen.

One after another she went through the list of gifts, writing like a fiend, channeling her inner Sylvia, knocking out thank-yous. There were notes for bottles of wine, for autographed baseball gloves—Anton was a fan—and for an antique jade vase from the Kremlin. Jeez, did the Simonov household really need another vase, another set of crystal glasses, another set of mono-grammed cuff links? *Cuff links?*

She backtracked over the list, just in case she'd read wrong. Why was Anton getting cuff links?

Rose studied the maid's tidy handwriting and flipped the paper over to find the name of the gift-giver on the following page.

Rose swore, loud and completely improperly.

Blair Rapaport? Hussy, with a capital *HO*.

By the age of twenty-one, Blair had written a tell-all book on her breast augmentation surgery and had financially exploited seven sex-tape scandals—and the clock of misdeeds was still ticking. On the last television interview, her parents defended her, saying that drunken voice-mail messages over the Internet was "all part of growing up."

So why was Blair giving a Christmas present to Anton? Rose checked the list again. Cuff links? Seriously? Did Blair even know what cuff links were?

This couldn't end well. Rose looked at Helen, who remained stubbornly silent.

No, Rose. Keep out. This was none of her business. There was probably an easy explanation…actually there was no easy expla-nation that wouldn't end with Sylvia pitching a fit, and Rose didn't like it when Sylvia pitched a fit.

She didn't like it when *anyone* pitched a fit.

Opting to do nothing except her job, Rose inked a bland note. Although, maybe, if Blair was smart enough to read between the lines, she'd notice the overuse of the word *we*. And the "such a grown-up gift from such a young girl." That was a definite dig.

Rose reread the card and in the end, tore it up into tiny pieces and dumped it in the trash. Blair was getting no thank-you card from the Simonovs, and if Rose had her way, she'd get a bitch-slap instead. Well, probably not an actual bitch-slap, but if Rose were inclined, if she were *truly* channeling Sylvia, she could do it. She curled her fingers in a fist, wound it up and slammed it down on the desk—killing her hand.

Okay, no bitch-slaps for now, but tomorrow was another day.

By the time she'd finished the list, it was 2:00 a.m. and she was no closer to wanting to sleep. She could hear her computer calling her, a languid come-hither hand inviting her to only peek and see if maybe…

What would it hurt? Honestly. And how would she know otherwise? A gazillion to one. Not a chance in the world.

Tiny goose bumps appeared on her arms. Not fear.

Even though she was alone, she looked both ways before hitting the keys. Navigating Craigslist, she arrowed in on Missed Connections, scanning, scanning, scanning…

Who knew that so many strangers hooked up on New Year's Eve? There were four pages of—

Oh.

My life started on the first second of the New Year…

Magic.

Rose jumped out of her chair, knocking over the pile of thank-you cards, and then immediately picked them up.

He was looking for her. His name was Ian. Her feet slowly touched the ground. Ian was not Dr. Remy Sinclair. He was a stranger in Times Square who had really good shoes and an expensive coat. That coat was a triple-word score, spelled *A-R-M-A-N-I*.

Rose knew that justification of a wrong was a dangerous game, but she wanted to play. Her loins ached to play, and her loins had never ached before.

Under her parents' eagle eyes, she hadn't dared stray, and after Child Services had removed her to a group home at age fourteen, the environment hadn't been conducive to activities of a sexual nature.

However, at fifteen, on a cold December night, she'd learned to explore. Quietly, hidden under the blankets of her bunk so her roommates couldn't hear…

Those dark silent moments were instructive to Rose. She wanted to learn about pleasure, to create it, to control it, to deny it. Pleasure led to impulsiveness, which led to mistakes. Mistakes were not tolerated.

On those dark nights, with the scratchy wool on her thighs and her hand between her legs, there were never any fantasies for Rose. Men didn't arouse her with their arrogance and their games. Rose knew the prison-warden side of the alpha male—the rules, the constraints, the dominance.

Rose hated it.

But last night when her hand had crept beneath the covers, she had seen him, felt him, remembered his mouth on hers, trailing down her neck, teasing one breast then the other, sliding farther…

Rose stopped that line of thought and fanned herself, surprised by the heat on a cold January night.

Ian—she rolled his name off her tongue—turned her on with something else. Her fingers slipped between her legs, beneath her panties, and she found herself wet, aroused.

Odd, yet fun. Curious, she pleasured herself, conjuring his face, remembering his mouth. Her finger stroked faster, her body flushed, and for tonight, she could imagine a man's hands on her, feel his gentle caress, sure, easy, hungry yet restrained. Her breathing staggered, and this time she didn't see the dark of the ceiling. Instead, she saw deep brown eyes burning with a light she couldn't understand. She tasted the heat of his mouth on hers. A tiny moan escaped from her throat. Pleasure. Stealthy and sly. The pleasure teased her, beckoned to her, testing her control. Warily her lashes drifted shut, and she surrendered to the fantasy, finding her rhythm, sensing the orgasm chasing after her.

The first flutters of pressure increased, building more, and her heart began to race at the challenge to cut it off before it took control of her.

In the end, it was no challenge at all. Here, no man would follow her, and Rose closed off her mind, banishing the twinkling eyes, blocking the feel of that devouring mouth. Here, no one followed but Rose. The warmth pooled over her, and there was only a second—never more than one gossamer second—that her muscles contracted and her body flooded with pleasure. Deliberately, Rose shut the pleasure down.

Here was her secret place, the quiet blanket in the dark where the blustering voices had never entered, where only Rose could hide. She'd been quick and careful and silent because little ladies didn't touch themselves and little ladies were not to be touched, and Rose needed to be the world's most perfect little lady.

In the blink of an eye, her cheeks had cooled, her heart had calmed and Rose had smoothed the silk pajamas. Gracefully she took her seat and typed out an appropriate response on the keyboard. When she was finished, she allowed herself one tiny punch into the air, all while keeping her feet firmly on the ground.

His name was Ian.

THIS WAS WRONG. BECKETT never trusted sex, it was too full of complications and emotions, but he trudged after Phoebe, ignoring the eight thousand logical and rational reasons that this would be a mistake. He'd been in her long and empty apartment many times before, but not like this. Not with his cock painfully full, and images of her plastered in his head.

Foolishly he followed her over scuffed, golden oak floors, followed her into the dark recesses of her bedroom. She had five seasons of *Family Guy* on her dresser for late-night watching. He kept rolling over that mundane fact in his mind, but when she began to strip off her clothes, suddenly he was obsessed.

He wanted to touch her. Badly. His blood burned with it, but his brain—the part that was still functioning—held him back.

The sweater came off, exposing a sheer bra and the dark nipples underneath. The air smelled of pine cleaner, burned soup and Beckett's lust. His breathing grew ragged as he watched her shed her shoes, her jeans. The glasses were removed, dropped on the nightstand near the bed.

Through the window, the Upper East Side slept quietly in their beds, a ship's horn bleating, a truck honking and somewhere a siren screamed.

Beckett didn't care. Tonight, the entire East River could burn and he wouldn't budge from this place.

In his mind, he'd never considered a naked Phoebe. Yet there she was. The half-opened slats of the blinds pushed light into the darkness of her bedroom, her skin flashing gold, then shadows as she moved.

She walked forward, bare feet padding on the thick rug, and from the living room he could hear the crazed cackle of her parrot, scolding him. Still, his eyes didn't stray. She was…not exactly beautiful, but something that fascinated him even more. The long, lean curve of her that ran from the high breast to the arch of her hips. His gaze drifted lower to the sleek muscles of her thighs. The dark shadow between.

When they were a whisper apart, Phoebe raised her head and stared, and those normally shielded, practical gray eyes were blurred with confusion. Beckett hated confusion, but his mind wasn't thinking, or more likely, he didn't want his mind to think. Furious, with her, with himself.

Complications and emotions. He could feel them swirling in the air, smelled it, stronger and more potent than the musky scent of desire. If they did this, they could never go back.

Complications and emotions.

There was a clanging in his brain. A bell. A foghorn.

A phone.

"Do you want me to answer that?"

NO! "You should," he stammered. "Get that. Now."

"Whatever you want, whatever you say," she muttered. "Get the phone, Phoebe. I'll get the phone, Phoebe." As she walked, he watched the miraculous perfection that was her bare ass, until she selfishly wrapped herself in the duvet covers and picked up her phone. *"WHAT?"*

He nearly laughed, but then she would glare, so he kept quiet. Beckett needed the break. He was nervous and desperate—never a good combination. Fate had thrown a kink in their plans. Why the kink? Was fate trying to tell him that this was a bad idea? It hadn't seemed like a bad idea earlier.

"Who wrote you?" Phoebe was talking into the phone. Without her glasses, she looked so different, so unsure. Okay, this *was* a bad idea. The duvet cover slipped, his eyes tracked the movement…

"Why didn't she tell you her name?" Phoebe glanced at him, mouthed the word, *Ian.*

She was talking to Ian. Naked. She was naked, talking to Ian. Beckett tried to follow the conversation but *naked* kept getting in the way. He turned, futzed with the *Family Guy* DVDs on the dresser, doggedly studying the nefarious face of Stewie, knowing that behind every innocent expression lurked the mind of evil. Beckett looked at her reflection in the mirror, now doggedly studying the V between her breasts, and felt his tongue start to swell.

Her eyes met his, but she wasn't wearing her glasses. She wouldn't notice. Her brows furrowed. She noticed. Quickly he refocused on Stewie, because somewhere in the world, the Fates were laughing.

And if he didn't get it, her parrot started cackling, as well.

She put her glasses on, her eyes magnified, the confusion magnified, his guilt magnified. Damn it.

No, he was above all this. Carefully he moved toward the bed, step by step, inch by inch, and then balanced precariously on the very edge. "What he's saying?" he whispered.

Phoebe hit the mute button. "She e-mailed."

"She didn't give her name?" he asked, his mind resuming function.

"No name, no number, but he still set up the date. Jane Doe agreed." Her voice was brisk, businesslike, as if nothing had ever happened. As if she wasn't sitting there bare….

"No good," he cut in. "What if some other strange woman saw the listing and decided that Ian sounds like an easy mark? Or worse yet, what if he shows up and she's a serial killer, or like, a cow?"

Phoebe glared, and he sighed with relief. Okay, this felt normal. This felt right. She unmuted the phone. "Ian, listen. What if some other strange woman saw the listing and decided you sounded like an easy mark? Or worse yet, what if you show up, and she's a serial killer, or umm…mean?" There was a pause. "No. I'm not channeling Beckett, thank you very much. I'm just concerned."

Beckett beamed at her. Silently she shot him the finger.

"No, I don't think she's trying to protect herself. *You're* not a serial killer."

She sighed, bosom heaving. Beckett sighed, too, then looked away. "No, you couldn't be a serial killer, Ian."

Beckett snickered.

"I'm not trying to mother you. I give you my word." She stared at Beckett pointedly. "Yes, if you wanted a brutal evisceration of reality, you would have called Beckett."

Insulted, he stood up and went back to studying the DVD. Mostly.

"I'll try to be positive. How about this? It's a huge sign and you're right to be over the moon." Ew. Beckett frowned. Really, she needed to come up with better lines than that.

"Yes, I firmly believe it's the same hottie who kissed you and the two of you are going to live happily ever after.

"No. I'm not just saying that to make you feel better.

"Ian," she warned.

"You're not needy. Okay, you're needy. Good night, Ian."

With a click she hung up, and they were back to being alone. Beckett held the DVD to his chest like a shield. "I have to go. Can I borrow this?"

"Do you want to find out about Ian, about his date, about how excited he is?" She sounded ticked; he knew she'd be ticked, and it was better this way. Safer. No complications. No emotions. If only she'd get…dressed. Until then, he was screwed. Metaphorically, not literally. If he meant literally, he wouldn't be having this stupid conversation with his brain.

Manning up, he met Phoebe's eyes squarely, prepared to set things straight between them. "He's screwed. It won't be the same chick, or if it is, he'll get punked on some reality prank show. Life doesn't work out that good. Nothing works out the way you want it to." He held up the DVD. "Mind if I borrow this?"

Okay, he'd settled nothing, but she wasn't looking at him all soft and confused anymore. Now she looked pissed. "Just go, Beckett."

She was proving his point. Beckett ran for the door, clutching the DVD, her parrot's crazed cackle echoing behind him.

5

THE MANHATTAN OFFICE for Employment Displacement. It was the tenth floor of a worn midtown building with an elevator that sometimes went wonky. All around the three-room office were signs of encouragement, pictures of eagles soaring in the sky, posters that proclaimed: "Yes, you can." Yet inside the reception area were also the faces of the employmentally displaced, and it was hard to reconcile them with the pictures of soaring eagles when all they wanted was to find work and pay the rent.

For all the wisecracks Ian made at the eagles' expense, he did his part. Jeans and goofy T-shirts were the uniform here. His boss, Sal D'Amato, said it made people feel less out of touch. Privately, Ian thought that a T-shirt that said, "Practice Safe Lunch—Use a Condiment," didn't do squat, but he kept an encouraging smile on his face and his prelayoff wardrobe stored in his closet. "Interview clothes," that's what Ian called them now.

Although, tonight "interview clothes" would morph into "date clothes," because tonight he had a date, and not just any date. This was the date of a lifetime. With a woman whose face had been embossed on his brain, in his dreams. He could remember her smell, the silken touch of her skin, even the feel of her fingers pressing against his neck. He looked at the eagles, wings outspread, images frozen in time, and he gave them an encouraging smile. *Tough luck, dude. Tonight, it's my turn to fly.*

Alas, today he had to actually work like a turkey before he could fly.

The hiring project of the day was Mitchell Unger, an unemployed ad man, forty-nine, with a family of three to worry about.

Adding to his misery, the oldest boy would be starting college soon, and Mitch was starting to sweat not only food and rent, but tuition, as well.

At precisely 9:13 a.m., Ian started on the phones—because true New Yorkers took precisely thirteen minutes to get down to business. The first three calls went straight to voice mail, the next number had been disconnected, company number five believed that marketing was overrated, company six had just hired someone new, but on lucky call seven, Ian finally hit pay dirt and the negotiations began.

Without any remorse in her cold, cold heart, Mary offered the lowest of the low. Mail room. Ian jumped all over it, because any opening was progress of the very best kind.

"What about this? You pay him the mail room salary, but throw him some creative work. Think of the cost savings alone. Imagine the visual. Your managers sitting around a table, and you're pitching Mitchell's ideas, and they're all looking at you as if you're a goddess. This is your moment, Mary. Humbly you explain about Mitchell, explain how little he's costing the company and how much he's bringing to the table. And then the suits crack a smile—nay a broad-bowed grin that is going to crack the Botox right off their faces. Imagine it, Mary—suddenly you're the hero."

His hero wasn't completely buying it. "No, I don't write fiction. Come on, Mary. Give him a shot. I'll do anything."

And those were the magic words she'd been waiting to hear. Ian wondered if he ought to feel cheap, pimping out his investment skills in exchange for work, a habit that was marginally illegal since he wasn't employed by a licensed broker, at least not presently. On the other hand, it was for the greater good, the ultimate sacrifice, and best of all, his skills stayed razor-sharp.

"Altriva? The dog food company. You heard something?" Ian hunched over the keyboard, fingers flying as if they were born to soar. "Maybe. Give me a second." He scanned the numbers, catching the six-month-long uptick. "You know this is going to cost you, right?"

Mary knew.

"I don't come cheap. But the Portland Scientific recommendation panned out, right? The numbers are solid. Liabilities are low. Recently a lot of insider trading, all buys, but I don't see any clues in the news. It's definitely trending up. The P/E looks sweeter than my mom's apple pie, and they have new management. Go ahead, buy. You have my blessing." Sensing victory within his grasp, Ian strolled back over to his desk and kicked up his feet. "I'll send Mitchell over for an interview today. Clear the schedule, Mary. You're going to love him."

After he rang off with Mary, Ian punched in Mitchell's number.

"Mitch, my man, it's Ian. You need to turn off the daytime talk shows and break out the suit. Interview at Scholstein, Harden, today at four. It's a junior position. Sorry about that, dude, but I have great faith in your abilities to turn a silk purse into something even silkier. After all, you *are* in advertising."

For the next five minutes, Mitch cooed and oohed, expressing his undying gratitude until, embarrassed by the compliments and accolades, Ian made up an excuse and hung up.

The gratitude always hit him between the eyes. When Ian was in banking, his clients were smug, taking their ten percent returns with a clipped nod and a bottle of aged scotch at Christmas. At the employment office, this gratitude felt off. Ian didn't deserve it. Honestly, there were no miracles working here, none at all. Not like in finance, where miracles occurred by the trillion on a daily basis.

Thinking of his prelayoff life was not a good way to start today. Automatically his hands reached for the polished rock that sat on his desk, tossing it up and down like a baseball. When Ian was seven, he had wanted to be an astronaut. His father had sat by his bedside and solemnly told him the stone was a moon rock. After that, every single night he had slept with the tiny fragment of the galaxy under his pillow. By the age of nine, he wanted to be a basketball player, and his father had said that it was a piece of foundation from Madison Square Garden. However, by the age of nine, Ian was smarter and wiser, and called his dad a big, fricking liar. His father had gazed at him, man to man, and told him the rock's initial place of residence didn't matter. The most important thing, according to his father, was to think about the rock's final destination. A rock could be moved from place to place, but where it ended up was a lot more important than where it started.

Being a cocky nine-year-old, Ian had rolled his eyes and drawn out *Da-ad* to a long two syllables. But when his father wasn't watching, Ian took the stone and casually tossed it in the air before tucking it in his pocket.

Ian felt his dad's smile, rather than saw it, and to this day, Ian found myriad uses for his stone. Maybe this wasn't his final destination, but for now, for today, the victories were starting to smell sweet.

One file on his desk was not smelling so sweet. There were no victories for Hilda Prigsley. For four months, he'd beaten every bush in town—and a few out of town—but sadly, in New York, very few individuals saw the wisdom of taking on an over-fifty teapot-shaped immigrant from the UK. She typed well over one hundred words per minute, one-twenty-two to be exact, but unfortunately believed that computers were the handiwork of the devil. Ian had tried his damnedest to find her something, but positions for a portly Mary Poppins weren't as plentiful as some might think.

Once a week Miss Prigsley stopped in the office, bringing him a tinful of handmade English biscuits. Ian always called them cookies, because then she would correct him in her proper English way, and he would pretend that he'd forgotten, and she would giggle and smile and he felt as if he'd just charmed his grandmother. If he could only figure out a way to market a sentimental lexicologist, she would be *so* employed, but reluctantly he pushed her file aside and focused on the nonlexicologist extraordinaires.

By the end of the afternoon, Ian had found two more positions. One for a budding young medical assistant, Deirdre Synder, and one for Mortimer Haswell, a fifty-eight year old mortgage broker who wasn't happy about a secretarial job and came down to the office to whine in person.

After a few seconds of polite listening, Ian paused for dramatic effect and then held up his stone. He looked Mort in his basset-esque eyes and asked, "Do you know where this came from?"

Mort shook his shaggy gray head.

"This stone is from my first job. Recycling. Now, if you've ever worked recycling in this state, you know it's not a pretty job. It's not elegant. It's not one of those run-out-and-brag-to-all-your-friends job. But I did it. Dirty, crappy and I smelled like bad fish until I went to sleep with that smell on my pillow. I stuck my hands in things better left unidentified, and my friend, in garbage, ignorance is the only thing keeping you sane. After my first month, when I was one refuse load away from quitting, I found this stone, winking up at me like a talisman. For seven years I shoveled trash, saving up for college. And let me tell you, on the bright, shiny day I graduated from Harvard, this little stone was tucked under my mortarboard. It was my lucky charm. You gotta see the big picture, Mort. It's not where you start, it's where you end up."

Mort's unibrow furrowed deeper into his forehead. "I don't know, Ian. I can't type."

Ian was used to the objections and nodded sympathetically. "Yes, you can, Mort. You can do anything you want. Go in there. Make yourself indispensable. You'll be fine, wait and see. Within a year—tops—you'll be back in finance where you belong."

It took a little more convincing, but eventually Mort left—almost satisfied. Ian picked up his polished rock and put it in the drawer. Wasn't going to need any props tonight. Tonight was all about the shimmer and shine.

When five o'clock rolled around, he watched as the civil servants left before pulling out his suit and studying it with a critical eye. The lapels didn't have quite the spiffy stiffness that Wall Street required. Some wayward lint had wormed its way under the cuffs, and even an untutored nose could detect the faint aroma of mothballs. Okay, lots of work to be done here.

For the next thirty minutes, Ian toiled away at mothball-scent-removal. Using a combination of high-dollar cologne, an emergency container of Febreze and a twist of lemon, he finally transformed mothballs into something resembling the elusive, yet highly potent, scent of success.

When the cuffs were straight, the collar was angled exactly

right and the shoes were shined, Ian admired the finished product in the men's room mirror. This was the Ian Cumberland of yesteryear, maybe a little skinnier. His chin rose, his smile got slightly harder and his eyes sparkled with that familiar devil-may-care glint. Yeah, that was it. *Absolutely perfect.*

Watch out, world.

Ian Cumberland was back.

THE RESTAURANT WAS IN the financial district, on the thirty-second floor of the Liberty Towers. The view was spectacular—the lights from the tankers on the Hudson, the skyscrapers across the way, the Statue of Liberty in the New York Harbor—but it was nothing compared to her.

She was standing by the window, waiting, and his breath caught, held.

He'd never seen a woman whose face was so exquisitely formed. Would it always be like that? Did the curators at the Louvre ever stop gawking at the Mona Lisa?

Up to now, Ian had always made fun of the pretentious types who had season tickets to the symphony, idling their time in pursuit of cultural beauty. He never quite "got" that. Growing up in Scranton warped a man's artistic perspective. But this woman's perfection stopped his heart.

She turned, smiled, and he wiped the goofy gobsmackery off his face before she saw. Tonight he was the investment banker, a confident man who never caught being gobsmacked at all.

"Ian Cumberland, at your service for the rest of your life." He meant it as a joke, but his voice sounded serious. Serious and gobsmacked. He tried to get the devil-may-care look back. Failed.

"Rose," she answered. "Rose Hildebrande." Her smile was shy, blushing, and he thought Rose was the exact perfect name.

He took her elbow, twirled her, admiring the flair of her little black dress, the way it crossed over the straining perfection of her breasts, the way it set off the long line of her legs. Sexy, simple. *Hot as hell.*

"You know, all the guys in there are going to want to kill me."

Her cheeks flushed, her lashes lowered. "Sorry," she told him, a bit of hesitation in her voice.

And now he'd scared her. *Dude, get on your game.*

"No, I'm the one with the apologies. You look lovely," he told her, leading her inside, seeing the eyes follow them, follow her. *Yeah, eat it up, New York. Tonight, forever, she's mine.*

The evening had been meticulously planned, perfectly arranged, each step designed to turn her glorious head. Ian figured that tonight he had one shot to seal the deal. One shot for him to recover his prelayoff charm; it could be done.

The maître d' greeted him by name, leading him to the designated table, the prime spot at the apex of the windows, where all of New York awaited her pleasure. She looked at the table, stared up at the vent and then—so delicately that only a man attuned to her every smallest movement would notice—shivered.

"Is there a problem?" he asked, praying to God there was no problem; he'd given the maître d' an extra C-note for that table, and he knew the man wouldn't give it back.

"No," she answered, but there was a tiny quiver in her voice.

"If you want to sit somewhere else, honestly, it's no big. You get cold?"

Her soft blue eyes filled with anxiety. "I'm sorry to be such a pain. My internal thermostat is crazy. I'm hot, then cold. Do you mind?"

"Of course not," he said, and then gave the ever-efficient maître d' a commanding nod. "What else do you have?"

"A small table in the back, sir," he responded, a stodgy whiff of England in his accent. "By the kitchen. Unless you'd like to wait at the bar."

"I don't mind the kitchen," she told him, then pitched her voice low. "It will probably be warmer anyway."

"Tonight, whatever you want," answered Ian gallantly.

After they were seated, she balanced her chin on her palm, eyes wide and liquid. She had ridiculously long lashes, shuttering against the golden sheen of her cheeks. "I'm the world's biggest idiot."

"Nonsense," he answered, because he would fight her for that title. Probably win.

"So, Ian. Do you come here often? It's gorgeous. I love all the flowers." She sniffed the heavy perfume of the nearby vase of lilies, her glorious breasts filling, creamy skin beckoning to him.

Ian leaned close, ignoring the flowers, his hungry gaze following the line of silken skin, his fingers itching to touch. She noticed, and her mouth twitched with humor. Charmed, Ian shrugged, just as any good investment banker would. "Busted. Sorry. I'm not usually such a carnal-vore. Actually, really, I usually am, and it's been a long…" *Shut up, Ian.* Quickly he changed the subject. "My building's around the corner," he explained, forcibly removing his eyes from her chest. "We take a lot of clients here."

"Clients? What sort of clients?" she asked innocently, leading him into the very subject he really should avoid. But why should he be so determined to avoid it? If he was truly a courageous man, he would be honest. Let her evaluate him on his own merits, charm and roguish good looks, rather than his bank account.

Ian hesitated for only a second. "I'm an investment banker," he lied, opting not to be evaluated on his own merits, charm and roguish good looks. Immediately he glanced around, waiting for lightning to strike. None did. Ian smiled, relieved.

"Still on your feet, I see. No pesky recession to strike you down?" There was respect in her eyes, and Ian knew he'd answered correctly. He loved that flare in a woman's face, more powerful than a beknighting sword to the shoulder, more satisfactory than when the tellers at the bank had greeted him by name. He exhaled, his chest swelling with pride, completely undeserved.

"I survived, but it's been tough. A total bloodbath, but they like me. I do a good job for the firm. What about you?" he asked, getting the subject away from him. He didn't want to talk about his prelayoff job; he didn't want to talk about his postlayoff life. That pretty much limited the conversation to her, which was fine with him; he wanted to know everything about her, every secret, every dream…every inch underneath her dress.

"I'm a personal assistant. Not as glamorous as you."

"Still, I bet it's a cool job."

"Someday I'm going to do more."

"Like what?" he asked, reading the uncertainty in her face. He saw it all the time in his world. People adrift, not sure which way to move, frozen into doing nothing.

She shrugged, a small lift to an elegant shoulder. "I'm not sure. Nothing feels right. How did you know that banking was for you?"

"I've wanted to be in banking for…pretty much forever. Dad didn't make much money, and I wanted more. Greedy, I guess."

"I call that ambition."

"See, this is why I like you. With spin like that, you should consider a career in advertising." Automatically his brain shifted to job-finding mode—there was an agency in Park Slope, small, boutique and… *Stop it, Ian.*

Rose glanced toward the doorway where a waiter appeared carrying a large porcelain vase of two dozen perfect white roses. Handpicked by Ian only two hours before. Every woman's eye was drawn to the bouquet, longing to be the one, and Ian's smile got a little more cocky. The man started toward the window.

Walked closer to the table by the window.

Walked even closer to the table by the window.

Finally, with a continental bow, the waiter presented the two dozen perfect white roses to the elderly woman seated at what used to be Ian's table. Her husband, a white-haired man with silver glasses—and most likely, a fat bank account—beamed, as if he'd given her the world. The wife blushed. Ian seethed. Quietly, unobtrusively, so no one would notice.

"Is something wrong?" asked Rose.

Ian blanked his face. "No. He looks like a VP that I once worked with. Really didn't like him. Always took credit for the slog he didn't do. You know the type—they haunt every office of every industry in America."

"Of course," she said, but she was watching the couple, her heart in her eyes. "It's fascinating. He still orders her flowers. Why?"

"Maybe there's no reason." Not every gift needed an occasion; sometimes it was just because.

"I don't think so. There's always a reason, even if they don't realize there's a reason. People don't give without expecting in return."

"Wow, beautiful and cynical, too." He'd assumed that men paid homage to her, built temples and monuments, wrote odes and symphonies. But contrary to her hard words, her gaze was firmly glued to the sight of those white roses and the contented smile on the other woman's face.

So it was flowers that were her raison d'être? One more piece of data to put in the Rose file. *Bring flowers for no apparent reason.*

Eventually she looked away, her eyes more firmly entrenched in the here and now. "In the long run, pretty isn't the big whoop that everyone thinks it is. There are levels in the world. Pretty will get you invitations, five dollars off on your laundry and maybe a free pass on a parking ticket, but that's as far as it goes. But the man at the top, the one who sits fifty stories above the masses, that's the pinnacle. He lives life on his terms, and no one tells him what to do."

Ian felt a cold knot in his gut, and wondered if she had guessed at his sorry truth. "You're talking about money, aren't you?"

She nodded once. "Sure. Money, power, control."

Something flashed in her face—pain? And then the moment was gone, the shutters in place. The impassive Mona Lisa was back and the light began to dawn. This wasn't about him. This was about her. "He did a number on you, huh?"

"Who?" she asked sharply.

"I have no idea."

Immediately the wistful dreams reappeared like magic. "I'm not sure what's bothering me tonight."

"Don't want to talk about it? I'm a good listener, and I know absolutely nothing about you."

"Not much to say. Personal assistant. Moved from nowhere to New York. I manage."

With a pile of men trailing after her with their tongues hanging out. Like Ian. "So what happened with your date?"

She didn't pretend she didn't understand or play coy, and he admired her for that. He liked that. She might sell herself short on brains, but she could read people well. Including him. Politely he dabbed at his mouth, in case his tongue was hanging out, as well.

"His name is Remy. It was our fourth date. He's very nice. He's perfect."

"How perfect?" asked Ian, now surreptitiously checking for hidden cameras, in case this was reality TV at its worst.

"He's a heart surgeon. Pediatric. Saving small children is a line on his resume. Good-looking. Family money."

"Cheats on his taxes?"

Sadly she shook her head.

"Undisclosed porn addiction."

Rose looked at him and laughed. "I don't think so."

"Wow. I don't see anything wrong there."

"I know," she told him unhappily.

"Rose? Why are you here?"

"Do you believe in it?" she asked him, her face serious and nervous.

"What's 'it'?"

"Fate."

He could invent something really romantic and magical, something to make her sigh, but she'd probably heard all that before. Instead Ian went with the unremarkable truth. "In the past, I didn't. I mean, I wanted to, but it never went my way, so it was a lot better for my mental health to think it wasn't out there."

"Why not?"

There were a lot of ways to answer that question. Ian chose the least incriminating. "There was this kid in third grade, Kevin Trevaskis, and his parents were a total pain because every year he stayed up waiting for Santa Claus and he never got any presents. But he still believed in this great concept of goodness, even though nothing ever came his way, either. I always felt sorry for that kid. At least, if your parents perpetuate the Santa Claus myth, you have those formative years to hang your hat on, but Kevin didn't even have that. It was sad."

"You didn't tell him the truth?"

Now that he thought about it, it was becoming completely obvious that Ian had issues with truth, even as a young child. Yet now was not the time to dwell on past—and possibly present—indiscretions.

"Who am I to take away his hope? And before New Year's I'd been thinking about Kevin, thinking maybe he had it right. What if we were the ones who had it all wrong? I went down to Times Square, drinking the enchanting elixir, because for one day, for one second in time, I wanted to believe in that hope, too. I wondered if I'd been missing out. Then I saw you, and I knew. Kevin *was* right."

Rose turned a little pale, her eyes wide. Definitely fear.

"Why is that a bad thing?" he asked, not wanting to be insulted, but worried that once again, this was not going to end well, especially in light of Dr. Pediatric Perfection.

"Destiny implies an absence of choice. It means that my decisions, my choices, my words don't matter. Somebody somewhere is playing chess, and I'm the pawn."

Relieved, Ian exhaled slowly. "You don't have strings. You just follow the open doors and see if you like where it leads."

"Doors aren't good. Doors can be shut."

"Doors can be opened."

"But you're an idealist," she pointed out. He'd never thought of himself as an idealist before, and she was wrong, but he liked that she saw him that way.

"So you don't think this…is fate?"

"I've thought a lot about it since that night. I'm not a big romantic. But you make me want to believe in something nice."

When he looked at her, he could see the ghost of Kevin Trevaskis. Hope and fear battling it out. Ian's feelings were much more defined. Rose made him believe in a better road ahead, in soul mates bound by a single kiss—and then, of course, getting her naked, not specifically in that order. Prudently, Ian shook off the lust and then deflected the conversation to her.

"How come you've never married?" He couldn't wrap his head around the fact that she'd stayed single, sexy and beautiful for this long.

Again she fiddled with the silverware, hesitating. Eventually she decided to trust him. Rose looked up, her eyes not so hard, now almost wistful. "I keep thinking that something better is out there. Like I'm missing out. You ever run up to the crosstown bus stop just as the driver's pulling away, and you know that was your bus, but you can't see the number, so you stand there for a minute, not sure if you need to start walking. That's the way I feel about the men in my life. That I've just missed the bus, but I don't know if I should start walking or wait for the next bus."

Self-consciously, she pushed at her hair, the long strands falling, covering her eyes. Hiding.

Ian didn't say much, watched, wondered, until the waiter appeared at their table in all his tuxedoed splendor and presented the wine list to Ian. "Would you care for wine, Mr. Lawrence?"

"It's Cumberland, not Lawrence, and I've already—" Ian stopped and watched the wine steward moving toward the table by the window. His table. His wine. Champagne, actually. Dom Pérignon, four hundred a pop. Ian managed a weak smile for the waiter. "Give me a minute to decide," he said. The waiter left silently, efficiently, most likely having a really good night, unlike Ian.

Frustrated, he gazed up at the magnificently painted ceiling where all the angels were watching, pointing, laughing.

He should have told Rose the truth.

"Quite an evening they're having."

Ian looked over at the other table, where the older woman sat laughing then leaned over to plant a shaky kiss on her husband's lips. Ian heaved a regretful sigh. "Yeah."

Resigned to his fate, he gestured, and the waiter reappeared. "You've decided, sir?"

"I'll have what they're having."

6

IT WAS SOMEWHERE BETWEEN dinner and dessert that Rose found herself getting drawn into the land of Prince Charmings and magic wands. She'd never seen a real magic wand, only a twelve-inch ruler that hurt like hell on her knuckles. The memory was always there, ground into her marrow, but tonight, it didn't make her sit up straighter. When the waiter clattered the silver lid, she didn't jump in her seat.

It was Ian. He had such a nice face. The way his eyes watched the world with a light all his own, not afraid of what he would see. Hope, that's what he'd said, and when she looked into those sparkling eyes, she wanted to see it, too.

There was something else in his expression, something more basic that made her nerves tingle and stir. He wanted her. Sometimes it flared in his face, the way his gaze skimmed over her, her mouth, her breasts. But there were no innuendos, no sly remarks, no expectation that Rose would play the game. It was desire without strings, and she could feel an answering prickle on her skin. The longer she was with him, the more she relaxed, the more her body opened up. Tingled. *Desired?*

She was forgetting her training, forgetting her lines.

When he quietly listened to her rant for over ten minutes about the cost of living in the city, there was a staggering moment when she imagined his hands cupping her shoulders, sliding the dress down her skin. When she sent back the chocolate torte because they'd forgotten to take off the raspberry sauce—an extra one hundred and twenty calories—Ian smiled indulgently, and Rose felt a hard pulse between her thighs. Her face flushed, and she crossed her legs tightly.

She tried to summon an enthralled, sophisticated air, wide-eyed, pursed mouth and a fawning hand to his shoulder, but all she was managing was inching her chair toward him, absorbing his scent, and a trampy hand to her own cleavage. When she realized what she was doing, she sat up straight, her back glued to the chair.

Yet the exquisite allure remained. Over coffee, she slipped off her shoes. Like a child hypnotized in a toy store, her impudent foot glided over the polished mahogany floor, flirting closer to his chair.

Her mother's voice echoed in her brain. A woman who made fast moves was a slut and a whore. Yet closer and closer her foot moved. Nearly there, a toe's breadth away, when a shadow fell over the table.

"Ian? Ian Cumberland?"

Shocked, *shocked,* Rose pulled her foot home and into her chair, curling it up under her in case the appendage decided to roam again.

The man was alone. Mid-thirties. A high-dollar business type with a narrow-lapelled suit that looked custom, no tie, and sharp blue eyes that oozed over her, assessed her, appraised her. His wolfish smirk said that she passed.

Ian stood, they clasped hands, one firm shake to test who would flinch first.

"I was wondering about you the other day." The man's smile blasted Rose with his well-practiced charm. "I can see you're doing fine."

"Rose, this is Michael O'Leary, aptly named for his voracious appreciation of the female sex."

"You were always jealous." Michael covered his heart. "But now I think I'm the jealous one. Rose. *Rose.* You should leave this loser."

Her smile was open yet satisfied, a slow, subtle curl to the mouth, exposing a flash of dimple on her right side. "I'm happy where I am." *Happy.* She rolled the word in her mind, enjoyed it.

"Where did you land?" Michael asked Ian, and Ian grinned, that carefree smile that so impressed her. He didn't care what people thought, merely content to be who he was.

"I'm at Caldecott Capital. You've probably never heard of them. European. Small. Very—" he waggled his fingers "—private."

"Congratulations. I knew you'd do fine. We'll have to do

lunch. Call me." He gave Rose a last, slow once-over. "So fine. If he mistreats you, you call me, too."

As he walked away, he flipped his card on the table with the casual confidence of a man used to having women call. Rose took his card, and once the cutthroat Michael O'Leary was out of sight, she tore it into little pieces.

"He's not that awful," defended Ian, which only made Rose like Ian more, because he wasn't critical or judgmental. He accepted everyone—flaws and all.

"Maybe he's not that awful, but that much ego in one room makes it hard to breathe. You're different. You've done so well, but you don't have to throw it around." It was a standard compliment, usually offered to men who needed to feel humble in their quest for billions. This time, it was sincere.

Instead of appreciating the compliment, Ian only seemed to grow more uncomfortable. "I don't deserve that," he said, the true definition of humble, which only impressed her further. Even Sylvia was going to be impressed with Ian. Rose couldn't wait to introduce them. Finally, she'd found a possibility.

"I think you deserve it. You're the exception."

He winced, placed his napkin on the table. "Rose, I need to tell you something," Ian began, his voice serious.

She didn't like the regret in his eyes, didn't like not knowing what to expect. She liked to know what to expect. Always. Underneath the table, Rose slid her feet back into her shoes, not wanting to have this conversation barefoot. "What?" she asked, now fully prepared.

For a few eternal seconds, he fiddled with his napkin, folding it into neat, orderly triangles, an odd trick for a man who didn't appear to be neat and orderly. Then his eyes lifted, met hers squarely. "I'm not an investment banker. To be fair, at one time I was, about ten months ago. I lost my job. But I got a new one. I'm an employment counselor. I find people work. It's not pediatric surgery, it's not well-paying, though the city benefits are nice. I have trouble reconciling my personal belief that some people are not meant to work with our mission statement of 'we find jobs for all.' But that's personal, and not germane to the fact that I lied to you. I'm not rolling in the dough. I used to, albeit not necessarily roll, but maybe wash, or loofah, or something, but it was definitely better than now—although I'm not starving, either. I'm getting by fine. I have trouble admitting this, I'm not proud of my current profession—on a lot of days I don't even like it. But it's what I do, and you should know that. You should know the truth."

His gaze never wavered, never blinked, never backed down, not once.

Rose took a moment, slipping words on her tongue, words that she'd practiced over and over again. Something earnest, where she told him that she didn't tolerate dishonesty, which was a nicer way of saying financial struggles were not in her plan and hell would freeze first.

She'd seen hell, she reminded herself. She'd lived it. She wasn't going back. Yet none of those warnings moved her as much as the defensive vulnerability in his eyes, that defiant bravado that said: "Go ahead. Get it over with so that I can move on with my life."

Oh, God.

She'd never possessed that bravado. Not once.

All her carefully practiced words disappeared, and her cool, polite smile faded like an old memory.

"I live in the Bronx," she confessed in a voice so low he had to ask her to repeat it.

"A three-story walk-up that's two blocks from the waste disposal plant. I hate the Bronx. I told myself I should move to Jersey and be done with it, but I'm too much of a snob to live there, so I end up calling myself all sorts of stupid. Did you know there are three hundred and seventeen synonyms for stupid? Over twenty-five hundred if you count hyphenated words."

"I bet I could come up with more synonyms for poor." He was so rueful and so endearing, so tempting.

A smile cracked across her face as something cracked in her heart. "Poverty can be overcome. Stupid is forever."

"I like you, Rose Hildebrande."

Of all the compliments that Rose had received in her lifetime, this was the first that made her grin—an honest, true grin created from happiness, not a wildly pleased facial gesture designed to foster the male ego.

"I like you, too, Ian Cumberland," she answered, and she stared into his eyes and breathing began anew. The night began anew, no expectations, no performances.

Slowly she talked, about different things. He wanted her opinion on which *Star Wars* movie was the best and they argued—*argued*—over the original versus *The Empire Strikes Back*. Rose had never argued in her life. It had been over twenty years since the word *no* had passed her lips.

Over the second cup of coffee, he wanted to know the best way to fix the world, and Rose, who had decisive, yet carefully closeted opinions on the world economy, found herself comparing and contrasting the philosophy of world aid against fostering economic independence. She was firmly on the side of independence, no shocker there, but Ian was a remarkably bulletproof marshmallow, telling her that fishermen couldn't fish unless somebody bought the pole.

By the third cup of coffee, she was captivated by the expressions on his face. Surprise, horror, shock, desire, everything shown through his eyes. The horror made her laugh, the surprise made her goggle, and the desire made her…hot.

A lurid image flared in her mind, that indulgent smile flashing in the dark, a tangle of bare limbs, those lean, extra-attentive hands tracing over the full curves of her breasts, pressing between her thighs. Inch by wayward inch, her hips moved, curled upward in the chair, like a flower seeking the sun.

Pleasure beckoned once again. Tempting her to see whether this bubbling magic truly existed. If her virginity was the price she paid, so be it. Her parents were out of her life. Rose was in control.

Tonight she wanted to invite him to her secret place. Just one night, that was all. For one night, she wanted to believe in so much. The goodness of Santa Claus, the ideal of true happiness, and most importantly of all, in giving herself up to fate.

The wispy voice in her head bothered her, with its weakness and excuses. Sun Tzu would not approve. But wouldn't this be the ultimate test?

The ancient Chinese general had said that a ruler must know if his army can obey an order to advance or retreat. If he didn't, misfortune would fall and the battle was lost. Therefore, if Rose didn't know if her mind could outwill her own body—if her own orders would be obeyed—then wasn't she setting herself up for failure?

Wasn't she *required* to find out?

Her foot slid across the floor, finding Ian's ankle, causing him to jump with a start. That single jump, natural and completely without guile, cemented her decision.

Tonight was a test, nothing more. Tomorrow morning she would walk away, completely in control.

IAN KEPT WAITING FOR the other shoe to drop. For the fickle finger of fortune to deliver another debilitating blow, but by they time they were at his apartment, the only shoe that dropped was hers. Along with the other one. Along with the dress, along with the bra, along with the stockings, along with the black silk panties.

Ian froze, fully clothed, one of his shoes clutched helplessly in his hand. Undressing further would require movement. Mental capacity. Right now, he was incapable of both.

The dropping of a shoe had never been such a brain-sucking event.

Rose stood before him, a pocket-size goddess, nude skin glistening in the night-lights of New York. He reached out to touch her, fully convinced that she couldn't be real, and his hand fell to his side, because he didn't want to know. He wanted to stay in the dream. But she took hold of his fingertips, skimmed them over a full breast, a taut nipple. His lungs refused to breathe.

"Will you kiss me?" Her voice shook on the words, and underneath his hand, he felt her heart beat. Too strong for a dream.

Still playing in this happy dream, he inched closer, until their bodies were a whisper apart. His hand slid upward, to cup her neck. There he found soft skin that was too warm for a dream. His head lowered, still terrified that he was going to wake up, but then their lips met and lingered.

Rose breathed against his mouth. A tiny sigh that was too audible for a dream. Not quite so terrified, Ian shifted closer still, burying his hand in the perfumed silk of her hair, the scent of honeysuckle following in its wake.

Please God, do not let me wake up. This is too good. Too real.

Slowly, warily, he kissed her, as if his future depended on this one moment, this one meeting of lips. Her warm breath stirred his senses, echoed by the soft rise and fall of her breasts. Naked breasts burned into his skin.

Not a dream. Not a dream. Not a dream.

Very real fingers slid up his chest, clenched his shoulder. Then the distance between them was gone, Ian was gone. The kiss turned, fast and deep.

Desperately he touched her, explored her, memorized her. A wise god would not grant a moment like this to a desolate man. With each pleasured sound she made, his hopes soared even higher. *Not a dream.* His mouth stayed on hers, sampling, feasting, savoring, not letting up for a second. Now that he had tasted her, now that he had tasted this happiness, nobody was taking it away.

He laughed softly when she tugged frantically at the buttons on his shirt, his fly. It was an odd dance—lips fused, his clothes falling ungracefully, all accompanied by a staggering shuffle toward the bed. In the end, they only made it as far as the couch before Ian fell on her. An ungainly flop. Thankfully, Rose— perfect Rose—giggled, finding a sensitive spot below his ear, above his ear—*hell, yeah*—in his ear. Every place this woman touched, his skin heated then burned. Already his cock was pulsing, prodding, arrowing between her thighs, but there were other things to be done first. There would be time. By now he had persuaded himself that he had all the time in the world.

Reverently his palm shaped her breast, testing the full curve, the plump weight of it. One pink nipple rose under his finger- tips, and he took the peak deep in his mouth, his tongue abrading the flesh. Her body shifted underneath him, her hips arching up to his, and suddenly he was the most powerful man alive. Oh, hell, yeah.

Her hands pulled at his hair, then harder, and pain had never felt so damned good.

Wanting more, his finger slid between her legs, between her lips, the passage warm, moist, heaven. Her muscles tightened, clenching, and he thrust his finger again, her body beneath him. His cock tightened, pulled, but he wanted to please her; he needed to wait. Ian bent his head, finding her mouth, settling in, matching the rhythm of his hand.

When he broke the kiss, he heard the sound low in her throat. One, single sultry moan that broke through the night. A sound that made up for an entire year of heartbreak.

"I can't think," she whispered. "Can't…think."

For Ian, that was it. No more time. His hand located the condom, sheathed, and with one ragged thrust, he was inside her.

Her eyes flared open, melted blue swimming with fear. *Fear?*

"Rose?" he whispered, because she still wasn't moving. "You've done this before, haven't you?"

"Yes," she told him, but her face looked unusually pale. A liar's shade of pale—or a virgin's.

"Oh, jeez. Uh, listen—" he started, but she stopped him with a kiss. It was no ordinary kiss; it was full-bodied, her mouth soft and welcoming, her arms locked around his neck and her nipples were conducting ten thousand volts against his chest.

Ian thrust once.

Rose arched her hips, pulling him deeper inside her, and Ian thrust again. Her face was buried in her shoulder, but he heard a small gasp of pleasure.

Ian stilled at the sound. The tiny sound that ripped through his heart. He wanted to stay here like this, waiting, hoping, praying that this…this very best second of his life would not end. That would be worse than ten thousand pink slips. Frankly, death would be easier. Gently he pushed the tawny silk of her hair away from her face. He needed to see her eyes. Needed to see the fear gone. Needed to know that she was okay.

She sighed, a long, shuddering nonending sigh, and then, with the strong grace a dancer would covet, her legs slid over his hips and locked around him like a vise. Her lashes fluttered up to reveal diamond-bright seduction, glinting brighter than gold.

Oh, thank you. Thank you, thank you, thank you.

At heart, Ian wasn't a man to let opportunity go to waste. This time, he tempered his motions. A slow, gentle glide rather than a sharper thrust, taking the chance to savor the magnificent details of making love to one Rose Hildebrande. Apparently, one Rose Hildebrande was an opportunist, as well. Her hips pushed upward then pivoted, causing all oxygen to leave his brain. He gasped. Pleasure, tremors of pleasure, remained.

"You can't move like that. I will die. You don't know how good this feels. If you move like that—"

She did it again.

Ian rose up on his elbows, glaring, as much as a man could glare in midcoitus. There was something wrong here. He was supposed to be gentle because she was supposed to be a virginal lamb. "You did that on purpose," he accused, not completely upset.

Proudly Rose beamed at him, more foxlike than lamb. "I did."

"Why?"

"If you attack when your opponent least expects it, he is most vulnerable. And," she added slyly, "he likes it better."

"Did you read that in *Cosmo?*"

"The Art of War."

He laughed at her joke, and swept a hand down the curve of her spine.

"Let's forget a moment about what you think I like better. Honey, this one's for you. What do you want?"

Nervously she licked her lips. "Anything?"

There were few words that energized a man's sexual imagination like the word *anything*. But Rose was a virgin, he reminded himself. Inexperienced in the carnal arts. To her, *anything* implied a back massage, or a kiss on the neck, or maybe, if he was lucky, a little muff-diving would be involved.

"Anything," he assured her.

"I want to be in charge."

In charge? Ian rose up on his arms and studied the Cinderella-blue eyes, the cupid's-bow mouth—his gaze slipped lower— and those *Penthouse* breasts. "How in charge?"

She hesitated, her teeth worrying her lower lip, and Ian's

mind raced ahead to handcuffs and *Penthouse* breasts in black leather. Holy shit. Rose was no lamb. He was the lamb.

"Go ahead," he urged, praying no pain was involved.

"I want to be on top," she whispered, and he breathed a sigh of relief.

Gently he touched his mouth to hers. "I have been thoughtless, pig-brained and, for lack of a better word, a total nudge for not noticing sooner. If you want—no, if you *need*—to sit on top of me, showing no sexual mercy at all, it would be selfish of me to refuse."

Rose tilted her head, mulling the possibilities. "I would like that, I think." Her eyes held an audacious glint that might have scared a lesser man. Ian found himself…curious.

Curious he might be, but he was now prudent, as well. He took her hand and led her to the larger confines of his bed. "It will be safer here," he said, before pulling her down on top of him, deciding that being the sacrificial lamb had a lot of perks he'd never realized before.

"I get to be in charge?" she whispered, her voice husky with possibility.

Heroically, Ian restrained himself from jumping her. "Whatever you want. My body is a mere tool to be used and abused."

All humor died when Rose settled herself over his thigh, seeming intent on both pleasure and torture, all at the same time. Her sex brushed close to his cock, sliding, riding, but not quite there. Completely intentional. Completely shameless. His body bucked, but she stilled him with a surprisingly firm touch. Then, with bold eyes, her hands stole over her breasts, teasing her nipples to hard peaks, and against his thigh he could feel her wet, wetter… *Oh…*

His cock jumped, searching for that moist heat, but she wasn't done. Her lips feathered his chest, her teeth scraping with exquisite purpose over his nipples.

"Rose…honey…sweetheart…" His voice strained, and she froze. She looked at him with wide, innocent eyes, then slowly, her mouth curved into a smile, the eyes no longer innocent. Her body shifted, rose. Then, inch by heated inch, she lowered herself, filling her, surrounding him. Killing him.

She watched him, aware, curious, as gently she began to move. Slow, languid strokes, her body gliding over his, up and down. Her fingers teased his chest, dancing, caressing, and she leaned down, taking his mouth in a long, open-mouthed kiss. He reached for her, craving more, but she pulled away.

Okay.

"You want?" she taunted, her hands settling on her breasts, and her body arched, hips riding him faster now.

I want.

Quickly she moved, and his hips pistoned up and down, matching her rhythm, until he was at the point of breaking, but he didn't touch her. No, Rose needed this; he would not deny her. Her gaze locked with his, sapphire-bright, until he was drowning in the blue of her eyes. His body pulled, his balls tight. Her smile was the devil. Her muscles clenched him, and she stopped. He thought she was going to come, but then the lashes fluttered open again, and there was something driving her. Something that he couldn't understand. Helpless, he caught her hips in his hand and thrust inside her, higher and higher. Rose gasped, her body clamping down on his cock, and he needed one…more…

He was ready to move, ready to drive in there one last time, but then she pushed down on him, until he was buried deep, too deep. Her body froze, tensed, and before his eyes, she shattered.

Too much. Too much.

His cock pulsed once before his body shuddered, finding its own release. She collapsed on him, her body slick, her breathing shallow. Carefully he stroked the length of her spine, wondering what she kept locked up inside her—and wanting to know. He wanted to know everything about her.

Ian lifted his weak head and pressed a kiss to the shoulder of a Valkyrie. "Now I have truly lived. Jessica Alba? She's dead to me."

Against his chest, he felt her mouth curve up in smile. "Jessica Alba?"

"I was young. Impressionable. A gullible fool." He shifted their positions, liking the way her body curved into his. Fate. "Rose? This was your first time?"

"You weren't supposed to know. I screwed up."

"No," he said, stroking her hair. "You were perfect. Better than perfect, actually. Quite…inventive at the end. So, how did you know all that?"

She stirred, tilting her head, and Ian found himself distracted by the erotic shelf where her shoulder met her neck. Rose slid upward on him, arousing him even more.

"Know what?" she asked.

"The way you were, um, touching yourself. You didn't read that in *The Art of War,* did you?"

"Not *The Art of War. Cosmo.*"

Then her mouth took his. The kiss started slow, but not for long. Her tongue glided between his lips, in and out, in a movement lovingly copied by her hand on his cock. But now Ian was clued into her tricks and he tumbled her beneath him. "You're mine, my pretty, all mine."

And for the next hour, while the city of New York burned and beamed, Ian poured himself into Rose, heart and soul. At least for tonight, he was king of the world and she would be his queen.

ROSE AWOKE TO THE unfamiliar sensation of an unfamiliar bed, an unfamiliar ceiling. Through the window she would see the lights of New York, not the diffuse lights of the Bronx. She could feel the warm heat of his body calling to her. Just like last night.

Last night.

He lay on the bed, his hair tousled with sleep, his hands outstretched, reaching for something that he'd never have. Ian Cumberland was a beautiful man in sleep, and last night had been a shock. She'd never known that her knees could buckle under the lightest touch of a hand. That her heart could weaken with the taste of a kiss. That her mind could go thoughtless from the pleasure of a man. His heart had been so strong, pumping wildly against her own.

Stronger than her own.

Rose had told herself that this was a test of strength and will. One night, and then she'd be able to walk away.

If she was as strong as she told herself she was, all she had to do was leave now and not look back. If she wanted to be in control of her life, her destiny, all she had to do was walk away. She wasn't that little girl who was forced to obey. She wasn't that young teenager in the military-style barracks eating peas off a green plastic plate. No, Rose Hildebrande had dreams.

Quietly she pulled on her clothes, tried to smooth her hair. Could she make it to the bathroom without waking him? Of course, Rose was an expert sneak, silent as a shadow.

When she eased the bathroom door closed, a small night-light clicked on, and Rose blinked at the reality she had created.

The mirror reflected so many things, bad things, and Rose felt her hands tighten before she forced them to relax. Who was that person staring back at her? The hair was in tangles, her makeup smudged, and the eyes were too vulnerable. Even in the feeble light, the faded bruises of her soul were too exposed. Still, she made herself look, made herself study the imperfections that were there, planning how to fix them. Battles were not won by making mistakes, only by eliminating them. Eventually the weakness dimmed from her eyes, resolve in its place. Then she began to work in earnest.

In less than ten minutes, her makeup was repaired to a flawless pale gold and her clothes were neatly in order. But she needed to escape.

Last night she'd forgotten everything, woozy with the force of his smile, weak with his kiss. It wasn't a mistake she would repeat. Her eyes searched in the mirror, her chin lifted. No one was better at being a stone than Rose. She knew what she had to do.

Break the woks, sink the boats, burn the bridge. Every army in every language had some equivalent of the actions that would make retreat impossible. All Rose had to do was light the match.

She reached into her trusty makeup bag and brought out True Love Shimmer, a subtle pink lipstick with flashes of gold. Efficiently she scrawled out the words *Please don't call* on his mirror.

The lure of Ian Cumberland was strong, but she'd worked too

hard to rebuild herself, and she wouldn't be broken down again. She liked this Rose Hildebrande. The strong one that made her own way. He would find someone new; the world was full of women who didn't mind being torn apart.

But Rose knew better.

7

IAN WOKE SLOWLY, COUNTING the beeps of the sanitation trucks outside. Normally it annoyed him. Today he didn't mind. Unless of course, last night had been a dream. Happily, the scent of honeysuckle hung heavy in the air. The glorious musk of sex wafted from the sheets. Ian reached out one arm, searching, finding…

Searching…

Finding…

Searching, searching, searching…

He threw the duvet aside and looked.

Rose was gone. Ian rubbed his eyes because he was sure that he hadn't dreamed last night. The dinner, the dessert, the quiet pillow talk, and yes, hallelujah, the sex. A man did not hallucinate wild, unrestrained sex like that. Well, some men might, but not Ian. Postlayoff, he wasn't that vain. To be truthful, last night exceeded prelayoff fantasies, as well. It had been…whoa. Now he was making himself dizzy again.

Quickly he sat. "Rose?" he called, but by now he knew she wasn't there. Her essence was gone from the room. That quiet glow that followed around her like a moonstruck shadow. Silence remained, except for his lonely sigh.

One more time, this time with feeling.

Gathering all his energy, Ian stood up, stretched and stared at his bed—the rumpled covers, the shallow dent where she had slept. He should have the whole thing bronzed and framed above the mantel, cherishing the accomplishment, the very pinnacle of his happiness. But then people would think he was shallow. Rose would think he was desperate. There was truth in that, but he could hide the desperation from her. After all, he'd already told her about his job situation. And still, she'd stayed. And still she'd made love to him.

No, the crazy-talk needed to stop. Ian had to quit reliving last night and get on with today. After he got to work, then he would call her. He was practicing what he would say, grabbing a towel for the shower, when he stopped, frozen in the doorway to the bathroom. There he saw the words. *Her words.*

Ian blinked twice, because he knew he was reading them wrong, the letters scrabbled up in a mishmash that had to be wrong.

His hand went to the sink, held there.

Please don't call.

The room grew so quiet, so insanely quiet, three words sing-songing round and round in his head.

Briskly he wiped at the mirror, keeping his mind carefully blank, but the lipstick only smeared, leaving his hand stained with pink. Ian pressed at the glass harder, but Rose·Hildebrande must use the world's most indelible lipstick, because the words wouldn't go away. A towel didn't work. Glass cleaner didn't work. Finally he shoved his fist into the glass.

Much better.

Blood streaked over his knuckles, down his fingers and into the sink. Finally the pain started to settle in, his hand, his heart, the hole in his gut. Ian hadn't expected to be sucker punched again. But here he was, his hand wrapped in a towel and one fucked-up mirror. But at least he didn't have to look at those words anymore.

After a long, cold shower, Ian got dressed and bandaged an old T-shirt around his hand. The buzzer sounded, and his first thought—his first pathetic thought—was that Rose had changed her mind. That she'd somehow realized the utter betrayal of her actions and come back, begging forgiveness.

He ran, *ran,* to the button next to the wall and jabbed it twice before pain took over and he realized that he'd have to stop using his right hand for a while. "What?"

"It's Phoebe. Buzz me up."

Two minutes later she was upstairs, tossing off her coat,

wiping the sleet from her shoulders and the fog from her glasses. Then she scanned the room, for what, he didn't know. "Is she here?" she whispered, dramatically loud.

"No one's here, Phoebe."

She noticed the bloodstained shirt on his hand. "Your hand is bleeding. Getting crazy with the Ginsu knives again?"

"Yeah. Why did you come?"

"Are you kidding? I have to get the dish on last night. Was it awesome?"

A bell sounded in his head, louder than the pounding pulse in his forehead, harsher than the throbbing from his hand. "I don't know what you're talking about."

"Don't get all innocent and noncomprehending here. Hello, Mystery Date?"

"Can we not talk about this?" Ian glared. Phoebe didn't get it and plopped on the couch instead, the same stuffed leather couch where he'd had Rose underneath him….

Honestly, Ian had to work on his glare.

She leaned forward, her eyes curious, but Ian didn't want company. Not even Phoebe.

"Go away. I can't do this right now."

But at least she finally got it. "I'm sorry," she said. "I don't understand. You were my great white hope for happy endings, 'cause I knew I wasn't getting any." Her eyes turned sad, and she looked at his hand. "Do you have a bandage or something? You need clotting here. Serious clotting." Gingerly she unwrapped the cloth, saw the scarlet streaks of blood and pulled a darker face. "Ian. What the hell? Come on." She grabbed him by the arm and led him into the bathroom, not saying much until she saw the mirror and was hit with the full extent of Ian's idiocy. "Oh. Dude. We should go to a clinic."

He didn't like the pity in her eyes. Another time, he might have soaked it up, but today he felt stupid and raw. "Phoebe, it's not a big deal."

"It's a big deal," she insisted. "You put your hand through a mirror."

"Into, not through. The proper preposition is important. There's a Duane Reade around the corner. I'll buy a roll of gauze. I'll be fine. No clinic."

Phoebe blew out a breath, stared at him, stared at the mirror. Apparently she began to put two and two together. "Ian, what happened?" she asked gently.

His gaze cut toward the wall, and he shrugged. "It was an accident. As I said, not a big deal."

"No. Not the hand. What happened with Mystery Date?"

Yeah, good question. What the hell had happened? Ian called forth his cocky investment banker's smile. "Her name was Rose. No sparks. Nothing was there."

Her eyes narrowed, not quite calling him a liar, but he could see the suspicion. "After all that—the anxiety, the public kissing, the great moment of time when your lips met—and there were no sparks? I don't get it. Your face had sparks aplenty. I could have charged a lightbulb with your—your—" her hand gestured somewhere in his pelvic region "—that energy. Your feet did not touch the ground. You were sparky."

Another time he might have laughed, but right now, Ian didn't want to be sparky. He didn't want to rehash last night with Phoebe. He wanted to be numb and pain-free, and get on with the rest of his life. Obviously he needed to think up an even bigger lie. "She was really boring. Very little personality. I was shocked," he said flatly, adding a sad shake of his head for effect.

Phoebe cocked her head, but she seemed to go along with it. "Okay. That's your story, we'll stick with it." She tapped him on the shoulder. "You're better off without her. Men get so hinky around gorgeous women. Here's a test for you. If you knew that her personality had been deficient ahead of time, would you still have taken her to dinner?"

In a heartbeat, he thought, before he told his heart to shut up. "Not a chance."

"Speaking for average-looking women everywhere, my hopes are restored. You're a good man, Ian Cumberland."

And a total patsy for a great pair of tits and wistful blue eyes.

"See, everything works out in the end."

"Got that right," Ian told her, putting an extra shot of cheer in his voice. "Now, go to work. I'll talk to you at the game tonight. Wait— Why *are* you here? Just because you were curious? I mean, couldn't it have waited?"

Casually she shrugged. "Probably. I just needed to see a friend. And hey, I saw a friend." As she walked out the door, she waved. "Take care of the hand."

Ian's smile was full of bullshit, and if Phoebe had had a full load of caffeine, she would have noticed. But he was glad she wasn't fully aware. That was one inquisition he didn't want to have.

THE MORNING'S WEATHER WAS cold and miserable, much like Rose's general attitude toward life at the moment. She slid into her sturdy wool coat, pulled the wool cap over her ears and headed out into the sleeting rain. On the way to the station, she made the route down one block, over two and past Rudy and Thom's Paradise of Pets.

She stopped under the awning, out of the sleet, and huddled close. The puppies were out this morning, yipping and tumbling over each other, and she almost smiled. In the pen to the side, the big monster watched her carefully, but she didn't look at him, she fixed her eyes firmly on the cute and cuddly ones. Puppies that couldn't hurt a fly.

"You want to see one?"

The man stepped out from the door, a rough-looking gentleman with a large dragon tattoo on his arm, a flannel shirt that needed ironing and what she hoped was a tomato stain on his jeans. God, please don't let it be blood. Carefully, Rose kept her eyes off the tattoo.

"No. I just come to watch them."

"You like dogs? They need a home."

"I can't have dogs. Building regs," lied Rose.

The gentleman shrugged meaty shoulders. "You should move."

"Someday. You know how it is," she said, her gaze drawn back to the one puppy who was careening over another.

The man nodded once, scratching behind his ear, just like the fur ball in the window. "Yeah. I do."

"My boss is holding a benefit for the humane society," she said, because she didn't want him to think she was a dog-hater.

"Does he want to hold one for Rudy and Thom's, too?"

"It wouldn't have the same impact."

"You should have the dogs there."

"It's a dinner and auction," Rose explained, shuddering at the idea of dogs and food and crystal and pristine white tablecloths.

"Still, the dogs are the stars."

No, she thought to herself. The bachelors were the stars. Those little puppies were cute and fluffy, but they couldn't provide either security or shelter. Puppies were a decoration, much like her. "I'll think about it," she promised.

Her part said, all expectations met, she turned to go, but then stopped. Firmly Rose pushed her hair from her eyes, and gave one curt nod toward his jeans. "White vinegar. It'll take that right out. Nontoxic, too."

A few minutes later, she made the transition from the unkempt Bronx to the rarified Upper West Side. She hung her coat and cap in the closet, then checked her hair in the mirror until the waves looked perfect.

The cream-colored serenity of the living room always calmed her. With three windows that looked down upon the city, it was like a fairy tale, she thought, humming to herself. Outside, the world was cold and sleeting, but here, it was a perfectly moderated, perfectly humidified seventy-two degrees. Here, it was so easy to forget about last night. Forget about bare skin and bared souls, primitive emotions laid out for the world to see, to examine, to judge. Rose stopped her humming, frowned and picked at the flowers. This morning, the delicate aromas didn't help.

Last night, there had been so many mistakes. If she hadn't slept with him, there would have been no fear. If there had been no fear, there would have been no bitchery. Writing kiss-off messages in the mirror? She'd never done anything like that before. Oh, yeah, she'd dreamed about doing it lots. She'd seen it on television, where the kick-ass heroines told the world to take a hike. But not Rose. Never Princess Rose. Sometimes, when her dates went sleep-inducingly bad, when she smiled like an angel, her mind had schemed the worst sort of rejections, but not once had she ever delivered one. Not Rose.

Until Ian. No man had stripped her bare so fast without her even suspecting. It had been a long time since she'd felt that powerless, that loss of control. Her leg began to shake. Even in the perfectly humidified seventy-two degrees, she began to shiver.

Music filtered through the hidden speakers in the room, something classical and soothing. But she wasn't soothed. Restlessly, she grabbed a rag and wiped down the spotless piano, rubbing and buffing to remove marks that weren't there.

The only marks were on her skin. A hickey on her breast, a bruise on her thigh. Rose threw down the rag and swore. No matter how busy she kept herself, her mind was determined to remember, and her body wasn't ever going to forget.

All that tautly muscled male strength constrained under her thighs. Ultimate possession. Ultimate control. Ultimate power. Ian hadn't minded. He had let her lead willingly…. She snickered and corrected herself. No. *Enthusiastically.* He let her lead enthusiastically, his smile so disarming, unabashed sin.

No wonder she'd resorted to bitchery. The man was lethal. Surrounded by his trappings, the classic restaurant, the crystal and champagne, he was no threat to her. But without them, when they disappeared…

The damned flutters started all over again.

Rose ran for the security of the cream-colored love seat, covered her face with a frilly throw pillow, and screamed her most silent scream.

"You know, if you're trying to exercise the neck muscles, there are much better ways. Morning, Rose."

Sylvia. Rose shot up, ceased fluttering and giggled in the manner of a woman who had been caught doing facial exercises instead of fantasizing about a man's—

"You're exactly right. You should teach me."

"You're too young to worry about your looks. He called, didn't he? I see it in the overheated gleam of your eyes."

Overheated gleam? Rose stopped overheating and frowned.

"No. He didn't call. I wasn't exercising. That was a silent scream of frustration. He didn't call. There was no call."

"So now you're disappointed, aren't you? Why do we women do it to ourselves? Build up the impossible with hearts and flowers and then we get crushed when it doesn't fly into our lap with little pink wings and a cupid's arrow." She snapped her fingers. "You know what you need? A new dress. Something sexy and adorable—currently available for twenty-percent off at Saks. I love being frugal. Anton gets such a charge out of it. And we'll get shoes. White, with killer heels. You have to try the Louboutin shoes, darling. I know you've resisted, but they're the perfect pick-me-up—or pick-you-up, as the case may be."

When it came to fashion, Sylvia was beyond generous, but Rose didn't want her employer buying her clothes simply because she was depressed. Sabotaging a man's dreams, being the kick-ass heroine of her fantasies, wasn't what it was cracked up to be, and the last thing she wanted was to go shopping. But when Sylvia was determined to shop? Rose knew the stubborn gleam in Sylvia's eyes. Sometimes it was easier to give in; Rose was a professional at giving in.

An hour later, Sylvia was dragging her through Saks, holding up dress after dress, clicking her tongue, and then shaking her head with a regretful sigh. "The Kellehers' party is Friday night. Are you going with the doc?"

"He didn't ask," explained Rose.

"And why not?" Sylvia looked indignant at the thought.

"Because my heart is involved elsewhere and it's not like he's going to stage a full-frontal assault while I'm supposedly pining for someone else." Rose bit down on her tongue, because that was rude and mouthy and something that she wouldn't have said if she'd had more than three hours of sleep. And if she didn't have his marks on her body. And if she hadn't spent the night losing her virginity to a man she could never see again.

Sylvia didn't even notice. "With the right dress, you bet he would. For instance, something innocent, classy, sexy. Not black. That's too vampy for you. You need princess. Think Cinderella. Blue? It would show off your eyes."

Rose was prepared to argue. She hated Cinderella blue, but then Sylvia's head snapped, her eyes narrowed—a hunter spotting the prey. With what was best termed a war cry, the Countess of Simonov dived for the rack, ripping the white dress from an unsuspecting teenager's hands.

The girl looked as though she wanted to fight over the spoils, but Rose touched her arm and slipped her a twenty. "You don't want to do that," she warned. "Last time there was blood."

For a moment the girl studied Sylvia, probably seeing the scary echoes of a Brighton Beach catfight and then swallowed. Quick fingers snatched the twenty from Rose and off she ran.

Sylvia beamed at Rose proudly. "Now, see? That efficiency and attention to organizational detail is what I pay you for."

Next up was the fitting. Mutely Rose stood while Sylvia held up the lacy fabric, oohing and ahhing, and then calling over the sales assistants, commanding them to ooh and ahh, as well. "It's perfect. We should have a tiara."

Rose felt the beginnings of a headache. "No."

"You're right. Subtle, subtle, subtle. Nothing showy for you, my darling. You don't need accessories."

Once she was alone in the fitting room, Rose studied herself in the full-length mirror, discarded the blue and reverently pulled out the white concoction from the pile. Her parents had dressed her in something similar for the Dream Princess U.S.A. pageant, but that cheaply sewn rayon had nothing on the gossamer layers that floated around her now. The silvery beading almost disappeared until the light caught it just so. It had been the only pageant they could ever afford, and cheap fabric and thrift-shop shoes hadn't been able to compete with the other girls.

Rose had lost.

Cinderella, she thought with a frown.

After the dress came the bag, even the requisite white, princess-length coat. Rose objected, but Sylvia was in a mood. "Do not argue, missy. You have to be perfect. Absolutely perfect. After you're married, after Dr. Sinclair snatches you up, then you can pay me back with a six-figure contribution to the charity of my choice. Until then? Let your fairy godmother get a little crazy." She snapped her fingers, a flash in her eyes. "Let's go find some shoes. Something tall, a killer spike."

This time, Rose didn't even pretend to protest, allowing Sylvia to go wild. They ended up with a Christian Louboutin pair that Rose thought was mildly trampy, but Sylvia disagreed. "Trampy? You think? More courtesan. Those were the days, weren't they? Gorgeous clothes, men falling all over themselves to scramble into their beds, and those dresses. Good lord, to have such cleavage. I'm so glad Anton isn't a boob-man. If I thought he was straying toward double-wide Winnebagos, I'd have to worry, and I hate to worry. Or I'd have to castrate him."

Sylvia looked absolutely unconcerned about the possibility, and Rose kept her head low, the worry out of her eyes. Blair Rapaport had cleavage aplenty. Artificially augmented cleavage. Rose should say something. Like: "Blair is giving your husband cufflinks."

Yeah, sure. That's what she should do. Today, of all days, when every time she opened her mouth thoughtless words flew out in abundance. Maybe she should, but she didn't have any concrete proof of wrongdoing. It wasn't her business, and she wasn't going to worry Sylvia about nothing. No. For Sylvia, she would do something more, and as a plus, distract herself from the pit of shame in her gut. "Is Anton going to the Kellehers' party?" she asked, oh, so innocently.

"He'll be there. He bought me a new set of diamonds just for the occasion. I love my Russian count, I do, I do."

Sylvia radiated happiness, so blissfully sure of her Russian count, and Rose hid her frown. Hopefully Sylvia wouldn't have to castrate him.

8

WHEN IAN GOT TO WORK, everyone asked about his hand. He joked about learning to juggle with knives. No one seemed to notice that his laughter sounded forced. On his desk, three files were waiting for him: Sarah Cooper, an investment analyst; Charles Dowd, former VP of financial products; and Harley McFadden, cook. None sounded appealing, or easy. But he had a job, people needed this, and dammit, he would not let a minor disappointment spill out and ruin it for everybody else.

Sadly, he managed to ruin it anyway. He called Albany, talked to some manager in the state's office of labor, and got so furious with the tight-assed twit, he ended by hanging up. Strike one. Next he phoned personnel at Municipal Life and got a "I really don't have time for this." Ian told the man he was a heartless bastard who had no business working in HR. Strike two. And the best part of his morning was when his own mother called his cell, Ian put her on hold and then forgot her. It took him ten minutes of solid compliments and shameless bribery in order to make things right.

He needed to clear his head. He needed to find something positive. He needed to take positive steps. Encouraged, he dialed his old boss—keeping the foot in the door was always a plus. For a few minutes he hedged, making polite conversation, asking about the wife and kids.

"We miss you around here, Ian. I'm glad you found something."

"That's what I was thinking about. I miss the bank. What's the situation there?"

"We're dead now, but I'll keep my ears open. You were good. I'd love to have you back."

"Thank you, sir," Ian answered, feeling better. After he hung up, he took a deep breath and promptly spilled coffee all over his desk. Apparently his desk contained no blotting material, because he was still rifling in the drawers when Beckett called.

"What?" he yelled, possibly more rude than he intended.

"Oh, touchy. Want to have lunch?"

Ian mopped at the dark liquid, swearing ripely.

"Is that a no?"

"Coffee spill. I'm overcaffeinated."

"Yeah, you and Phoebe."

"What do you need, Beckett?"

"Hello, lunch? You could tell me about last night."

"I already told Phoebe."

"I didn't talk to her. Don't assume that I talk to her all the time. I see her at the basketball games. And I don't even like to talk to her."

"Beckett?"

"What?"

"I don't want to have lunch. I don't want to go over last night."

"Well, what if I wanted to go over last night? Does it always have to be about you?"

"Look, I appreciate the concern, but it's not a big deal."

"This is about me. *I* want to talk."

"I don't."

"What the hell is wrong with you? I'm having a crisis of logic and reason, and you get all pissy."

"What crisis?"

"It's not a crisis. That makes it sound bigger than it is. It's just an…issue."

Ian abandoned his cut-rate cleaning efforts and sat. "What kind of issue?"

"I have this thing, and I want it, but it's not a healthy thing, and I think if I actually had sex with this thing, I could do some permanent damage."

"What thing are you considering have sex with, Beckett?"

"It's a woman."

"A woman is not a thing. It doesn't matter if you actually believe it or not, but you can never say those words aloud."

"Trust me, it's better if I think of her as a thing. Objectify. Tits. Ass. Nothing more."

"What sort of permanent damage could she do?"

"Bad. The bad sort of damage."

Ian glanced at his hand. "Is this because she's not interested?"

"I think she's interested, but I think it's an irrational interest. Like when you're at a party and everyone's drinking, and you start asking stupid questions, and then people sit there, contemplating the stupid questions because it was one of those things you only think about when you're drunk."

Only Beckett could be emotionally stupider than Ian, which cheered him up even more. "Did this start when she was drunk?"

"No. She was sober."

"Were you?"

"Unfortunately. It would be easier if I was aroused under the influence."

Yeah, men were suckers for sex. "Do you want to make love to her?"

"I think I want to have sex with her."

"Then, if she wants to, you do it." *Go ahead, run with the scissors, play out in traffic, use the dynamite with the Acme label.*

"And what about the consequences?" asked Beckett in a voice that said he wasn't going to pay attention at all.

"Wear a condom. You'll be okay," Ian lied.

"You're sure?"

"Absolutely."

IT WAS FRIDAY NIGHT, THE FIRST Friday of the New Year, and the ballrooms of the St. Regis were decorated in seasonal splendor. Pine boughs and berries hung from wave after wave of arched ceilings that belonged to a grand age long past. A towering Christmas tree filled the main hall, decked with shimmering pearl garlands and fat velvet bows. Crystal stars caught the candlelight, reflecting it back with a holiday wink.

The ballroom bustled with elegant men in distinguished

tuxedos, and beautiful women who shone and sparkled with color and jewels. From every corner, from every crevice, laughter and good cheer spilled forth.

Rose smiled, a slight smile, because she knew this place. Her fairy tale, her wonderland, the place that had always kept her safe. A deferential two steps separated her from Anton and Sylvia, because she didn't want to be in the spotlight anymore. She didn't mind, it was never the attention, only the light that called to her. As the band struck up a lively tune, the count turned and gave her a wink. Dressed in black formal tails, Anton was tall and handsome, every bit the aristocrat. Next to him, Sylvia stood, surveying the room, stunning in maroon silk and an elaborate choker of diamonds.

For a long second, Rose closed her eyes, inhaling deeply, searching for that elusive scent: happiness, joy, life as it should be lived. Her eyes opened as she reached for the old familiarity that always comforted her.

The frilly dresses, the bubbling smiles, it all took her back. When the Hildebrandes had dropped her off at Little Princess School of Charm, her parents had been so...*parental* when other people were around, as if they loved her. To Rose, those dreamlike days were tiny moments that she had clung to like a security blanket.

But tonight, it all seemed off. The knot in her stomach, the nerves dancing on her skin. Feeling. *Guilt.*

"Rose, you're looking so gorgeous. The shoes are exactly perfect." Sylvia nudged her husband in the ribs. "Anton, tell her she looks gorgeous."

The count took Rose's hand, lifting them both to his lips. "A work of art." Then he turned to his wife, eyes warm and amused. "But when your hand begins to dabble, perfection follows like a shadow."

Rose spied the emerald cuff links on his arm and her stomach tightened even more. He never had, as far as she knew, worn the monogrammed present from Blair, making her worries seem silly.

Straying? Anton? It should have been laughable. When he was with Sylvia, he didn't seem bored, or itchy or roving. He was a man in love. No reason to worry. None. Okay, so maybe she trusted Anton. But Blair? That was another problem entirely. A problem that Rose intended to handle tonight.

The three of them walked the room, Sylvia air-kissing the world and directing traffic, Rose planting a quiet self-satisfied smile on her face, and Anton laughing at the appropriate intervals.

Under Sylvia's watchful eye, everything was easy. After several years of working for Sylvia, Rose had gone to a lot of these events, and she was familiar with the drill. Sylvia was the current and Rose followed in her powerful wake. Rose knew the crowd; she knew the names, their position on the social register, their birthdays, the favored wine and the amount of the last contribution to Sylvia's charities. It should have been a habit by now, nothing more than a paycheck and a job, but for Rose it had always been a sleepy dream.

Not anything like the charged dream that haunted her; a mouth at her breast, her body arched into him.

Please don't call.

Instantly her spine stiffened, her back rigid, her chin pointing up. Once again, she was in control.

"There!" Sylvia bent low, shoved a glass into her hand. "Twelve o'clock. Leaning against the marble pillar. He looks lonely. Go!" whispered Sylvia, giving her a hard push.

Rose frowned over her shoulder, but she obeyed. On paper, there was a lot to like about Remy Sinclair. The gossip rags tried their best to paint him with the scandal-brush. Club sightings, the woman of the month, but nothing really juicy. There were no arrests, no public fights, no drunk and disorderlies. He knew the line, and never stepped across it. Controlled and content and rich. Remy Sinclair was perfect. All she had to do was toss aside her lifelong behavior of poised female restraint and hook him like an Upper West Side, diamond-bellied trout. Easy.

Rose took a sip of her champagne. Then another. Lifelong behaviors were tougher to shake than one might suspect.

Except with Ian, her brain reminded her, and she promptly reminded her brain to keep its nose out of her business. Tonight, she had a diamond-bellied trout to hook.

Automatically her shoulders squared and her smile was a picture of radiance. "Excuse me, is this wall taken?" she asked, gliding up beside him.

He grasped her hand, raised it to his lips, and her smile widened. "If I had known you were going to be here, we could have come together."

"Surprises are so much more exciting," she lied smoothly.

"Are you searching for new bachelors to torture?"

"Excuse me?"

His grin was almost innocent. "For the auction."

Her heart started again. "Tonight is all about fun."

"Then why the sad face?"

Quickly she adjusted. "No sad face. In this place? Impossible."

"Even sad, you still look beautiful. That dress suits you. Sexy. Vulnerable. Aloof."

"Exactly what every woman wants to be."

"Really?" he asked, and she noticed where his eyes landed— on the Sinclair matriarch who stood there, amusing her subjects. "Have dinner with me tomorrow?"

"I have to work," she told him, not exactly untrue. "The benefit's less than a month away. I think I'm going to have dogs there."

He laughed. "My mother will love that."

Rose glanced at his mother, noticed the look in their direction and smiled politely.

"She approves of you," he said, not a surprise. Everyone approved of Rose. Her smile tightened. "Dinner on Monday, then?"

"You're much more persistent tonight."

"Blame it on the dress," he answered. "If I were really persistent, I'd take you out for a drink later. I know the perfect place." There was an unusual heat in his eyes, and she didn't think it was all because of the dress.

"Dinner on Monday."

"I'm crushed," he mused.

She cocked her head and studied him. Tonight, everyone seemed to have their battles to wage. "But you'll survive." *And speaking of survival.* Rose turned and scanned the room. "Have you seen Blair Rapaport?"

"How could I see any woman but you?"

"Seriously."

"Seriously." He lifted his glass, watched her. "Why Blair?

You don't seem—how can I say this and be polite—suited for each other."

Rose smiled vaguely. "No reason."

Remy studied her, intrigued. "You look like there's a reason. But I'm too well behaved to pry."

No, he was too well behaved for everything. He was, quite simply, the perfect man. Except… No, she corrected herself. No exceptions. None, none, none.

So, why was she in such a hurry to leave? Because she had a job to do, nothing more.

Politely she nodded at him. "It was wonderful talking. Monday. Looking forward to it," and then she was off, leaving Remy Sinclair behind. As she moved across the room, there was a new, more confident spring in her usual, elegant glide. Almost jaunty. Heads turned. She pretended not to notice. Sylvia would approve.

She had a date, and it was all of her own finagling. Happily she allowed herself a self-satisfied smile. She searched through ballrooms and salons, finally coming across a tiny reception area. Dim, candles flickering, a smaller Christmas tree casting the room with silvery lights. Much more intimate. Much more private. Blair Rapaport would have to die.

Quickly she spotted the count leaning against the dark wooden bar with Blair close by. Too close by. The long black dress was cut insanely low. Trampy. Definitely trampy, thought Rose, wishing she had the cahones to pull it off. Maybe she didn't have the daring fashion sense, but she could recognize the fawning little touches on the arm, the wide-eyed, "oh, big boy, the better to eat you with" expression. Truly, Rose did it so much better. Subtlety? Hello?

Then there was Anton. The idiot. What the heck was he thinking? Where was Sylvia? Oh, God, this was a mess. What was Rose thinking? She reversed course, racing out, fully prepared to drag Sylvia back toward her husband and let the woman see the goings-on that were possibly going on right under her nose.

In the main ballroom, Rose spotted Sylvia, chatting, laughing, looking gloriously content with her life, and now, the dragging-Sylvia plan didn't sound so appealing anymore. Rose had nothing but dire suspicions, a pair of insanely inappropriate monogrammed cuff links and a deep distrust of women with more cleavage than her.

Rose would handle this herself, no Sylvia-involvement necessary. Her parents had thought she couldn't do anything right. They were wrong. Dead wrong.

It was a new year, a new life. Rose had been with a man, she'd rolled in the sheets—barnyard immorality at its finest—and she'd survived with no scarlet *A* or a screeching lecture from her mother. Why was she still jumping at shadows that couldn't hurt her anymore? Her parents had long been removed from her life. It wasn't about them. This was about her.

One night, but she had walked away, strong and sure. All this week she'd seen the changes. Her claws were sharper, her aim was more sure.

She'd taken the test and passed.

With steely resolve, Rose took a deep breath to elongate and strengthen her spine. Then she walked, no, she *marched* directly to the other room. Sylvia Simonov had taken care of Rose. Tonight, Rose was going to return the favor, and for Blair Rapaport, payback was a bitch.

Her mind seethed with all those unused comeback lines, those dramatic scenarios never played, all those imagined put-downs that she'd never said. When she spied a tray of champagne, Rose politely stopped the passing young waiter, snagged a crystal glass and drank. Bubbles tickled her brain. In fact, for Sylvia, she would go to hell and back, kicking ass and taking names. As the young man waited patiently, Rose downed another glass, mainly because she knew it was a good idea. When she was done, the man smiled at her, impeccably politely, completely nonjudgmental. Rose nodded once, rubbing the pad of her velvet gloves to polish a tiny print until the crystal was restored to its proper sparkle. Then she handed him the glass. "Thank you," she added. "It's a very lovely party. You're doing a fabulous job."

Now, on to the carnage of war.

With bold steps she approached the couple, as if she had just as much right to occupy this darkened corner as anyone else.

"Anton. There you are. Have you seen Sylvia?"

"Sylvia? The last time I saw her, she was gossiping with her friends like little chickens. Some time ago, I lost patience and abandoned her for a glass of well-deserved champagne."

Rose looked pointedly at Blair. Held out a hand. "Rose Hildebrande."

"Blair," said the other woman, sizing up Rose, dismissing her. Rose was in no mood to be dismissed, and her smile became a little thinner, not that anyone would notice.

"So, are you enjoying the evening? It's a great cause. Sylvia is a huge champion for literacy. Do you have a cause? Homeless, food pantries, protecting the sanctity of home and marriage and supporting the very foundation of this civilization as we know it?"

Blair threw back her head and laughed. A move designed to draw a man's eyes to her throat, her neck and even lower to the double-wides with the For Rent sign nestled snugly in between.

Oh, cattiness. Rose grinned to herself.

"I'm too young for a cause," Blair replied. "That's for old people." *Like you.*

Under the velvet gloves, Rose's hands tightened into fists. "You're selling yourself short," lectured Rose. "All you need is a little grit and something to believe in. People always think they can't do anything, that they can't make a difference. But you have money, connections and time. You have the world at your fingertips. Why don't you use it?"

This time it was Anton who laughed. "My darling wife has been spreading the propaganda."

At that, Rose nearly popped him one. *Propaganda?* "If more people listened to your darling wife, this planet would be a better place. That's all Sylvia wants. To take care of people and see that no one's forgotten. Speaking of, the auction is starting soon. You and *your wife* should talk. I bet she'd adore that emerald necklace. Maybe an early Valentine's Day present, hmm?"

"You think I should?" he asked, his face worried as if he'd been derelict. Not guilt, but not so innocent, either.

"Trust me, she'll love it," Rose told him, giving him a hard nudge toward the other room, where his wife was waiting. If the count stayed here any longer, Rose couldn't be held responsible for her actions. She'd had two glasses of champagne and was loaded for bear.

"She told you to tell me, didn't she?" Anton asked, stubbornly not moving.

"Sylvia? Subtle and secretive?" Rose threw back her head and laughed. Okay, her white dress had cleavage, but it hinted discreetly. It did not bellow.

Finally Anton seemed to get with the program. "What was I thinking?" He placed his glass on the bar, where it was efficiently whisked away, and then nodded to them both. "Ladies. It pains my heart to leave such beautiful companionship, but when the countess beckons? What can I say, I am her slave."

And he was going to remain that way if Rose had anything to do with it, which she did.

After he left, Rose stuck around, fiddling with her gloves, stalling for time, waiting to hear the prime MO of one Blair The Ho Rapaport.

"Love the shoes," said Blair, unleashing her claws right from the get-go. "Cinderella's got a wild side."

Rose reached for a glass, took a sip and eyed her prey over the rim. "Cinderella can kick your skinny ass."

She shoots, she scores, the crowd goes wild....

"Go back to your mommy, little girl. The pigtails and the bows, the cute Mary Janes? You don't belong. You're the hired help, nothing more."

Rose ignored the sting from the dig, but slammed down her glass a tad more forcibly than she intended. "What do you want from him?"

"It's a bet. One night. If I can seduce him, I win," Blair answered, not even bothering to lie.

"What do you win? Miss Congeniality? Miss My Vagina Can Swallow Idaho?"

Apparently, back-alley insults were the only thing that struck a nerve. This time, Blair looked at her, annoyed. *At last.* "What is your deal? Why do you care?"

"These are people. You can't just rip them up and then throw them away." Her own words tripped through the anger, through the champagne, falling flat on her conscience. *Please don't call,* blazed in her brain. Oh, God.

Blair watched her with cold eyes and a bitchy smile, and Rose desperately fumbled for something to say. Sadly, all those dramatic scenarios, all those imagined put-downs disappeared along with her judgment.

Blair merely rolled her eyes. It seemed fitting, and Rose found her tongue.

"Leave Anton alone. He's happy. He loves her. She loves him. Go find…someone else to toy with."

"Rose, sweet little Rose, I don't like to lose."

Rose got up in her face, not so sweet. Not so nice. "You're going down, sister," she blurted and then immediately wanted to slap herself. She'd been on a roll. Clever, witty…kick-ass, and then—blah. That was the best she could come up with?

Blair laughed, and blew her a kiss. "Going down? Yeah, I think I am."

Rose watched her walk, that sultry little side-to-side, and seethed quietly. She didn't know who made her angrier. Blair or herself.

After a minute she called Sylvia, choosing to avoid a physical meeting because Sylvia would sense she was ticked. The physical signs were all there. Heaving bosom, shaking hands and the look of death in her eyes. Sylvia would want to know why.

"Sylvia. I've got a headache. A real pain in the… Anyway, it's a big pain. I'm heading out."

"Sorry about the head. Go home, relax. Did you talk to Remy? I saw you two chatting. A little back-and-forth, a little this and that, before you know it, a little hootch and cootch, but not too soon. Always be the little lady. You make such a great little lady."

"A date on Monday," Rose answered, buffing her nails.

"Oh, my little girl is growing up. I knew it. I have remarkable instincts when it comes to matters of the human heart. Speaking of. Anton's asking about the necklace, Rose. Look at you, setting it all up. Every day…oh… It makes me proud. Monday night. We'll have to shop. I fully expect you to knock his socks off."

Rose smiled wearily. Sometimes Sylvia exhausted her. "No

more than the socks. I have standards and morals and most of all, a strategy."

Yeah, she had a strategy, to mend a bridge that she had burned.

Yeah, now there's some socks you want to knock off. You go back there and you'll be doing a lot more than mending bridges.

So, she argued with herself. She wasn't a precious virgin anymore, she didn't have anything to lose. It was only sex. Now that she was an experienced woman, Rose could walk this line. Not that he'd talk to her anyway. Heck, he might not even let her in the door, so why was she worried?

And if he did let her in, if things got a little steamy, so what?

She'd already proven that she could handle it. Sex wouldn't change anything.

She'd started something with her life and it was working. Finally. Finally she was where she wanted to be, she had her target in her sights, and she was proud of what she had accomplished.

Her eyes surveyed the ballroom, reveling in all the beautiful things, all the beautiful worlds.

Ian Cumberland was merely another beautiful thing that she wanted.

And one she intended to have.

9

IAN STARED BLINDLY at the television. He hated television. The buzzer sounded and he so badly wanted to ignore it. Tonight he didn't need Phoebe or Beckett babysitting him. Not when he felt like this. Tonight, he wanted to sit and watch mundane blather and get slowly, blindly drunk. He was even prepared; the bottle of Scotch nestled snugly into the cushion of his sofa as if it was his long-lost friend. He hated Scotch.

Annoyingly, the buzzer blared again, and Ian shot a loving look at the bottle. Not yet, but soon, my pretty.

"What?" he bellowed into the speaker.

"It's Rose. Can I come up?"

Well, well, so she had decided to revisit the scene of the crime, to find out how badly he'd been damaged. Ian took a long swig of Scotch and jabbed the button with his good hand. See, he was already learning.

He opened the door with an elegant bow, mainly mocking; he hoped she got the point. "After you."

Instead of entering, she stood nervously in the open doorway. Apparently tonight's attire for genteel bloodletting was cocktail wear with long white gloves and a matching white coat. She looked young, innocent, ready for her first winter cotillion. Wow. You really couldn't judge a book by *that* cover.

"What do you want?" he snapped, noticing her wince. Ignored it. He propped the door open with his foot in case he did something painful, like wanting to keep her there.

"I'm sorry," she said, sidestepping his body, moving farther into the room, invading his domain. The honeysuckle smell trailed after her. Not that. Anything but that. He'd spent two nights trying to get honeysuckle out of his brain. Now it was back.

Stubbornly, Ian refused to shut the door. He was not, *not,* going to fall for this again. "Okay. You can leave now."

"I had a really nice time with you."

Realizing she wasn't going to leave, Ian slammed the door, loud, enjoying her jump mainly because now he was really pissed. "By nice time, I guess you mean great sex, a couple of orgasms and a really good laugh."

"I can't see you." Her eyes kept dodging his, staring at the floor, the wall, the bottle of Scotch in his hand.

"Funny. I can see you. Why are you here?"

At that, she raised her head, lifted her chin. "Because I'm not very smart."

"That makes two of us." Then Ian laughed, one of those loud, awkward laughs, made by people who have things to lose. Already she was messing with his head, and dammit, his head didn't need this. He held out his Scotch. "Want some? It helps."

Gingerly Rose took the bottle. Without hesitation she took a long swig and then coughed. Yeah, too cheap for her blood and her virginal white dress. She'd probably lied about the virgin thing, too. Another act. *So why the hell was she here?*

He didn't need this pretense, he didn't want her to ease her conscience. He didn't need to have his body poised, his skin warmed, as if… Dammit. Ian shut off his brain. "You've apologized. You can go."

"I want to stay." She wet her lips, his gaze tracked her tongue. Ian had another long drink, then proudly shook his head. See, he could reject her.

"Oh, no. Maybe I look like a masochist, but no." He stalked back toward the door, because the awareness was still there, hounding him. Even now, he remembered being inside her, and the rotting smell of honeysuckle was killing his brain.

Rose didn't follow. Instead she stood in the middle of his apartment, her hands wrapped around her stomach, and he stared at her gloved hands. A stripper's gloves.

Oh, damn.

"Why can't we do this?" she asked, not getting the whole rejection thing.

"Do what?"

"Sex. Why can't we do sex?"

At the word *sex,* Ian could only stare, slack-jawed, engines starting to fire. Obviously forgetting that last crash landing. "You're fucking kidding me," he said, mainly to himself.

"No. There are things I won't give up. I assumed you wanted something more than sex, and that was arrogant and conceited and unfair."

Now she'd done it. He stopped worrying about the door and collapsed on his couch. "So you're willing to fuck me?"

"Yes." Nervously she remained a statue, not moving.

He didn't like that look on her face. Fear and vulnerability, as though she was putting herself on the line. Ian scrubbed his eyes, wiping it away. "Why?"

"Because I want you. And I like the sex."

"And that's all," he asked, still thinking, still hoping, still wanting to believe. She stood there like a debutante, those sexy gloves, little white shoes and that glorious face that even now was still feasting on his heart.

"Yes."

There were men who would jump at the chance. Men who took sex wherever they could. And if his mirror hadn't accidentally bumped into his hand, if he hadn't spent last night dreaming of her—again—if his life weren't postlayoff and not getting any better, he would put his pride behind him, screw her once and then say adios, washing his hands of her. But here he sat, actually…considering it.

It was official. This was the worst moment of his life. Okay. Fine. Yeah, he would do it. But she wanted to wring him dry? Oh, no, honey. Two could play that game. He leaned back into the cushions, and took another drink of alcohol, the burn much nicer than the burn in his gut. "Strip," he ordered, grinning to the entire world. See, he could be a bastard.

Rose blinked, completely missing his proud moment. "What do you mean?"

"Show me what you got. You want sex? Get naked." He shrugged, negligently crossing his legs, and waited to see how low she would go.

Quickly she shot up and headed for the door, her spine looking ready to crack. Apparently the mighty Rose had more pride than he did. Her hand grasped the door, but then she hesitated… turned…and came back.

Her hair formed a curtain, but he could tell when her chin lifted. Ian froze. Forgot to breathe.

Her little beaded purse dropped to the floor like an anvil, and Ian didn't want to get turned on. This was humiliation. This was about revenge. His body shouldn't care.

She took off her coat, folding it neatly before laying it over the back of the chair. That tidy gesture tweaked him, as if she could keep herself unmoved and dignified. Carefully she removed her shoes, tucked them next to her coat.

Then those gloved hands moved to the back of her dress, pulling the zipper and slowly the fabric fell away. Why couldn't she look like a slut? Goddammit. Underneath the top was a white satin bra, creamy flesh spilling out. Okay, enough with the innocent act.

Guilt kept rising in his throat, but then she met his gaze, pushed her hair out of the way—her eyes were blank, emotionless. This was nothing to her. *Nothing.*

Ian had another swig, but the alcohol wasn't working anymore. A hole was rotting in his gut and it wasn't from Scotch. The fancy dress slid to the floor, and now she was clad only in shimmering stockings and white lace and stripper gloves. Like a five-star, top-dollar debutante. Ian fisted his cut-up hand, pain radiating out, and he reminded himself that this was the same woman who had written a kiss-off on his mirror, the one who had robbed him of pride. No guilt necessary.

Uncomfortably Ian shifted against the cushions. However, when she remembered the gloves and peeled them back, he knew enough to leer in a completely soulless manner. The gloves dropped to the floor.

Next, she unclasped the bra, and he was happy to notice her

bare hands were shaking. The scrap of satin panties followed, and then she stood there, clad only in stockings, taking it.

It wasn't fair. An angel's face, wide empty blue eyes, but the body... He knew those breasts, intimately. The fullness, the hard peaks burning into his chest. One night, and he wasn't sure he'd ever forget. Again, his fingers curled, and this time he welcomed the pain. All those sleek, fair curves sliding into long legs, and a tiny shadow of gold between.

His cock jerked in ignorant bliss. A man's cock had no pride, no morals, no conscience. None, at all. At the moment, Ian envied that piece of his body that didn't care. Silently he waited for her to do something. Say something. Try and seduce him. Yell and scream. She did neither. Rose merely stood, as if she wasn't sure what to do, either.

Fine. Somebody had to put this goat-rodeo on track. "Turn around. Bend over," he ordered, and he saw the fury snap in her eyes.

Finally, he could breathe again.

She almost obeyed him anyway; then her feet poised to turn, or to run. Ian should have been celebrating, but he heard something break from her throat. Not a laugh, not a sob. Choking. Hastily she grabbed her coat, wrapped it around her and then gathered her clothes.

"Thank you," she said quietly. A lot of dignity from someone who had just been deliberately dehumanized. This time, the guilt exploded like a bomb, empty blue-eyed shrapnel embedding itself deeply in his heart. But he told himself he didn't deserve to feel like a heel. *Stupid shit.*

"What are you thanking me for?"

"I needed this. Sometimes the price is too high. I needed to see you as a son of a bitch. I burned my bridges, and now you have, too. We're done."

His hand began to throb, his conscience hurt even worse. Ian had never been that guy. Never. "Rose. Wait."

"No. Thank you." She headed for the door, her stocking feet skimming the floor. Quiet, elegant. Beaten.

"I'm sorry," he said.

That seemed to stop her. Whether it was his words or the self-loathing in his voice, he didn't know. For a long time, an eternity, she remained at the door. She didn't look at him, and he was glad. Right now, he didn't want to see her face, he didn't want to see her hurt.

"You decimated me that night," he continued. "I don't think you know what you did." Ian put the accusation out there. Partially as an excuse, and partially because he *wanted* her to know. In his world, you didn't go around ripping people's hearts—like what he'd just done to her.

"Yes, I know," she admitted quietly, and he was glad. Glad he heard the ring of guilt in her voice, as well.

"Why did you do that to me?" he asked.

She opened the door, but Ian was faster and he shut it, blocking her exit. This was too important. "Why did you do that to me?" he repeated. There was no reason that could justify it, but he wanted to hear it anyway.

When she moved her head, her hair fell over her face, hiding her from him. Dammit. *Hiding her.* He needed to see her eyes. He needed to know if they were blank and expressionless, as well. "I can't do this."

"Do what?" he yelled. He realized he was yelling and lowered his voice, trying to maintain sanity, calm, reason. "We had a date. We had great sex. I didn't ask you for anything."

Rose dug a hand through her scalp, lifting the curtain of her hair, and now he could see the tears. Oh, God. Tears. He was a bastard. He didn't want to be a bastard. He'd never been that guy, either.

"I won't give up. My life is my own. I choose. I decide. I rule. No one takes that away from me. Never."

Ian stared, confused. Where had this come from? Now he was determined to understand. "Rose?" He took her hand, put her on the chair—not the sofa—then sat across from her, safely away, where he couldn't do any more harm. Silently she huddled in her cotillion-white coat, her hair in her face, not saying a word, not moving.

"Talk to me, Rose. Please."

Carefully she sniffed, and lifted her head. Tears swam in her eyes before she wiped them away. As he watched, her hands twisted in her lap. "It'll take a long time."

Ian leaned back. "I've got all night."

WHEN SHE SPOKE, SHE WANTED to keep her voice carefully void of emotion, but the trace of the mountains crept in, the piece she'd worked so hard to scrub out.

"I grew up in the shadow of the Appalachians, poorer than dirt, but there it wasn't that uncommon. You didn't see money, didn't see fancy cars. Not like here. My dad, he was a big, quiet man, and he didn't talk much. He didn't know much but his job. Every day he worked in the mines, and Mom kept the house, puttering around, making pies and watching her shows."

Her smile was dreamy, because this was the life she'd made up. The family she'd made up. Those long hours, sitting on the floor in the dark, she'd had a lot of time to think about what kind of family she'd pick if she could.

"The mine was dangerous and Mama always prayed every morning when he left. Seemed like she was always praying about something. Not that they ever did any good. I could have told her that."

That part was true. Her mother had been a devout woman, and as far as Rose knew, she still was. But her mama's heart was as black as the soot from the mines and no amount of praying changed that. It took a few years before Rose realized that not every kid had to walk with a book on her head, or got her knuckles rapped smartly when her smile wasn't just so.

"I was the princess. That's why they called me Rose, or at least that's what Mama always said. Everywhere I went, people would ooh and ahh, and tell me that I was going to have a great life because I was so pretty. Mama liked to dress me in pink and white, and put bows in my hair. At first I thought it was dumb, but then it just began to seem normal 'cause I didn't know anything else."

Rose sniffed and looked down at her hands where slowly and methodically, she was pulling at the skin around her nails. Her mother used to hate that. Her mother wasn't in her life, so why should she care anymore? But it didn't matter. She folded her hands and stopped.

"Three years running, I was the lead in the high school play. Couldn't sing, sounded like a wounded dog, but nobody seemed to mind. Mama was smart, though, and strict. She told me to be careful of the boys because they were gonna want things, and I needed to hold out because I was destined for something big. Something better than a coal miner and a waitressing job. So I kept my eye out for something better, and as soon as I turned eighteen, I headed for New York. Determined to make it big, determined that I wouldn't be poor anymore."

There was no way to dress it up, no way to make it more appealing. Oh, hell. He thought she was a heartless bitch. What difference did vain or stupid make? But they did, she whispered. What he thought was frighteningly important. She raised her eyes to his and met them, firmly, evenly, no backing down. "I won't be poor again."

"Is that all?"

"What do you mean?" she asked, and heard her voice break nervously.

He looked into her, looked through her, and he knew. She could hear the words in her head: *Tell him. Trust him.*

Instead, she smiled automatically because she didn't want him to worry.

"After I moved to the city I got a job as a secretary, because I've always been good at details and organization. You should see my makeup drawer. Labeled, expiration dates, what works with what." She was starting to ramble, the accent getting thicker, and her leg started to shake. With her right hand, she latched on to her thigh and held. The shaking went away.

When she spoke again, there was no more trace of the mountains at all. "I won't go back to that life. It was hell."

"Why was it hell, Rose?"

Rose rubbed her hands on her knees, felt the current run through her again. She lifted her head and fixed her shoulders, looking Ian right in the eye, because this was the one moment that she held above all. That time in her life when she came into her own. "I want pretty things. I want soft music. I want laughing and joy and people who aren't afraid."

"Not everybody's afraid," he said gently, as if he didn't think she was the hardest bitch alive.

"Not everybody likes to be poor," she reminded him, because he shouldn't like her. He should hate her.

"Come here," he said, his voice so gentle, so tender.

Automatically she walked to him, started to take off her coat, but he stopped her, held the material together. "This isn't what you want?" she asked.

"Yes. But it's not what I'm going to do. I'm sorry for what I did. I'm very, very sorry." He talked to her, slow and careful, as if she was an idiot. She hated that tone.

"I don't want you to feel sorry for me. Lots of people were born poor. Lots of people get over it."

He trailed the back of his hand on her cheek. "Can we start over?"

Rose shook her head; it wasn't that simple. "You can never start over. Everything builds on the foundation you've already got."

"Then go out to dinner with me. Tomorrow." He looked at his watch. "Tonight."

He still didn't seem to understand what she had said. Why couldn't people listen to her? Before, when he thought she was some model of perfection, he had listened, but now he was only hearing what he chose to hear. "We can't do that."

"Why not?"

"I'm not that girl anymore. I'm a lot smarter now. I know what I want out of this life and I'm going to get it. I won't be that girl."

"I don't want you to be," he said, staring at her as though she was the princess.

Rose pulled away and began to pace around the room. "Yes, you do. Maybe you don't want me to be stupid and a big lump of clay, but you don't like my dreams."

"What dreams?"

"I want money, Ian. I don't want that stress in my life." She wetted dry lips, because when she talked about this with Sylvia, they laughed about it, and Sylvia understood. Rose didn't think Ian was going to be that easy. "I'm going to have the life that everyone always told me I could have, but I wasn't strong enough to latch on to it. I'm strong enough now. I told you I was a personal assistant, but I didn't tell you everything. I work for Sylvia and Anton Simonov. What I want, it's there. It's close. I just need to be patient and not so eager to jump at everything that looks good."

"And I look good?" he asked harshly.

Rose flushed, embarrassed. "It wasn't meant to insult you."

"Thanks. I feel better."

"I'm sorry."

He held up a hand. "No. Ignore me."

"I could never do that," she said. It was the truth, but she had said it to make him feel better. All it did was make him swear under his breath. So she waited.

"You want money?" he asked. "You want to marry well?"

"I can do it." And she could. People expected it from her, and she was tired of people being disappointed.

For the first time he looked at her, into her, and she let him see those pieces of her that she hid. They weren't nearly as pretty as the rest. Men didn't like women who could stare into the darkest parts of the world and be honest about it. They would call her a gold digger or a whore. But if a man sought money, he was ambitious. Everybody wanted money. Everybody needed money, but nobody liked to say it, and Rose was getting tired of tiptoeing around reality.

Ian stuck his hands in his pockets, and she didn't like the way he watched her. Then she told herself to grow up. For way too long, she'd worried what everyone thought of her. Everybody had bad in them, even Ian. She'd just had a first-class demonstration. But even knowing that, she still desired him. That thought cheered her up.

"So what do you want from me?" he asked.

This was trickier, and she knew that she was walking a minefield, but tonight she'd already walked through one and survived. "I liked the sex. I like being with you."

"For how long, Rose? After you're married?"

That shocked her. "No."

Slowly he shook his head. "I can't do this."

Of all the scenarios she'd run through in her mind, she'd never considered him saying no. She knew that men loved sex, and when men were offered it without strings, no wasn't a part of the vocabulary. Sylvia had told her so, and Sylvia knew all.

Silently Rose met his eyes, wishing he were a little weaker. But if he was, she didn't think she would want him so badly. Her heart clutched, because there were few things Rose wanted badly, but now there was nothing left to do. She gathered her clothes a little closer to her chest, hiding the wound she was leaving behind. All she had to do was turn around and leave.

Leave him?

What the hell was she thinking? How long had she worked for Sylvia, and in that time hadn't she learned anything?

Furiously Rose stamped her foot. Not once, because the first time wasn't that great. But the second time? That one was good. "Why the hell not?" she demanded.

"I think too much of myself," he said. "When you decide you want *me,* I'll be here. But I'm worth more than you think I am, Rose."

He believed she thought he was worthless? Oh, heck. She was messing it up again. "That's not what I'm saying." Sweet heaven, she was offering him free milk along with the cow. Why wasn't he jumping?

"That's exactly what you're saying."

"Ian…"

He stood up, walked to the door, and Rose stared after him, confused. He wasn't supposed to do this. "What do you want me to do?" she asked. Yes, her voice sounded weak and helpless, but she wasn't leaving. She wasn't moving from this spot until she was ready.

"I want a chance. There's this thing between us. It's magic and good and it's supposed to be. And okay, I didn't realize exactly what was going on in your head, but now I know more, and sure, not everything is simple, but it can be okay. But you have to trust me. I'm the good guy here. And yes, I screwed up earlier. God, did I screw up. And okay, that was me, too, but I was pissed, and you did bad, too. But you didn't screw up, Rose. Truly. Trust me."

Trust me. Her whole body screamed to collapse, to fall in on itself, because those were the two deadliest words in the world. "No. You haven't earned it."

It was a little white lie, because she could never trust him, but she didn't say that. This way, if he thought there was hope, she could keep him in her life. It was a rare occasion when she could pat herself on the back. Mentally, she did.

"I can earn it. You have to let me."

She didn't like the easy confidence in his voice. He thought this would be a walk in the park. Oh, well, she wasn't about to disillusion him, not when she was getting her way.

He put a hand to her face, so extraordinarily gentle, as if she would break. Not anymore. No one could break her anymore. Shyly she met his eyes, nearly blinked at the things she glimpsed there. Magic. The most dangerous sort of magic. Her eyes closed, shutting it out, and then, because she couldn't wait any longer, she pressed her mouth to his.

His lips were so tender, so careful, so…affably romantic. Honestly, Rose was getting tired of this damned princess bit. She liked when he saw her as flesh, as blood, as heart. Boldly she dropped the coat, rubbed like a cat in heat and tore at the buttons on his shirt. Tonight she wanted to fly again, and he was the one who gave her wings.

"Rose," he said, and there was desperation in his voice. Her smile was all power and the promise of the sex. Truly, the man didn't stand a chance.

IT WAS A LONG TIME LATER, and Ian thought Rose had fallen asleep. Worn herself out would be the more appropriate description. Her head was pillowed on his chest, one thigh buried between his. Every now and again her hands clutched at him, holding him there, as if he was planning to leave. Yeah, right. In sleep, she was closer than she'd ever been awake. Or when they made love.

Once again, Rose had been the dominant, needing to take charge. At first, Ian was nervous and tried to be gentle, but that didn't help. When he had rolled Rose underneath him, she grew still, lifeless. He asked her if she was okay. Rose had smiled and said yes, but he wasn't fooled; he was learning the Stepford look. A few minutes later, they rolled again, and like magic, wicked Rose was back, pulling him deeper inside her, her thighs tight, almost painful. Ian had felt odd, as if he was taking advantage. But when she was there, her body so open and willing, icy-blue eyes burning into him, burning him… All he could do was comply.

The lights from the building next door filtered through the window, and he watched the pale beams stroke across her bare skin.

What was her truth? He'd heard some tonight, but not enough. Her eyes were too blank when she talked. She was too quick to jump, too quick to please. She bore scars somewhere. He'd wanted to ask, but one step at a time.

Ian was in this for the long haul. Rose Hildebrande was his fate, and he knew it. It wasn't going to be an easy fate, but slowly Ian was realizing that life wasn't about easy. Life was about good.

The silvery light passed over her again, and she clenched her hands, stilled. That absolute stillness, like stone. It lasted for a bit too long, but then her chest filled and she stroked a line down his torso.

"You're awake," she whispered, and one of her hands slid down his body. Found his cock. Lingered. Ian took his right hand and placed it over hers. It was the first time in his life he'd ever reined in a woman's touch on his cock, but someone had to keep their head. Unfortunately, it would be him.

Her hand moved up, traced over the outline of his bandage. "What happened?"

He considered the truth, decided that was a big no. "I was running with scissors."

Rose looked up and met his eyes. Hers were cool and unbelieving. "Dangerous."

Ian tried to smile, but this was too new, and he had no idea what to say, what to do, how to touch her, how to make a joke. "I know. I have trouble with authority."

The magical fingers moved around his hand, glided up and down over him, and his blood throbbed and settled low. Slowly, very methodically, Ian felt himself being seduced. "I bet you have trouble with authority, too," he told her, his jaw tight.

One bewitched finger slid over his seam, and Ian closed his eyes, giving in to the pleasure because it was easy. Too easy. Eventually that voice in his head—some called it a conscience—was nagging too loud to be ignored. Very methodically, yet very firmly, Ian removed her hand. His body would forgive him later. Maybe.

He looked down at her, hair tousled, eyes sleepy and aroused, the curve of her breasts…

Damn.

"I'll be back," he mumbled, and tore out for his closet. There, he shrugged into a pair of old jeans and found her a T-shirt and sweats. He needed her covered, awake, with preferably twelve, maybe fourteen inches of space between them. Then, and only then, would she be safe.

When he walked into the room, suitably clothed, he saw the light dim from her eyes, and he hated that he did that. But what was he supposed to do? Wearily, he ran a hand through his hair and Rose laughed. He liked to hear her laugh, liked that moment when her face grew soft and warm. He was fast learning there weren't enough of those.

"What?" he asked.

Rose leaned back into the pillows, the covers falling away, in what was a very planned, very well-executed, very effective attack on his virtue. "You look like you're about twelve," she told him, her plump mouth curved enough to be dangerous.

Because he wasn't that easy, Ian kept his gaze glued to the white wall behind her.

"Mrs. Robinson, you're trying to seduce me, aren't you?" Then he tossed her the sweats and shirt, where they magically landed across her bare torso. Ian told himself he was happy. "I'll go find breakfast." It sounded like a good plan until he remembered his refrigerator and its usual complete absence of food. "I'll go hunt for breakfast," he corrected, and then turned his back, listening to the soft rustling sounds of Rose getting dressed.

He was such a stupid shit.

A few minutes later, his head was buried deep in the cabinet, where he salvaged a lone can of green beans, expiration date, 2004.

Rose came up behind him, not touching, but he could feel her, smell her. Honeysuckle was back. Ian smiled, and held up the can proudly. Those sharp eyes locked on the label, and without a word, Rose tossed it in the trash, ignoring the very real possibility that green beans had a shelf life that extended well into the next millennium. Apocalypse provisions, that's what he was talking about.

However, Rose had other ideas. She stood, hands on her very cute, sweats-covered hips, and contemplated his cabinets. "I could help you with that. I'm a master organizer," she said, and immediately started opening doors, frowning soon after. Cinderella in gray fleece, his Rutgers T-shirt clinging with carnal purpose. Very sexy.

Eventually she turned and raised a critical brow.

Still very sexy, but he wasn't so inclined to jump her.

"I don't believe in a lot of clutter in the kitchen," he answered by way of explanation.

"I've got this great system. I can take your spices, sort by alphabetical order and the date they need to be replaced. We can branch out into—" she glanced toward the lone can of beans "—food."

"I don't have spices. I don't cook much. I don't think the oven's ever been turned on." Ian leaned back against the counter, giving her his best Oliver Twist look, something he'd mastered postlayoff.

"Why didn't you ever have a girlfriend, a fiancée, a wife?"

"I don't know. There were some, but nothing ever felt right. It was like there was some voice in my ear, whispering for me to wait."

"Commitment phobic. That's what I call it."

"Yeah." *Or fate.* Ian frowned, wondering what the Fates actually thought of him. At midnight, January 1, when they had planted a beautiful, sexy woman into his life, he had assumed that meant that Ian Cumberland was back, hitting the fast lane, shifting gears. Instead, he'd been pulled into the life of a beautiful, sexy, slightly lust-crazed woman who had more issues than he did. Rose Hildebrande was a double-edged sword, a sword that knew how to draw blood, he thought with a glance toward his hand. Lots of blood. Honestly, Ian wasn't big on blood loss.

When she looked at him with those big pools of pale blue, he got dizzy and confused, and honestly, Ian wasn't big on dizzy and confused, either.

Ian blinked, realizing he needed to feed her before she thought he couldn't afford that, either. "I'll run out, get some orange juice—and food, too. Breakfast of champions."

"Please don't. You don't need to go out of your way," she replied cheerfully, and Ian wanted to shoot himself for saying the wrong thing. Everything he did or said seemed to hit some pre-programmed response in her. He had faced automated phone systems that were easier to get past. But she was lucky, because his automated phone system skills were now legendary. Mentally, he cracked his knuckles.

"Would you sing for me?" he asked, testing his new strategy: diversion.

"Uh, no," she said with horror—not, he was pleased to note, one of her five most popular preprogrammed responses.

Okay. Diversion is good. "Oh, come on. It can't be that bad." Ian used his coaxing voice, the one that had gotten past stifled bureaucrats, surly secretaries and main desk attendants with a mild Napoleonic complex. Rose was no match for the master.

"It's that bad," she told him, holding her own against the master. "Trust me."

"Come on, you've seen the dark secrets of my kitchen. I think I'm entitled. I think I've earned it," he said, testing out his second theory: outlogic-ing her own logic.

Her eyes narrowed, but she nodded. She cleared her throat, then gave him one last chance to change his mind. "You're sure."

Ian waved a go-ahead hand, watching with fascination as she launched into a glass-cracking chorus from "Everything's Coming up Roses." Fascination turned to sainted martyrdom as she hit notes that made his eardrums curl up in a fetal position, but Ian kept a rapt smile on his face. After she was finished, Rose looked at him smugly, waiting for his reaction.

"Wow. Just, wow."

"At least you don't lie and tell me it sounds like the angels. My mother thought I could hit it big on Broadway, and she made me practice that song over and over, until the pageant director set her straight. Mama cried for a week."

As he listened to her talk, Ian smiled, much easier this time. A pageant director? One more little piece of her life. Maybe it wasn't deep emotional insight, but they were talking and she wasn't jumping him—it was progress.

A few minutes later, when she started on the cabinets, Rose reached across him, her breasts brushing his back, not even on purpose. Didn't matter, his nerves popped awake and Ian jerked, thwacking his head on the empty cabinets.

Deep into organizing the empty recesses of his life, Rose didn't even notice. Definitely progress.

Discreetly Ian turned away, shoving his hard-on from the locked and upright position, into something less…obvious. "I'll go get breakfast. Bagels?" he asked, eyeing her ass as she rummaged through the cabinets.

Rose didn't look up, didn't see the lust in his eyes. "Bagels would be fine."

AFTER IAN LEFT, ROSE stood there, alone in his apartment, clad in his clothes. All morning, he'd worked so hard to make her feel comfortable. Instead, all he was doing was messing with her head. The T-shirt was like some ancient device of torture. Sure, it was clean and freshly laundered, but there was some intrinsic mark that he'd left behind, and it made her itchy, nervous…weak. She almost pulled the thing off, weighing that option against the white cocktail dress from last night. Reluctantly she stayed in his shirt, feeling the material stroking her breasts.

It wasn't the physical that worried her. It was the feeling of intimacy, the very intimacy that she wanted to avoid, because Ian was sneaky, nearly as sneaky as she was. Look at how fast he'd gotten her into his clothes?

And when had "just sex" transformed into breakfast and the sharing of clothes? Rose wasn't a clothes sharer. Heck, she'd never worn a man's clothes. They were big, bulky…comfortable.

Right as she was telling herself that she was being freaked for nothing, her cell phone rang—Sylvia—and Rose punched the button.

"Rose? Are you feeling better?"

Rose pulled at the T-shirt, trying to find that place where it didn't touch her nipples. There was none. "Oh, yeah. Loads. I don't know what happened last night." *Yes, she did. Sultry McSlut invaded her body and rode the F train to O-town. Over and over again.*

"I was worried about you, but now you're fine, so tell me… Remy? The date?"

Rose glanced toward the apartment door, feeling oddly disloyal, then making a face at herself for feeling oddly disloyal. This was the arrangement. Signed, sealed, cleared. No disloyalty when everyone was honest. Mostly honest. "I'm looking forward to it," she answered, noticing the bedspread was close to falling off. Rose bent, straightened the covers, smelled sex, Ian, sex and Ian. Abruptly she sat on the edge, getting the flutters down below.

"You don't sound very excited about this, Rose."

Excited? Rose stared at that bed with longing, a slow and insidious longing, a dangerous undertow pulling at her. "You'd be surprised at how excited I am." Before Sylvia could go any further and drag something out of her, Rose switched to a safer subject. "How was Anton? Did he get you the necklace?"

"Wasn't that delish? We spent most of the night in the sauna, making out like teenagers. Walter nearly walked in on us. I think I gave the man a heart attack, but sometimes…"

"I know," said Rose with an understanding nod. "Listen, I have to go. Do you need anything today?"

"No, be free. Take the day off. Get a facial. Or a pedicure. Something fun. I'll see you tomorrow."

"Sunday?" Rose frowned.

"Yes, Sunday, silly. Got the food drive to get started on. Can't let the grass grow under our feet, now, can we? People are hungry in this city, and they need to be fed, *muy pronto*. Unless… Oh, listen to me. Can you believe I'm such a Marie Antoinette. You'll be screaming, 'off with her head' before I realize. Do you want Sunday off? We can do everything on Monday. Truly."

"I'll be there on Sunday," promised Rose. "For today, a facial sounds divine. I think I'm going to call right now. I'll see you first thing in the morning. Bye." Rose rushed the words, disconnecting the call before Sylvia wanted to delve more into Rose's state of mind, which was currently as tone-deaf as her singing.

With phone in hand, Rose considered the insane impulse to sprawl on the bed, roll in the covers and replay last night. No, not the sex, which was great, but the torrential aftermath, when she had been curled next to Ian, feeling safe, sheltered, protected, letting him take charge of her life. She had felt his chest, his heart, and the light of the day was so preferable to sleep.

Trust me.

In the light of today, which, she realized, was yesterday's tomorrow, "trust me" didn't seem so impossible. Ian hadn't barked, or yelled, or snapped, or criticized…except for last night. And she'd deserved that.

Stop. It.

Rose would not make excuses for him. He was who he was, and she was going to follow the path that she'd decided on. Not Ian. Not fate. But Rose alone. She could sleep with him. He hadn't asked to marry her, to love her, to do anything but go out to dinner. Yet it was the dinner that terrified her.

When terrified, Rose called back those skills that served her best. Beauty and organization and an unnatural talent for cleaning. Beauty wasn't going to do beans for her, organization needed things—and Ian certainly didn't go overboard with the material possessions—so there was only one thing left to do. Rose headed for the bathroom, because when you needed to clear your head and tackle the world, the harsh smells of ammonia and bleach could work miracles.

Armed with paper towels and spray cleaner, she walked through the threshold then stopped, and stared. The mirror, or what was left of the mirror, stared back. Rose took a step closer, found her reflection crisscrossed with jagged cracks and gaping holes.

"Rose?"

It was Ian. Ian was looking for her, but Rose couldn't move from her spot, and that was where he found her.

This bathroom was really too small for two people. Terribly small. Her arms started to itch, the soft cotton scratching like wool.

He raised his hand—helpless, not violent. Rose flinched anyway, and Ian saw.

"It bothered me," he was telling her. She heard him speak, but the words fell on her ear with a distant echo. "I don't usually hit things. I've never hit people. Ever, except this one kid…"

Trust me.

Rose glanced at the mirror, and she could feel the sweat on her neck, beading there, but no one would ever know. Ladies did not sweat. She needed to move, but if she moved back one step, they would be touching. She made herself move back. Made herself touch him. Gently, she kissed his cheek.

"I know. You're a good and decent man, and we all have our moments. Sylvia called. I have to go into work. I'll do breakfast another time."

"Rose?"

The vulnerability was there in his eyes, the concerns and the worry. She didn't want to talk. She didn't want to hear explanations, or defenses, or excuses. She handed him the bottle of cleaner, because ammonia and bleach weren't going to help. She only needed to leave. "I had a lovely time," she told him, painstakingly polite.

"Later, we can have dinner. Go for a walk. There's a club…"

Her laugh was particularly happy. She was good at that laugh. Most people couldn't tell. His eyes narrowed. Ian could tell. Rose took one more step away, and then she managed to lift her face, meet his gaze evenly and decided to outline the situation very clearly, so that he would understand. It wasn't something that she'd ever done with her mother, and she'd always regretted that she hadn't been brave enough. Not anymore.

"No dinner. No walks. No clubs. We're having sex. You agreed. I'll see you later. Probably not tonight. Maybe tomorrow. I'm not sure."

With that, she left.

10

IT WAS A COOL, CRISP Saturday afternoon, and Ian pulled up a
bar stool, ordered a beer and objectively considered his current
miserable condition. This was supposed to be his good year.
And yes, some things were great, some things were awesome,
but the way Rose had watched him before she left? Like he was
Jack Nicholson wielding an axe? How could it get worse?

"What's up with you?" Beckett asked, sitting down. He
took a sip from Ian's beer, reached into the bowl of peanuts and
got cracking.

"That's my beer," Ian reminded him. Now people were
stealing his beer. Things were getting worse.

"So, what's wrong? You sounded really ragged on the phone."
Beckett popped a nut in his mouth and munched happily, looking
cheerful and unconcerned. Unaccountable rage suddenly built up
inside him, almost all currently directed at Beckett. That's what
friends were for.

Earlier, when Ian had invited Beckett to the bar, he had wanted
to confide, ask his advice, rag about his situation, and maybe, in
the end, come up with a plan. But now he realized that this was
Beckett he was talking to. Beckett would tell him that life sucks,
the world was a dank cesspool of misery and corruption, and Ian
should wise up and follow along like the rest of the lemmings.
Not exactly the sort of optimism that Ian wanted to hear.

"I'm excellent. How's your crisis?" asked Ian instead,
sounding more smug than he had any right to be. Feeling guilty,
he ordered Beckett his own beer. By the time Ian was finished,
Beckett would need it.

"What crisis?"

"The female thing," Ian reminded him.

Comprehension dawned on Beckett's face, and misery followed. "Still there."

"Sucks." Idly, Ian cracked a few peanuts, leaving the husks in his wake.

"Yeah." The beer arrived, but Beckett only stared into the amber liquid, and then sighed. "I remember what you said, and I've ended up on her doorstep a few times, but then...jeez. Sex is a big step. There are all sorts of complications. And emotions. And complicated emotions. If I hadn't seen her naked—"

"You've seen her naked, but you haven't had sex?" Ian popped a peanut in his mouth. Beckett's misery felt more cathartic than he expected.

"I can't have sex."

Ian gaped. Beckett looked up, noticed and backtracked. "I mean, I could, but I didn't. I *chose* not to. I should have just done it. Got it over with, but sex is... I don't know. It's this huge abyss. And you look into the abyss and it's dark, and you don't know what lies down there, and you could get sucked in and never return. An abyss is a scary-ass thing."

"I know," agreed Ian.

"Ian?"

"Yes."

"After you have sex with someone, are you intrinsically bound to that person, and does it alter your relationship forever, never to be forgotten until the advent of some form of memory-erasing device?"

Generously, Ian shoved the bowl of peanuts in Beckett's direction. It was the least he could do. "Yes."

Beckett ignored them. "Yes, you are intrinsically bound to that person, or yes, it alters the relationship forever, or yes, they have invented some form of memory-erasing device?"

"Yes, yes, no," Ian answered, cheerfully watching as Beckett thwacked his head against the bar.

"I thought that's what you were saying. I can't do this."

Ian slapped him on the back, not to induce pain, but to actually help. "Yes, you can, Beckett. Some things are worth it."

It was true. Rose was worth it. It was going to be hell. A dark abyss that would suck him inside, but he was already intrinsically bound to her. He had been bound to her even before the sex. After the sex, seriously, who was he kidding? Somewhere, somehow, the Fates were laughing at one previously cocky, self-assured Ian Cumberland. He looked up, mentally shot them all the finger and felt better than he had in days.

Alas, Beckett still remained miserable. "I don't know if it *is* worth it," he said. "It's the abyss. You don't know what's in the abyss."

Ian sighed, feeling old and wise and resigned. "But if you want to fall into it, then it's worth it."

"I'm not convinced," Beckett argued, still struggling with the inevitability of his destiny.

Hearing the doubts in his voice, Ian pushed Beckett's beer mug toward him. Destiny was best confronted with a cold beer, an overflowing bowl of peanuts and a good friend who understood.

Patiently he watched as Beckett drank, waiting until Beckett was done.

"You're convinced, but you're nervous," Ian rationalized with slow words, because Beckett had a Spocklike engineering brain, and the subjective caused him problems. "You don't know what to do, but you know what you *want* to do, and that's what you're going to do. You can't fight it."

It was a brilliant piece of philosophy, suitable for framing. In the face of such brilliance, Beckett didn't say a word, sipping at his beer and cracking peanuts.

For some time they sat in the bar, watching the Tar Heels stomp all over whoever the heck they were playing. Destiny. Truly, it was a game-changer.

Eventually Beckett finished his beer and stood, looking if not happier, at least more courageous. "You're going to be at the game tonight?" he asked, when the bartender slipped over the tab.

"Odds look good," answered Ian.

Beckett picked up the tab, glanced over it, put it back down. "I owe you a beer."

"You owe me fourteen," Ian reminded him.

"They won't let me buy you fourteen at the arena. I respect the law. I'll buy you one," he said, and tossed his jacket over his shoulder.

"Beckett."

"What?"

"Thanks."

"Dude, you've lost a million-dollar job and now you're thanking me for one beer? It's weak, man. I feel like I'm losing you to…estrogen."

Ian laughed, his spirits restored. Nothing like wallowing in the abyss and coming out alive. "Beckett?" he said, deciding to be even more generous.

"What?"

"Forget about the beers. I'm good."

SATURDAY-NIGHT BASKETBALL games drew a crowd at the RAC, lots of action and lots of cheers. Rose hadn't called, but Ian had known that she wouldn't. He would wait, be patient and let her lead the way, since that seemed to be her most favored state. In the interim, he was looking forward to Beckett, Phoebe and plastic nachos. Life didn't get any better than this.

But when he got to his seat, Phoebe wasn't there. "Where is she?"

Beckett looked at him, oddly guilty. "I don't know. I haven't talk to her. Do I look like her keeper? I'm not her keeper."

"Just asking," muttered Ian.

"I don't know why she isn't here. Why don't you call?"

Ian stared. "Why don't you call? First you steal the beer, now you want me picking up all the phone charges, too."

"I thought you were okay with the beer. You told me you were okay with the beer. If you're not okay with the beer, it's your problem, because I don't want to owe you anymore, and you said I didn't, so I'm not."

Ian considered arguing further, then decided that Beckett was acting irrational, and dialed Phoebe instead.

"What?"

"Phoebe? It's Ian. Where are you?"

"I'm at home," she snapped. *Good God, was nobody happy today?*

"Why aren't you here?" he asked in his nicest, friendliest voice.

"At the basketball game?" she answered, the words dripping with sarcasm, missing his nice, friendly voice.

Ian abandoned all pretence of civility. "No, I'm at frigging Tiffany & Co. What the hell is wrong with everybody? You know, I have a reason to be in a crappy mood. But am I in a crappy mood? No, I'm the Mr. Cheerful of this crowd, but nobody appreciates it. Why don't you appreciate it?"

"I don't want to be there, Ian," she told him, still not appreciating it.

"And why the heck not? Who died and made you princess of the universe? You're supposed to be here. I need you."

"Beckett doesn't."

"Beckett's a jackass. Why are we talking about Beckett? I want to talk about me."

Beckett grabbed the phone, muted it. "Is she talking about me? What'd she say?"

Ian glared, unmuted the phone. "Phoebe. Get your ass down here. Now. I need more nachos. I want a beer, maybe fourteen, and I don't expect to be treated like somebody's backwash."

He heard her sigh. California could have heard her sigh. "Fine. I'll be there in twenty."

"Make it ten," he snapped.

After he put away his phone, Beckett was watching the game, lock-jawed. "She's coming?"

"Man, I don't know what her problem is. Probably got dumped."

Beckett grunted, started in on Ian's nachos.

Twenty-two minutes later, Phoebe arrived.

"You're late," Beckett told her.

Phoebe stayed silent.

"You having a hard week, too?" asked Ian, feeling a little guilty because he shouldn't have been so mad with Phoebe. She looked pale and there were circles under her eyes, and Phoebe didn't pull off pale well. Not like Rose who pulled off everything well.

Instead of thinking of Rose, Ian stuffed another nacho in his mouth.

"Who's the guy?" Ian asked when Phoebe didn't answer.

"Nobody," she said. "There's no guy."

"Okay, so if there's no guy, then what's wrong? Problems at work?" Phoebe was a manager of IT at an insurance company. There were always problems at work, but usually they didn't bother her like this.

"Work's fine."

"Family?" asked Ian, running out of options here.

"Family's good."

"You're not going to tell us?"

"There are certain things that I'd like to keep private."

"Absolutely," agreed Ian, because private was code for PMS.

"I didn't want to come tonight," continued Phoebe, because she was going to talk more about private. Sometimes women were difficult. "I was looking forward to staying home and watching TiVo by myself. Alone. No company."

"I think we got that," said Beckett.

Her eyes narrowed to slits. "You have no right to be pissy with me, mister. None. I am the victim, and you are the…non-victim, and I get to be pissy. Do you understand? I have earned that right."

Now it was Ian who was studiously watching basketball. Phoebe was on a tear. Ian kept silent. Beckett? Not so smart.

"I am as much a victim of this as you are. Just because I don't look as depressed as you do doesn't mean I'm not disappointed. You have to be careful with the abyss."

Abyss? Ian crunched into the chip, missed, bit his tongue instead. His stomach began to curl and twine and finally, when it was knotted into a tight mass of nerves, the nausea kicked in.

No. He was leaping to conclusions. No leaping. Absolutely no leaping here.

"Are you calling me an abyss? And I'm not depressed. This isn't my depressed face. This is my relieved face. I knew exactly what you knew. Afterward we'd be stuck with a big, stinkin' pile of awkward, and I'm too smart for that."

Unable to keep the evil conclusions at bay any longer, Ian leaped up from his seat. "Oh, no. This is not going to happen."

Beckett and Phoebe looked up at him, confused, which was so much better than…

"I will not allow this to happen."

Phoebe grabbed his plate of nachos and stole one, crunching defiantly. "Who died you and made you princess of the universe?"

Ian noticed the irate glare from the people behind them and wisely sat. He took his nachos and leaned low. "Listen. This is not smart. I need both of you right now. I will remind you—since everybody keeps forgetting—I'm having a hard time of it. Now, I've tried not to whine and burden everybody with my problems, because you know I don't want to be Whiny Guy, but if I can't whine, I at least need to have the comforting knowledge that nobody is going to dare whine to me."

They didn't look convinced. Beckett looked stubborn, Phoebe looked mad. Ian tried a new approach. A happier approach. "We're the Three Musketeers. We have stuck through everything together. We drink, do the wenching thing—except for Phoebe, who does the male-wenching thing. And we do this because it's bonding. Ten years we've been together. *Ten years.* A full decade, and now, you guys are flirting with disaster. Did Athos and Aramis ever do the deed? I think not. They were too smart. They understood the rare gift that is friendship. You can't just toss that away."

"Uh, Ian," Beckett interrupted, "Athos and Aramis are guys."

"Don't be so close-minded. It's not the gender—it's the complications."

Beckett wasn't done. "You told me that if I knew what I wanted to do, then that's what I was going to do, and I couldn't fight it. I want to do this."

And *now* Beckett makes his decision? Ian glanced at Phoebe, and, noticing the gooey look in her eyes, felt his stomach loop even tighter.

"You want to do this?" she asked Beckett.

This was a mistake. A recipe for disaster. Over the arena

speakers, organ music began to play. Right now Ian craved continuity, and everywhere around him, continuity was going on strike. Desperately he tried one last time. "I'm not going to pick between you two. You split up, I'm not taking sides. You guys will be dead to me. Do you understand? Dead to me."

They ignored him, caught in the wonderglow that was ill-advised lust.

Idiots.

Ian stood up. "Leaving now. Going home. Can't watch mistakes being made."

Nobody was even listening.

ON SATURDAY, ROSE SPENT most of the day at the Empire Hotel, arranging details with the caterers. After that, she met with the florist, explaining in precise terms exactly how the table arrangements needed to look. She checked in with all the heroic bachelors who were donating their time for ungrateful animals that would never throw them a bone, or probably do something cowardly like run away at the least sign of conflict because they were afraid of being mistreated by people, even by people with sparkling eyes that saw the best in the world.

Rose settled in her hard-backed chair, stared into Helen the Rabbit's judgmental blue, yet still-sightless eyes and sighed like a baby. She wanted to see Ian. She was still in his T-shirt and sweats, prowling through her tiny apartment, getting used to the cushy softness of the cotton, getting used to the idea that she didn't need to suck in her gut, because frankly, in these baggy pants, nobody could tell if she was gutless or not.

It was in that gutless moment that she realized that she was wearing the perfect excuse. Reluctantly she doffed her own clothes, pulling on the usual black woolen pants and a coordinated knubby sweater and then left for the laundry room, where at 9:00 p.m., she was laundering Ian's clothes, using extra fabric softener to make them lavender fresh and not smelling anything at all like Powder Puff Rose. Fine, she would be a powder puff, but at least she was a well-bred powder puff.

Two hours later, she was at his apartment, his clothes neatly folded in her hand. When he opened the door, Rose shoved the pile at him. "I brought your clothes. I cleaned them."

He was smiling at her, and it was nearly as nice as wearing his clothes.

"I should go," she said and turned. Ian caught her arm.

"You don't have to. I'm glad you came back. Sit down. Want a drink? Orange juice. Bagel? I bought food." He sounded nervous, but a good nervous. They both stood there, not moving. Ian tucked his hands in his jean pockets and rocked back on his heels. Rose felt her palms start to sweat. Ladies should not perspire.

"It's late. I should have called, but there was laundry," she babbled, still not moving.

Ian broke the not-moving thing first. He walked to the sofa and then, in a bold commitment to relaxing in his own apartment, sat.

Oh, God.

Rose rubbed her damp palms on her woolen slacks, found them itchy and took the opposite end of the sofa. "How was your evening?"

"Really miserable. You would not believe." He stopped, winced. "Sorry. It was great."

And now he was the one who was on Rose Alert. Great. "What was miserable about it?" she asked, being polite and actually curious, as well. Her night hadn't been that great, either.

"You don't care. Honestly, I don't expect you to care. It's stupid and it's pointless, and I shouldn't complain. Two people decide to get together—it should be a time for joy and happiness and little birds singing, and instead, I start twisting up into knots...."

Rose frowned at that, because it didn't bode well for the future of this relationship, which was based only on sex, of course.

"They're going to have sex. I know it."

She stared, even more curious. "Who?"

"Beckett, Phoebe. My two best friends."

"You have best friends," she murmured.

"You don't?"

"The countess."

"But you work for her?"

"Yeah, but I spend a lot of time working for her, so it's convenient having her for a best friend, as well." Over the years, Rose had discovered that women didn't like being around her. She was too quiet, too pretty, too reserved, too everything. Sylvia was too everything, too, but she understood. And sometimes Rose suspected that Sylvia knew more than she let on. Amazing, improbable, yet most likely true.

"So, you think Beckett and Phoebe are, even as we speak, having sex?" she asked.

"Probably," he said, looking miserable.

"Why shouldn't they, um, get involved?"

Ian stared at her blankly, and then shot up from his seat. Rose's hand twitched, but it was a small movement, actually more of a tremor, and Ian didn't notice.

"You think it can work?"

"You don't think it can?" she asked, because this was a game. Guess the reasons a relationship is doomed for failure. Reason number one: Party A is a basket case who jumps at shadows and has a fondness for the smell of bleach.

"It probably could work," he answered, but he didn't sound optimistic, and she missed that undertone of optimism in his voice. She liked that about Ian. He was a glass half-full person. Rose, on the other hand, was a "Glass, what glass? I don't see any glass," sort of person.

"Maybe it can," she encouraged.

Ian went back to his end of the couch and collapsed. "They're doomed. It's Beckett. He's all black, white, death, taxes and we're all going to fall into the abyss."

Instantly Rose knew she would get along with Beckett.

"And Phoebe?"

"She's sensitive. Sometimes she gets in over her head, and we sort of take care of her."

"Does she have problems?"

"Phoebe? Are you kidding? She's got a great job, managing about a hundred software developers. Truthfully, she runs the place." Ian stopped. "We really don't take care of her. It's more the other way around. She's the stable one."

"You're not?" asked Rose carefully, because Ian struck her as very stable. Relatively stable. More stable than her.

"I used to be." He looked at her. "I shouldn't have said that, should I?"

"I think you still are," she told him, and meant it.

"I usually am. But now…"

"I hurt you," Rose whispered, uncomfortable with that bit of truth. Being on the blunt-force edge of a lot of pain, she went far out of her way not to do the same to others. Ian was a first.

"I shouldn't have hurt you. I'm sorry."

"No, you shouldn't. But you did."

She moved to sit next to him and took his hand. It was a bold action that flew in the face of her sex-only manifesto. Gently, Ian squeezed her hand. Rose inched closer, wanting to kiss him, wanting to lean in and nibble along his jaw, where the evening's stubble ran wild and free. It called to her, that lean line of his jaw, beckoning, tempting.

Gently, he moved her head, pushing it firmly to his shoulder. "I think we should talk."

"All night?" she asked, hearing a bit of peevishness in her voice. It wasn't an attractive sound. Talking was right up there with clothes-sharing and trust. She needed a set of rules for this relationship. He was supposed to fall in line.

"Not all night. Maybe for a while."

"I'm not a good talker," she explained.

"I think you'll do fine."

"I don't know about this."

"Rose? Trust me."

His dark eyes looked uncomfortably sure of her, as if *she* was going to fall in line. Quietly she nodded, letting him think what he would.

It was only talking after all. How dangerous was that?

Deep inside, she knew the answer to that question, but right now, it was a risk she wanted to take.

BECKETT RIPPED OFF HER jacket, and Phoebe wanted to yell at him for being so careless. But he was already attacking her sweater and then the bra, swearing until, finally, he had his hands on bare, naked Phoebe flesh. For a second, he stilled, eyes on her chest, hands poised on her breasts, an expression on his face she'd never seen before. Like a chocoholic diving into a hot fudge sundae, or looking up at the sun on the first day of spring. Heaven.

Phoebe smiled.

"Hey," she whispered.

A dark flush ran up his cheeks, an adorable dark flush. How did he manage to be studly, arrogant, rash-mouthed and adorable all at the same time? Tomorrow, she would ponder. Tonight was about great sex.

"Sorry. Lost myself. Does this feel weird?" he asked. His hands were still latched on her breasts, like a man lost, confused and frozen at the cantaloupe bin, testing produce. At this rate, they would never leave the bin, let alone check out, and in a flash of clarity Phoebe knew exactly why they'd spent ten years apart.

Throwing caution to the wind, she grabbed his sweater, yanking it over his head, exposing one bare-chested Beckett. Oh, gawd. Phoebe's mouth went Sahara dry. Yes, she'd seen him shirtless before, but not with Phoebe-lust burning in his eyes, not with all that power-pack musculature heaving and miles of golden skin happily within touching distance. And all this could be hers…

Like ice cream. Better than ice cream. Breathlessly, Phoebe slid her hands over the glorious firmament of his chest, over the wide breadth of shoulders. Under her touch, she could see the play of emotions on his face. Confusion. Pleasure.

Fear.

"Kiss me," she ordered, because she didn't want a discussion, a debate or a logical twelve-point analysis on why this was wrong. She wanted to feel those curmudgeonly lips hard against hers. She wanted to feel the slide of that bitter tongue mating with hers, and most of all, she wanted to be filled with that primal piece of Beckett that was currently burning against her thigh.

Her lady parts began to purr with eager anticipation.

Tentatively, gently, his hands cupped her face. Next he took off her glasses, and then they were kissing. Phoebe and Beckett were kissing. She waited for the universe to collapse upon itself.

She waited for God to hit them with lightning. It felt wicked. It felt right.

Phoebe sighed, pushing closer.

Beckett swore, lifted his head. "Oh, God."

His brain-freeze was back. It was there in the panicked green eyes that were selfishly denying her pleasure—long overdue. *Well-deserved* pleasure. "What now?"

"It shouldn't feel this good."

"It can and will feel this good." *If we stop quibbling about it.*

"I don't know," he said, and then his gaze locked on her naked breasts. Stayed locked.

Because she was a vile, malicious person, she took her finger, wet it and then hypnotically traced first one nipple, then the other, praying tarty and tawdry would work.

The sound that broke from his throat most resembled a wounded animal. A wounded animal that badly wanted sex. That, Phoebe understood.

She flashed him a smile—slow and sinful—the sort men understood.

It was all the inducement he needed. Beckett jumped her, and together they crashed to the bed in a tangled heap. Frantically, he kissed her, her body quivering, his hands running over her, hot and greedy. Her fingers locked in his hair, her legs fused tight around his waist. She was not leaving this. Not now. Not ever. It was more than she'd ever imagined, had ever fantasized. *Beckett.*

Her mouth was going to be numb tomorrow, and she knew there would be bruises, but oh, it was a small price to pay for *this.*...

His hands grabbed her fly, unzipping, pushing, down to her panties, and then, *oh, yes,* he cupped her. She shot upright, all that frustration bubbling inside her, building, pressing, until...

"Phoebe," he gasped, lifting his head. No, there would be no doubts, no chance to back out now. She would kill him if he did. Because she was such a good friend and it would be really wrong—as well as sexually unsatisfying—to kill him, Phoebe brought his lips to hers, whispering promises, wicked promises against his mouth. There was only one man she'd ever said these things to, only one man she ever would. This man.

He groaned, but he didn't pull away. "I can't survive this," he told her, furiously pressing kisses on her mouth, her neck, her breasts. Phoebe arched, pushing that ravishing mouth closer, sensations shooting from her breasts to her thighs, down to her toes. She wasn't going to survive it, either. And she didn't care.

Like a total wench, she ground herself into him, hips pressing, thrusting, feeling the thick hard piece of cock that belonged to Beckett. *Beckett.* She'd had dreams, fantasies, but oh, heaven… Her heart thudded, pounded. Louder. Louder.

Phoebe froze at the sound of the door. Beckett stopped, swore, his green eyes marvelously frantic. "Leave it. It's not important."

The ticking frog clock on the wall said midnight. People didn't knock on doors at midnight when it wasn't important.

A woman's voice called out. "Con Ed. Anybody there? We're evacuating the building. We think there's a gas leak." Now there were other sounds in the hallway. A flurry of agitated voices, clomping footsteps on the stairs. People were leaving.

Beckett shook his head. "It's nothing."

Oh. This was torture. Beckett was nearly naked. She was topless, unzipped, dazzled with the idea of having sex with the man currently lodged between her thighs. Alas, Phoebe knew how this was going to end. She paid her taxes, she didn't cheat at Monopoly, and she had only lied to her parents once, and that was when she'd blamed the olive oil spill on her baby sister. Deep in her heart of hearts, Phoebe wasn't a rule-breaker. "It's a gas leak, Beckett. We need to go."

"It's probably a fake." He sniffed. "All I smell is the scent of a desperate man who's one minute from having carnal relations with his best friend and moving to the next level—which is impossible to return from—but willing to go for it, because damn, you have a dirty, dirty mouth, and my head is going to explode if I'm not inside you."

The door pounding started again. "Hey. I know you're in there, and look, I'm not happy to be bashing doors at midnight. I got a warm bed at home, too, and a husband who's going to *still* expect breakfast on the table at 7:00 a.m. I might be out saving the city from a gas disaster, but does he care? No. So, please, whoever you are, stop pretending you're not there. I have a job to do and I'm going to do it. So get up, and get your ass out here before I get really nasty and start kicking down doors. City doesn't like us to do that, 'cause doors are crazy expensive."

Phoebe gave him her best managerial we-must-be-responsible-citizens look.

Beckett, understanding the look and what it meant, rolled over and groaned. "I stared into the abyss, I was ready. I was totally in the moment."

Phoebe pulled on her sweater and rushed to the door, tapping her foot as Beckett hopped to her, one shoe half-on.

"I'm waiting, folks. Zip it up, throw on some shoes and coats—it's cold as a mother outside. We need to get moving because I've got another fifty apartments in this building, and I'm feeling my PMS starting. You do not want to be around for that."

Beckett picked up his coat and flung open the door. On the other side was a short, squinty-eyed woman in a blue Con Ed uniform, requisite white hard hat with Charlene scrawled on it in black marker. In the hallway, Phoebe's neighbors were starting to swarm out. Mrs. Garretson in a pink housecoat, the cute little waiter who worked at the corner pub and always called her Chicky. Phoebe yanked her coat tighter and tried to look like this was an ordinary night. Beckett? Not so much.

He glared, visually condemning Charlene to the worst of public utility perditions. Phoebe knew exactly how he felt, but she wasn't stupid enough to mess with Con Ed, especially since the woman looked as if she ate small children for breakfast.

However, Mr. Well-Adjusted liked to live dangerously, especially around monopolistic enterprises that provided his heat and electricity. Frankly, it was part of his charm. "I was in the abyss, lady. I stared it in the face, and I would have done it."

The woman rolled her eyes at Phoebe. "They look into the abyss and they're so proud. They think they deserve a medal of honor."

"You have no idea, lady."

Charlene turned, stabbed a stubby finger into Beckett's chest and got in his face, not an easy task for a woman half his size. Half his size, but twice the attitude and willing to shut off all the heat for Manhattan without a second thought. Beckett was doomed.

"Try being a woman, pal. Try dressing up in three inches of itchy black spandex that leaves your ass bare, and then stare into the face of a one-eyed love snake and swallow it whole. That, my ignorant friend, is true courage."

With that, Charlene gave them one last glare of disgust before pounding her radio on the next apartment.

Beckett glanced at Phoebe and shook his head, leading them toward the stairwell. "I think she ruined me for life."

"Don't be such a baby," she told him, and locked her arm in his, trudging behind Mrs. Garretson, making sure she didn't fall. The woman seemed a little wobbly; she liked her wine with Letterman.

A few minutes later, they were all outside, huddled, most everyone in pajamas. Beckett stroked his chin. It was a good chin, begat from elitist *Mayflower* genes, with a slight "screw you" jut to it. Phoebe loved all the complexities of that chin.

"You have three inches of itchy black spandex?" he asked, a slo-mo gaze skimming over her, causing a shiver in the very best sort of way, in the very best sort of places.

"Doesn't everybody?" she asked, making a mental note to buy some.

Expectantly he looked at her, as if there were favors left to be discussed, as if their sexual relationship were to be some sort of equal partnership. Ha. Phoebe had taken women studies. Aced it.

Militantly, she crossed her hands over her chest. "You want me to stare into the face of the one-eyed love snake?"

The elitist *Mayflower* chin tucked into his chest, and Beckett had the grace to appear ashamed. "Maybe."

Pleased, Phoebe kept her smile to herself. No way was she letting him see the full extent of her heart in one night. She had suffered a long, long time, and honestly, if he suffered and had some doubts, in the end it would only make him a better person. "There are very orderly steps in relationships. First, you jump in the abyss and earn your medal of honor. After that, we'll talk about moving to the next level."

Soberly he nodded. "I knew that."

THE APARTMENT WAS DIM, full of shadows, and outside, the city was bustling. Inside, Rose could hear the sound of his heart. Peace and contentment. It was something she hadn't felt in a long, long time.

Ian's hands stroked her hair, and every now and again, his lips would press there. A woman could stay like this for a long, long time.

"So, after you abandoned your lifelong dream to sing on Forty-Second Street, what did you want to do?" he asked.

"I'm a very good organizer and a cleaner," she explained, which wasn't exactly an answer, but people didn't usually expect more. No one ever expected Cinderella to be a rocket scientist. Nobody wondered why Snow White spent her days with little men and singing birds.

"Oh."

Anxiety filled her chest, a balloon sitting there, waiting for the pin. Obviously in Ian's world, Cinderella was a rocket scientist, too. "You think I should have a career goal. Some sort of worthy vocation?"

Happily, he laughed, and Rose felt the balloon deflate. "As someone who got busted up on that one, I think career goals are overrated. I think flexibility is the key."

"But you don't view organizing and cleaning as a viable career option?" she prodded, because there was judgment. He had tried to hide it, but it was there.

"I didn't say they weren't a viable career option."

"It's what you thought."

"Reading my thoughts?"

"Sometimes I can. I'm good at that, too."

"Don't take this the wrong way—"

Rose never let him finish. "You know, that's one of those lines," she snapped. "'Don't take this the wrong way' implies 'I'm going to take it the wrong way.' It's like 'no offense intended.' Of course it's going to offend. If it didn't, there'd be no reason to caveat it ahead of time. Bah. They should be banned from language."

"You're right," he said, and then remained silent. Her mother would have yelled at Rose for giving her sass.

She waited, but Ian sat there, his mouth firmly closed, until she was curious to know.

"Go ahead. Say it. What shouldn't I take the wrong way?"

"I shouldn't have said anything."

"You haven't said anything," she reminded him.

"I shouldn't have thought about saying anything."

In a lot of ways, her mother was a lot simpler to understand than Ian. "But you did think of saying something, and if you don't want to make me mad, you'll tell me."

"Do you get mad a lot?" he asked, and she realized that she had actually gotten mad at him just now. She'd yelled. Nearly. He hadn't yelled back. Yes, it pleased her that he didn't yell back, but it worried her, as well. Better the devil you know than the devil you don't.

The devil she didn't know was waiting for her answer. Rose shrugged. "I hardly ever get mad. I'm very much a powder puff." At that, Ian snickered, and she promptly whacked him on the arm. Hard. Very un-powder-puff. "That was sneaky and underhanded," she said, but there was admiration in her voice.

"It almost worked."

His easy smile nearly diverted her, but now she was on to his tricks. "Tell me what I'm going to get mad about."

"Why don't you want to do something? You know, for pay, punch a clock."

It was a question that she dwelled on long and hard, and never came up with an acceptable answer. Rose chose to punt. "I haven't really been trained in much. I can organize, clean, look pretty and sometimes cook. My meat loaf is truly awesome."

"There's a lot of opportunity for meat loaf makers. Don't underestimate yourself."

Sadly, her expectations, and the world's, as well, were high. It was her less-than-stellar results that were causing the difficulty. This time when she shrugged, her hair fell into her face. Rose left it there. "I'm a helper. I'm a follower. Number two on the org chart, never number one."

"Did you ever want to be number one?"

"No."

"I did," he said gently, pushing the hair from her face. "Come on, you can tell me. I bet as a kid, you dreamed of being number one. I mean, you learned Ethel Merman. Not some pansy-assed folksinger, or a delicate warbler, but Ethel Merman? That's shooting for the moon."

"Maybe I did. Sometimes. But in my town, you didn't see a lot. There was the banker, the three waitresses, Zinnia at Curl Up and Dye and a handful of schoolteachers. And the mines."

"And Ethel Merman."

"Dreams. Nothing more. Mama would make me sit, glued to those musicals for hours. All the long gowns, the sweeping music. I think she thought I'd pick up musical talent through sheer force of will. She was disappointed."

"I bet not. Mothers don't disappoint easily. It's a pregnancy hormonal thing. It's impossible."

People always thought the role of parents was to protect. Rose, who had no protection until CHS stepped in, was always surprised at how wrong people could be. Everyone wanted to see the best, but sometimes there was no best to see.

"Ian?"

"Rose?"

"Can we not talk about this? You wanted to talk, and by my calculations, we've been talking for about two hours."

"A hidden talent for timekeeping, as well?"

"I have more hidden talents."

"I live to uncover hidden talents."

It was the signal that she had been waiting for, and Rose pounced. Now she dared to touch him, to slide his shirt apart and revel in the feel of his body. This was no powder puff. Sure, he had a quicksilver smile, but this... Her fingers stroked the hard ridges of his chest, absorbing the strength and the restrained power. Truly, men had it made. "You have a very nice chest. Rangy and sinewy and very explorable. I could spend a long time with your chest."

He nipped at her neck, his hands gliding between her sweater, starting to explore, as well, but Rose was too impatient. Shame-lessly, she pulled her sweater over her head, glad to be rid of the scratchy thing. His gaze settled on the black demi-bra, the fullness of her breasts. When he looked at her like that, hunger and heat, Rose felt her body swell, felt her nipples tighten, sharp with desire.

"You have a very nice chest, too. Personally, I think it's much better than mine."

She grinned, and without a speck of self-restraint, Rose tumbled into his lap and began to play in earnest.

Before this, Rose had very set rules about the displays of pleasure and restraint. With Ian, she didn't have to pretend because with him there was no Ever After, no tomorrow. Just this. There were few things as freeing as casting off the shackles of her own image. With Ian, her hands didn't have to be still or composed; she could touch, taste and in general, overindulge a sweet tooth she didn't even know she possessed. Happily Rose did.

Her mouth feasted on his, his heart racing under her hand. She did that. The hard length of his erection burned against the layers of her clothes, and the wool of her pants was creating an itch that urgently needed to be scratched. Rose shifted, sank onto him, sighing with the thick feel of him trapped between her legs. Because she could, her hips moved with a steady, succulent back-and-forth rhythm, and she delighted in the raw need in his face. Fascinated, she watched as he struggled for control and lost. Spurred on by her own success, her hands dived for his fly, teasing with soft whorls of hair that arrowed into his jeans.

"Rose, don't take this the wrong way."

Her hands froze. Nervously she licked her lips, and waited for it… Three. Two. One.

"It's a lot of fun being the ravage-ee, but sometimes—a lot of the time—I have an inclination to be the ravage-er. Would you let me?"

Not bothering to hide the hurt, Rose pulled away, because ap-parently she couldn't do sex right, either.

He caught her face in his hands and made her look at him, and she wished he were a little jerkier, because then, it would be so much easier to stick to the script. To pull her face into something pliant and serene. To nod at the approval internal. To keep everything locked inside. Those were the rules she knew. "I thought you would like that."

"Oh, sweetheart, I love that. But sometimes, you know, I want to be number one on the org chart, too."

Mutely she stared into his eyes, searching for some hint, some clue of what she was supposed to do. All she saw was painless concern.

"Trust me."

He waited on her, waited for her to decide, and she was torn between letting him take control and making a run for the door. For the past eight years, Rose had focused on molding her life as she wanted, but Ian... He knew exactly how to unravel her, how to get her to lose sight of everything: who she wanted to be, who she needed to be, who she could be.

Trust him.

Her insides screamed, telling her to run, but instead, she nodded slowly.

He didn't touch her; he studied her, looking very touchable and temptingly disordered with his shirt hanging loose, jeans soft and worn and that deceptive tenderness in his eyes. Rose tried to be patient, but it wasn't easy.

His hand reached out, stroked back her hair, gliding over her neck, her cheek, tracing over her mouth with the pad of his fingers. Rose took a nip, only because if he put it out there, she wasn't one to waste the moment.

Ian's response was a soft laugh. He bent his head, lips nuzzling her neck. The evening stubble that had tempted her earlier was warm and ticklish, and she tilted her head to one side to let him do more. She sighed, feeling the pleasure start to build inside her. The quiet current that kept tugging at her, pulling her low. He didn't rush her, didn't push, didn't force. Instead, his kiss warmed her, coaxed and tempted. Rose relaxed, giving over to the liquid sensation of being indulged.

For long minutes, they sat on the sofa, his mouth discovering nothing more than the silk of her neck, the line of her shoulders, the sensitive spot behind her ear. All the while, he murmured silly nothings that made her want to laugh, but she couldn't. Between her thighs, a hard pulse was beating, louder, more demanding.

Ian took her mouth, an easy kiss, slow, an exchange of breath, of sighs. With the tip of her tongue, she traced the seam of his mouth, teasing, and was inordinately satisfied when he groaned. For a second, the kiss turned, and he entered her mouth, thrusting in and out, a blatant foretaste of how this would end. The pulse at her center grew, thundered. Rose quivered, pressing closer, chest to chest, hard to soft. Ian to Rose.

She thought she had him when his hand slipped between her neck, underneath her hair, tangling there, pulling her to him. But he broke the kiss, struggling to breathe, and swore.

"I'm on to you now, Madam Satan."

Rose merely quirked a brow.

When he smiled, when he teased, when he coaxed, she could feel herself responding, feel her emotions romping inside her like an unsuspecting child, and she didn't know how to tamp them back down. Right now, she didn't know that she wanted to.

His eyes were sparkling in the dim light, lighthearted until they rested on her mouth, the edge of her bra. "You are so beautiful," he whispered, and there was something so painfully raw in his voice. She was used to men saying that, but it'd never stripped her bare before.

With one hand, he reached out, intently tracing the line between the black silk and white skin. Rose held her breath, forgot her requisite restraint, and silently pleaded with him to touch her. He met her eyes, held them, and before she suspected his plan, effortlessly picked her up in his arms.

For Rose, this was the pinnacle. The absolute, hands-down most powder-puff moment of her life, but, oh, mercy, it was worth it. She didn't want this sort of romance, this sort of seduction with Ian. For exactly this reason. The dull buzz in her brain, the heady thump in her heart, and the absolute certainty that he was going to take her well-planned, well-thought-out strategy and chuck it all to hell.

Her hands explored the strong sinews of his arms, and when

he laid her on the bed, she heard the thump, the booming sound of strategies being abandoned. Goals being ripped into shreds. Manifestos being torn asunder. Battles being lost.

"Rose," he whispered, and he bent over her, lowering the silk of her bra.

Her eyes shut because she couldn't bear to see his face, bear to see the pure desire in his eyes. It hurt, even while his mouth covered her breast and made her sigh. Sensation washed over her, drowning her, and Rose fisted her hands, curling them into the covers. Ian was in no hurry; he favored one breast then the other with his mouth, his tongue, conjuring a slow, sensuous coil that made her weak.

She felt his hands on her zipper, laying her naked in the worst sort of way. She was complicit. She was encouraging. Worse, she was begging.

The pants slid off, and she needed him to take her panties with them. Screw her and be done, but Ian wasn't close to being done. Reverently, *lovingly,* he kissed her belly, tarrying there, toying with her. His hand slid lower, playing between her thighs, and limply, her thighs fell open. She couldn't fight this. He stroked inside her, feeling the dampness there, finding her clit, and her body arched, taut and ready to explode.

With each stroke, each touch, her need grew. Need. Binding them together, knotting them tight. Rose bolted up, but with a gentle hand he pressed her back and put his mouth on her.

No.

His tongue was killing her, robbing her, and she buried her hands in his hair, pulling. But he didn't stop. It was exquisite. It was torture. "Please," she whispered. "Please."

That stopped him. He raised his head, watched her, and then he shifted closer, laying a soft hand on her face, wiping away a tear. He didn't ask, didn't demand an explanation, but instead pulled her into his body and held her. The tension was still inside her, the muscles cramped tight, her body screaming with frustration, with betrayal. Underneath her ear, his heart beat strong, steady. A victor's heart.

He was so sly, so tender, his eyes so dark and warm. *Trust me.*

When all is lost, when you believe that defeat is inevitable, you must choose your weapon wisely. You will have only one chance before you will be vanquished.

She had only one weapon to choose, and she would use it wisely. "I have a date on Monday night."

She could feel the precise strike to his body, the way his breath caught and held, the way he stiffened and then made himself relax. "Is this one of those, 'don't take this the wrong way' or 'no offense intended' sort of things?"

His voice was rough, raw, hurt.

Rose didn't like the sound of his hurt, but the claws of fear inside her were starting to loosen and ease, and she knew that her hard-fought control was back in hand. "I wanted you to know."

He rose above her, his dark hair tousled from the damage of her hands. There was fury in his eyes from the damage in her words. Exactly as she had intended.

"Leave." He got up, shrugged into his shirt and tossed her clothes at her. "Get out. I can't do this. I know you've got issues, and I'm sorry about that. But I can't do this. I can't keep taking this and pretending it doesn't open a vein. Go. Just go."

This time, she felt the precise strike to her own body, the way her breath caught and held, the way she stiffened and then made herself relax. "That would be best."

11

EFFICIENTLY, ROSE DRESSED, feeling his eyes on her, but she didn't meet them; she couldn't. She tried to sustain her poise, glide effortlessly across the room, composed and refined, but her feet were like lead. Her sweater was like thorns on her skin and the remains of her dinner were lodged in her throat.

When she got to the door, she tried to open it but her palms were damp and the handle twisted and slipped from her grasp. "Ian?"

"Don't say a word. You've done enough."

She rested her head against the door. Struggled to breathe. "I told you what I wanted. You didn't listen. No one listens to me."

"Fuck you," he said. It was fitting. It was what she had wanted; it was what every inch of her was screaming. Leave. Go, before it's too late.

But there was a piece of her that knew it was already too late.

Abandoning the safety of the door, the quick escape, Rose turned to face him, face many things. Her fingers wanted to stay locked on the door handle, but she licked her stone-dry lips, and forced her fingers free.

He stood in front of the window, the lights of New York at his back, and Rose met the anger in his eyes, because she could see the pain there, as well. "Would you ever hit me?"

The anger eased but the pain stayed behind. This time, she thought it wasn't pain for him, but for her. "No." Ian smiled, but it was a nervous smile, an oddly reassuring smile.

"Would you yell at me?"

"Probably," he answered, and she coveted the honesty of it. Yelling wasn't nearly so bad. It was the other things that leeched her of blood, flesh and heart.

"When I do something you don't like, what if I still want to do it? What if I want to ride you like a two-assed pony for the rest of my life? What are you going to do about that, huh? Are you going to tell me it's wrong?" Her words were quicker now, her hands fisted tightly at her side, but she was not going to run. Not anymore.

Outside the window, a light pulsed, on and off, matching the rhythm of her blood.

While she watched, his hands raised then fell. "Are you going to explain this?"

"No. Not yet. And you have to accept that. Can you?"

"Is this a game?"

"No."

"Then I can accept it. For now. I'll wait until you're ready. But you keep throwing these punches, Rose, and honest to God, you'd be surprised at how much blood they produce."

She'd never wanted to hurt anyone like this, never imagined that she could with so few words, and it didn't sit comfortably inside her. "I didn't realize."

"No one's told you before?"

"I've never done it before."

"I guess I'm the lucky one."

"I'm sorry."

"I'm sorry, too. I don't…" He met her eyes and shrugged. "I know it's not easy, but you can't keep throwing punches."

"Fair enough."

He nodded once. "Are you still going out on a date on Monday?"

"Don't push this, Ian. Don't push me." The words surprised her, but she was glad she had said them. She tilted her head, made her voice strong. "I'm going."

Surprisingly, he didn't argue. This was more courage, more confidence, all without the typical swagger. "Don't sleep with him. Can I ask that?"

"I wouldn't sleep with him anyway," she told him, because she never would have, but Ian wouldn't know that.

"Why?"

"Because he's not…" *You.* "We just started dating. I don't…" How to explain without giving away more than she was ready to? He had no idea what he was doing to her insides, giving her power with one hand, taking it away with the other. For now, she wanted to hang on to what she could.

"You don't what?"

"I don't think of him that way."

"Then why go out with him? Where's that logic?" His voice was so reasonable, so quiet, not yelling, but she knew what he was doing. Pressuring her to do things his way. Soft and gentle or strong and loud, the end result was the same.

"You want me to call it off," she taunted, mainly to bait him, to see what he'd do.

He shrugged. "Actually, I think *you* want to call it off. But it's your decision to make."

She wasn't going to be fooled. "But you're trying to make me do this. You're trying to get what you want."

"What do you want, Rose? What do you really want?"

"I don't know."

"Yes, you do. If you're not happy with what you're doing, stop doing it."

"I'm not doing anything."

He laughed, and it wasn't a nice laugh. "You're building the dream house, your anatomically correct man-mate, a convertible that you can drive with the top down, so that you can smile and wave and watch the world from behind a sealed cellophane package."

Her head jerked from the sting of the words, as accurate as they were. "That's insulting."

"Not if it's true. You're not her, Rose. You're tearing yourself up, building this world that's all peaches and cream, but that's not you."

That's not you. Someone else deciding who she was, who she wasn't. Rose clenched her hands. "You're just saying that because you wouldn't be a part of it."

"I don't want to be a part of that."

He was lying. She knew it. Every man wanted the brass ring. They spent years, decades, lifetimes chasing it, hands always outstretched. Men needed to be alpha. They needed to be the provider. And when external forces messed with the primordial ooze that beat within the breast of the male species, they grew unpredictable, irrational, lashing out at whatever was closest. For years she'd watched her father beat her mother because there was never enough.

Maybe Ian didn't want to admit it, but all she had to do was expose the ambition in him that was no different from anyone else's, and she knew just where to start.

"Are you happy, Ian? I listened to you complain about your work. Wouldn't you want your old life back? Wouldn't that make you happy? Why can't people be honest? Why is it so bad to want to be comfortable? To have money? To not worry about things?"

He laughed at that, his face hard. "There's always something to worry about it. I had money. I worried. Now I don't have money. I still worry. It comes with the territory. It comes with life. All your little friends, they deal with the same shit as everybody else. Maybe they gloss it over, maybe a winter tan and capped veneers can hide a lot, but trust me, Rose. I know. It's there."

She thought of Sylvia, thought of their life. They were happy. Ian was wrong. "If you were offered your old job, would you take it?"

"No."

"Tell the truth," she coaxed, because she saw the hesitation in his eyes.

"Maybe," he finally admitted.

Rose pounced. "See? Why is it different?"

"Because that's not the point, Rose. What I choose as a career, or what I don't choose, isn't going to make me eternally happy. I like me now. I like you, Rose. The woman under the cream silk and lace. The real you."

The real you. No, he didn't see the real her. He only saw what she let him see. "How do you know me? We just met."

"I know you like to climb on top of me, I know you like gifts for no apparent reason and I know you're terrified of loud noises. I don't like it when cars backfire, but I don't look like I'm going to throw up. Not like you."

Okay, that wasn't something she had revealed. That wasn't something she wanted him to know, wanted anyone to know.

Ignoring the warnings inside her, Rose brushed the hair out of her face and met those unflinching eyes. There, in those dark depths, just as she'd known she would, she saw the courage lanced onto that vulnerability which had drawn her from the first. Time after time, men had worked to impress her with their might, their power and their absolute superiority. Yet it was that open gash of humanity inside him that tugged at her most, and Ian had the rare strength to let her see it.

He wasn't afraid. She wouldn't be afraid, either.

"You're not like them," she stated, believing it. Behind Ian, a light flickered in the darkened sky, blazed and then burned away. An airplane, or a neon bulb failing, or possibly, the tiny shift of a woman's heart.

"Who?"

Rose stayed silent.

Ian nodded once, tacit understanding.

"I let you lay out the ground rules, Rose. I followed them, but I have one of my own."

"What?"

"You don't think I can soar with the eagles, but Tuesday night we try."

"Tuesday?"

"Compare and contrast with the Doctor of Pediatric Perfection who has the ability to buy you a small country, and who, knowing my luck, is great-looking and also nice."

Rose smiled. "You're very sure of yourself for a man with no food and very little organizational skills."

His mouth quirked, his eyes warm. Tacit understanding. "Now you're being bitchy. But I like it."

"I am, aren't I?" she said, surprised at herself, and a little...pleased. All the snarky opportunities that she'd squandered. All the little pings of satisfaction that she'd never known.

Bowing to the inevitable, she lifted one shoulder, not too much, not too carefree. "All righty, then."

He looked so proud of himself, as if he'd had no doubt he would get his way. Slyly, she swung her purse over her shoulder, and kissed him lightly on the cheek. "I'll see you then," she said, her hand on the door, feeling so much happier than before. Free. It was nice.

"Wait! You're leaving?"

Her face was carefully innocent. "Yes. We're changing things, shaking it up, right? All I wanted was sex, but you said, no, no, no."

She'd got him. Slowly, Ian shook his head, but his eyes were both rueful and respectful. Mentally, Rose cheered.

"You're a bad, bad woman."

She grinned, knowing she'd lost the innocent look, and Mrs. Lane from the Little Princess School of Charm would have howled in disapproval, but honestly, she didn't care. "That I am, but I'll still see you on Tuesday."

12

FOR THE NEXT TWO DAYS, ROSE worked at the penthouse and contemplated her newly unbalanced world order. Ian stayed in her thoughts, her dreams…her worries. When she was with him, she wanted to believe. Her heart actively functioned as any normal person's would, but her mind wasn't so convinced.

She told herself it was the lack of financial security. She ignored his solidly comfortable apartment, yes, not spacious, but adequate. Cozy. Nicer than hers. And yet… She quickly appraised the opulence of the penthouse, and knew that this could be hers, as well.

By the time she'd addressed two hundred handwritten invitations, she'd convinced herself that because he was dissatisfied with his life, he would eventually be dissatisfied with her. And to further that point, on Sunday, on Monday, he hadn't called. Not once.

It was late in the afternoon, her date with Remy approaching, when Sylvia came home after what must have been a brutal day. Her face was flushed, her hair more mussed than her stylist would like, and her mouth was set in a tight line.

"Bad day?" asked Rose, going for the direct route, putting the stamped invitations in plain sight in case Sylvia fastened the death-glare on her.

"Hell," moaned the countess, falling to the couch and kicking off her heels. "Food pantry donations are down another twenty percent. I checked the bottom line for the Simonov Educational Foundation and it's recovering, but with not as much heft as I want. Then The Teddy Bear Brigade snubbed me, asking Vivian Egan to be chair for the Pathways Out of Poverty Women in

Leadership Luncheon. Can you believe the nerve? Who rules the Pantheon of New York philanthropy? Sylvia Simonov, and that's a direct quote from the *Times*."

"Sorry," answered Rose, and then held up the envelopes. "They're ready to go out."

"And look at you, working your fingers to the bone while I'm wailing about the trials of nothingness."

"They're not nothing. I think everybody has a bad day, but usually you're very happy."

"Blissfully," sighed the countess, pouring herself an iced glass of lemon water.

"And the count," asked Rose carefully.

"Of course."

"How do you know? How are you always so confident?"

"You have to be confident, Rose. You can't let things drag you down. And why am I being such a mooncalf. You have a date, missy. Tonight, if I'm not mistaken."

"Remy," she answered.

"I approve." She took another sip and then glanced in Rose's direction. "And the mystery man?"

Rose hesitated, not sure what to say, not sure what not to say. But in the end, the knowing look in Sylvia's eyes made her choice. "We have a date on Tuesday. His name is Ian."

"And?"

"He's nice."

"Nice, nice? Make you smile, give you flowers, take you to the Bahamas nice?"

"Not that kind of nice."

"You're breaking the mold. For three years, I've watched you with exactly one sort of man. High-class, high-dollar, high-gloss. Still got the tingles from New Year's Eve?"

Rose met her gaze. "They haven't left yet."

"And Remy?"

"He's nice, too."

"He'll make you smile, give you flowers and definitely take you to the Bahamas."

"True."

"No tingles?"

"Not a twitch."

Sylvia poured another glass of water, plopped it onto the desk and Rose promptly retrieved a crystal coaster. "You have a quandary, Rose. A very quandrious quandary, and I'm surprised."

"Because of the mold?"

"High-gloss, high-class, high-dollar, those are tough shopping list items to cross off. Whatever you do, pick what's going to make you happy."

And that was the problem. Rose wasn't exactly sure what happiness was, but she knew what nice was. Nice was smooth music, silky aromas and the quiet veneer of peace. Nice was the steady beat of a man's heart against her own. Happiness was her decision, nice was her decision. All she had to do was wrap her hand around it and shape it into whatever she chose. Maybe the quandary wasn't that bad at all.

THAT EVENING, REMY PICKED her up from the penthouse, taking her to a preconcert reception at Carnegie Hall. A world-famous violinist from a world-famous violinist-factory country was performing a world-famous concerto, and the gilded reception hall was filled with the world-famous of New York.

All in all, it definitely qualified as nice.

Rose made sure to talk up the bachelor auction, and yes, people did seem more enthused with the idea of having live dogs present than live, bid-on-able bachelors, which surprised her. Remy took her arm and introduced her to the governor, one Connecticut senator and the chief of staff from New York-Presby. Rose knew her lines, knew her facial expressions and performed them perfectly.

Rose shook off her moment's hesitation, focused on Remy, focused on her dreams, focused on everything she wanted.

From across the room, Blair Rapaport was holding court with an entourage. When she saw Rose, she waved. Stealthily, Rose checked to see if anyone was watching. When the coast was clear, she stroked her eyebrow with her middle finger and pointed directly at Blair, who never noticed.

"You're having a good time? You seem distracted," asked Remy, his nicely handsome eyes concerned.

"It's quite a turnout. Everyone who's everyone, and some people who aren't anyone at all."

Remy looked over at Blair and grinned. "Why don't you go over and pull some hair or rip some clothes? A catfight would make the papers, and it'd be great publicity for the auction."

"Why do you have to be such a man?"

"At some basic level, Rose, we're all alike."

Little did he realize how wrong he was. Ian wouldn't have suggested that. He would have handed her the champagne to throw in Blair's face.

"Why are you doing this?" Remy asked.

"It's for a good cause. Raising money for the humane society. Hey, what's not to like about that? What sort of person would I be if I didn't care about small animals that can't protect themselves?"

He shook his head. "Not the auction. This," he said, pointing to her and then to himself.

Rose laughed, an elegant sound that resembled bells. "What sort of a woman would I be if I didn't enjoy the company of Manhattan's Most Eligible?"

"He's still got your heart?"

"Who?"

Those nicely handsome eyes narrowed. "The one who you're still getting over."

Mentally she flogged herself, blaming the champagne, not wanting to blame Ian. "I'm doing better," she told him, keeping her face adequately enthused, one strand of hair falling in her eyes.

He stole a kiss but her mouth was cold, her heart was cold, and he might have been nicely handsome, but unfortunately, he wasn't nicely stupid.

When he lifted his head, he met her look. "You make a man want to hope. You make him think he can have you. Make him think those pale eyes will flash with something that resembles life or love. I don't want to hope for things I'm never going to get. I don't have to."

"Don't give up on me yet, Remy. I've been busy, this stuff for the countess, and I want it to work out between us. You have no idea how badly I want us to work out."

"Do you mean that?"

"All my life, I've dreamed of a man like you."

"Rich?"

"It's more than that. It's pretty. Like a dream, but it's not. This is real."

"And where does the man fit into the picture, Rose?"

That made her think for a moment, because she didn't usually have a man in her picture. Usually the princess was alone, asleep or worse. But Rose was learning, coping, hoping. She stumbled, her mind putting words to thoughts, to ideas and to a new set of dreams. The same, yet different.

"They're a set. A yin, a yang. A sun, a moon. For every person, there's a match." She pointed to her heart. "Somewhere in here, there's a piece that's missing, a shadow that needs light, and somewhere out there, is that light."

Softly he touched her cheek. "So why do you look worried?"

At first she schooled her features, but then Rose stopped. "You said you didn't want to hope for things you're never going to get. I don't, either. I used to want things that I never got and it hurt like hell, every day, over and over. I did learn, because sometimes I was a little slow. There are things I will never get. Things I don't deserve."

"Why don't you deserve them?"

She almost lied, but across the room Blair Rapaport was laughing and joking and making a mockery of who Rose wanted to be. "Because I don't have a heart."

Remy put a warm arm around her shoulders and smiled. "It's not so bad. Cardiology is my specialty."

ON THE WAY HOME, ROSE stopped by the pet store window, pulled her coat tighter and stared into the empty glass. All the animals were asleep, snug in their little puppy beds, dreaming of dog biscuits, chasing cars, slow-moving cats and all those things that cute puppies dreamed of.

In the corner of the case, the shadows stirred and she took a step back, hoping it was one of the cute fluffy fur balls who wanted to play and leap and grin with little puppy smiles. Instead, the black creature rose from the corner and crawled into the dim light.

"Get away," she scolded, and he obediently retreated on all four paws, belly dragging the ground. His midnight eyes mirrored her own, wary and weary, disillusioned with the dark corners of the world, the dark closets where black dogs were sent to hide, where little girls were sent to refine their behaviors, where monsters lurked and dreams died a small, quiet death.

Dr. Remy Sinclair was the dream that she'd never thought she could actually possess. Ian Cumberland was no dream. He made her feel, he made her cry, he made her hope.

Slowly she raised her hand to the glass, but the black dog was too smart to fall for her voice once again. He was a wise dog, adapting quickly. Survival.

"You're a good boy," she whispered, knowing he would ignore her. His ears perked, but he lay like stone, not moving in her direction. "I'll see you tomorrow," she told him, and if he were smart, he would know that humans were a coldhearted bunch. But Rose meant what she'd said; she would see him tomorrow, and maybe, if she were brave, she'd bring him a biscuit.

IAN SPENT TUESDAY in the office, working and getting ready for Tuesday night. This time, he was smarter, more prepared. He'd researched Dr. Remy Sinclair—his competition—and realized that on the basis of wealth, looks and contributions to humanity, Ian was toast. However, this was no ordinary ordeal, this was for Rose, and Ian was ready to plan the courtship of a lifetime. Yes, because he wanted her. Yes, he firmly believed that fate had thrown them together, but now there was something new. She needed him.

The only problem being that she didn't know she needed him. But Ian knew. He'd watched her in her sleep, watched the clenched fists and the rapid beat at her throat. He'd seen the mindless obedience in her eyes. Sure, money smoothed the way, it might smother the fear, but it wouldn't conquer it. As a man who used to believe that money could leap tall buildings in a single bound, being with Rose had opened his eyes.

Money wouldn't fix her. Money wouldn't fix Ian, either.

However, he'd made dinner reservations at the Waverly Inn and had arranged champagne on ice at the Crystal Room because yes, money wouldn't fix anybody, but the two-dimensional eagles on his walls were staring at him, prodding him into something that was a little extra.

His two o'clock was Hilda Prigsley, a conversation he was dreading. Ian knew banks, he knew advertising agencies, he knew IT organizations, but how to find a spot for a sixty-year-old woman whose sole talent was typing more than a hundred words per minute? For three hours he scoured the online requests, looking for something, anything that would match. Two hours of searching and useless calls, and he was ready to drink himself into oblivion.

Until his cell rang, and his caller ID said Rose.

Suddenly the impossible was possible, the gray clouds were blue and Neil Armstrong had once held the rock on his desk.

"So are you counting hours?" he started with, hoping she'd laugh, hoping she'd admit that she was.

"Hours to what?" she asked, but he heard the tease in her voice and it cheered him.

"We have a date. That's *D-A-T-E*. A social engagement where two people strive to have lively, sparkling conversation, indulge on a feast that will stagger the palette, and then, if somebody decides that someone else looks pathetically frustrated enough, they have passionate sex wherein souls are shared, stars are touched and in general, both parties are ruined for any future with all other people thereafter."

"I can see you've given this a lot of thought."

"You have no idea, and no, I'm not going to tell you exactly how much thought I've given it, because then you would think I'm the most sexually frustrated man on the planet. And so, Ms. Rose Hildebrande, how are you this most glorious of days?"

"Quite well, thank you. Planning the benefit, trying to get the cook to understand that the count doesn't like asparagus, no matter how artfully she prepares it, and I think I need to hire a dog walker."

"They have a dog?"

"No. But I'm putting dogs in the auction. I need a person who's comfortable with dogs. Do you have anybody?"

Ian glanced at the Prigsley file and sighed. "I don't think so."

"That doesn't sound like the voice of a man anticipating this most glorious of days. I would think that soul-sharing requires a certain amount of happiness."

"Talk to me after I find a job for a sixty-year-old woman from London who can type one hundred and twenty words per minute, and then I'll show you happiness."

"Surely people want that sort of superhuman productivity now?"

"On a typewriter, not a computer."

"Oh. I see your dilemma."

"How's the countess?"

"She's got the hairstylist coming in two hours."

"Rough life."

"She's earned it."

He wanted to ask her about last night, wanted to know if Dr. Dreamboat had touched her, if Ian was going to have to kill him, but he knew all those questions were a bad idea. Instead, he forced a laugh. "I'll pick you up at seven."

"I should meet you."

"I insist. Besides, I love the Bronx."

"You're a nice liar."

"That's totally not a lie. My most favorite thing is in the Bronx."

"What?"

"You."

MISS PRIGSLEY APPEARED precisely at five to two, not that it mattered because five minutes wasn't going to change the outcome.

She settled herself in the chair, her sensible feet planted firmly on the floor, and looked at him with great expectations in her eyes.

"I'm still working it," he explained, and then, to twist the knife even further, she handed him a cookie tin.

"You don't have to do this," he started, pushing the tin back toward her, because she thought he could deliver miracles.

"I don't have to, but I did, Mr. Cumberland. You're working

very hard on my behalf and it'd be awfully churlish of me to not to come up with some small whatnot to keep you in good spirits. So…there's still no takers for this old bird?"

"I won't give up," he promised, picking up his rock, thinking of a story to tell her and immediately realizing he'd told them all before. Her eyes sparkled behind her silver frames and Ian knew she was on to him, and even nicer, she didn't mind.

"You could learn the computer."

"And I could happen on to the winning lottery ticket and buy myself a nice warm flat. It's not me, you see. I need the feel of the typewriter, the keys pecking back at me, one whack of the roller and ding, you're off to the races again. I have to be who I am, and can't be any more."

"Yes, you can," Ian argued, because a person was only limited by the scope of his dreams.

"Mr. Cumberland, if the pool of potential employers can't appreciate who I am, then what good am I to them, trying to be someone I'm not? My great-aunt Hilda, second cousin on my father's side, used to always tell him that not everyone gets to be an astronaut when he grows up."

Ian stubbornly eyed his rock. "But Britain never had a space program."

"That's exactly what my father said, but then she'd fix him with her evil eye and tell him that if Parliament cared two hoots about a little boy's dreams, they'd have funded space exploration long ago, but instead they spent her hard-earned tax dollars on the Concorde, and we all know how that turned out."

With a regretful sigh, Ian stared down at the sheet of paper that had the phone number for the Waverly Inn, and firmly scratched it out.

"Miss Prigsley…"

"My darling boy, you can certainly call me Hilda."

"Hilda…"

"Yes," she asked, eyeing him with an obstinate lift to her brows.

"I'll keep looking. We'll find something."

She gave him a saucy wink and patted his hand. "I know

you will, Mr. Cumberland. You don't know what you're capable of, but I do."

After she left, Ian contemplated the hunk of rock on his desk and glared at the soaring eagles on the wall. He now had a new favorite motivational saying: Until you spread your wings, you'll have no idea how far you can walk.

13

Rose wasn't accustomed to people in her apartment. It was her space, her domain, and it wasn't so much that it was located in the Bronx—yes, that was some of it—but more, it was the belief that when someone stepped inside they would see all the things that she saw. The blinds that should have been dusted, the sofa slipcover that was ten years out of date and the sad sheen of a solitary woman who had very little life.

However, with Ian, there was no reason to worry about his judgment, to steel for his disapproval; with Ian, she didn't have to care. Which did nothing to explain why she vacuumed like a lunatic, why she made apple pie so the apartment would have that "homey" scent and why she tucked her rabbit carefully out of sight in case it made a grown man laugh.

When the buzzer sounded she checked herself in the mirror. The royal blue dress made her eyes look more vibrant, her makeup was flawless, every single hair was in place but her insides were plunged in mayhem. For a moment, she closed her eyes, searching for her peace, but when she opened them peace had still gone missing.

After she opened the door, Ian was there, black slacks, white polo, Armani coat and scuffed shoes. Breathlessly she waited while his gaze inspected her apartment, passed sightlessly over the slipcover and then ended on her face.

In the twinkling of an eye, Rose forgot the dated slipcovers altogether.

She held out the pie in her hand. "I baked you a pie."

"I think you look better than the pie."

"You don't like it?" she asked, putting the plate back on the table. Baking had been a stupid idea.

"I love it. We'll take it with us," he said, as if everyone carried food while commuting.

"I should have thought—" she started, but he covered her mouth with a kiss.

"I love the pie."

"Enough to drag it around Manhattan—complete with falling crust, gathering flies and strange looks? It's stupid. I won't make you take it." Quickly she stopped rambling. "Next time, I'll bring it to your office."

"Are you sure?" he asked. "It's your decision."

"Positive," she answered, very sure of herself, and she felt like he'd given her the best present ever. Yes, Ian Cumberland was a very sneaky man. She liked it.

They took the subway into the city, and this time she didn't mind the long ride, the swaying train. She stayed fascinated by the glow in his eyes, and yes, his scuffed shoes made her feel oddly comforted.

He asked about her day, carefully avoiding brining up her date last night. She answered him in great detail, trying to impress him with her dog-trainer-interviewing skills and carefully avoiding saying a word about her date last night.

As the lights of the city approached he looked at her, studying her. She put her hand in his, forgetting every ladylike rule in the book. "What?"

"I thought a long time about how to go about tonight," he explained to her. "Plan A was to impress you with the Waverly, champagne at the Crystal Room. But then I realized that you were too cynical for that."

"I was?"

"Oh, yeah. How many times have you been to the Waverly?"

"Seven."

"And where's the fun in number eight?"

Slowly she smiled, her fingers curling over his. "I see your dilemma."

"Instead I opted for Plan B."

"Which is?"

"You think no one can be happy unless they're rolling in money."

"That's about right."

"I'm here to shoot holes through that little mercenary life-theory."

"You can try," she taunted.

"And I will win," he said, pulling her up from the subway seat. "This is where we get off."

The weather had decided to cooperate—the temperature a mild forty degrees—the moon was full and the streets filled with the last of the holiday stragglers. Those gullible fools who didn't want to see the last of the New Year. Like Rose.

They walked to Eighty-Third Street, a street row full of dark awnings and tiny neon signs, and she watched curiously to see where they would land.

She didn't have to wait long. "First," he announced with a flourish, "we have the pièce de résistance of New York City cuisine. That succulent fusion of sweet and tangy that was first perfected in New York, circa 1905, and changed the culinary world forever. May I present the New York slice."

Her mouth fell open, only slightly, before she shut it. "Seriously? You're trying to impress me with pizza?"

Ian was not discouraged at all, one of the things she most adored about him. "And not just any pizza, but the finest the city has to offer. Fontini's."

"I don't know Fontini's."

"That's because, my darling debutante, you've lived a sheltered life. Follow me and let your taste buds discover culinary Utopia."

Inside was a small dining room filled with tables covered in red-checkered tablecloths and topped with straw-wrapped bottles of Chianti. The flowers were yellow plastic and the music was a grainy Frank Sinatra, but there was something special in the air. Garlic. Definitely garlic. Rose began to smile.

"Two slices, Fabrezio. Plain."

"But what if I wanted a salad," Rose blurted out. Not that she wanted a salad, but maybe she wanted the option of a salad. How did anyone know unless they asked?

Fabrezio looked at her, insulted, his voice starting to rise above the crooning strains of "It Had To Be You." "Excuse me, Miss Whoever You Are, here is buffalo mozzarella that does not melt into oblivion, here is fresh basil gently nestled among ripe Italian tomatoes, here is a bubbly crust perfectly cooked in a century-old coal-fired oven… You ask for salad, when I present you with…*capolavoro!*" He slammed his hand on the table, and Rose jumped.

"I'll have a slice," she told him demurely, deciding this was not the place to pick a fight—not that she would, but who knew? Ian looked at her as if the real world was a fine and shining place, and well, heck, tonight the sky was the limit.

After the man left, Ian put a concerned hand over hers. "You're okay?"

Determined not to be intimidated by a surly Italian who didn't like unenlightened plebs, Rose nodded firmly. "Of course. Although if this pizza isn't the greatest thing since sliced bread, I'm going to tell him."

Ian grinned at her proudly. "You'd break his heart."

"I'm a very hard-hearted woman."

"No," he told her, his thumb sliding over her palm, warming her all over. "I don't think you are."

The pizza was as perfect as Ian had said it would be, and when Fabrezio hovered nearby as she took the first bite, Rose smiled graciously. "It's delicious."

"That is all you can say?"

"Magnificent, a tribute to Sicilians everywhere, with cheese that shames my inferior palette."

Fabrezio nodded with approval. "Ian, she's all right. A little prissy, but every woman can be forgiven when she has the face of a Botticelli."

After dinner, they sipped on the wine and he made her tell him about working for the countess. She told him about her secret plan to dunk Blair Rapaport in the East River, and he laughed and made her think she could. She asked about his day, asked about the English typist, but he shrugged and looked away. Rose didn't press, but she wouldn't forget, either. Ian wasn't a man to shrug something off. He buried it inside, just like her, and it worried her to see it.

It was nearly ten when he paid the check and took her hand, leading her back into the night.

"Where now?"

"Dancing at the Rainbow Room," he answered, and she was too polite to tell him how many times she'd been there before.

Two subway stops later, they were outside Rockefeller Center, where they rode the elevator to the sixty-fifth floor. A sign outside read "Gibraltar Reception" and Rose pulled him back. "You didn't tell me we were going to a wedding reception. I didn't bring a gift. I don't even know these people," she whispered.

"I don't know these people, either," he whispered to her.

"Ian!" She looked at him, shocked, *shocked.*

"Rose!" he mocked, looking completely unshocked.

"You can't do this. It's…it's…not done."

"Oh, you are an innocent, but tonight, you get to sample some of my most favorite things. Over the past ten months as I have mastered the art of living responsibly, I have scoped out happy hours, free movie screenings, food samples at Trader Joe's and one really crazy bar mitzvah, sometimes because I missed the social life, and sometimes because it was a kick. It's only one night. Why don't you walk on the wild side?"

"The wild side, yes, but Emily Post will not approve."

His eyes darkened, lit with something wicked and wily.

"There's nothing I have planned that Emily Post would approve of."

Her stomach curled with anticipation, and Rose moved a step closer, drawn to the wild side. "We could just go back to your apartment and have mad, passionate sex and possibly an exchange of souls," she offered in her most seductive voice.

"After we dance," he insisted.

"You're going to make me do this." She was learning to recognize the hard determined face, and it didn't make her freeze the way it used to. Progress.

"I'm not going to make you do this. That would be wrong of

me, but I will be disappointed as hell if you don't," he said, standing his ground.

Oh, that was such a low blow. Admitting the strategy right up front and counting on her to step up to the plate, for him… *No, this was for her, and she knew it.* Rose frowned, scowled, an un-attractive face that would cause early wrinkles, all while Ian watched patiently and waited.

He wanted to get his way, wanted her to do his bidding, but he wasn't yelling, or glaring, or worse. He was giving her a choice. Rose bit her lip, the lilting strains filtering outside. She wanted to dance with him, and it only took one small, slightly unbecoming step.

"They won't throw us in jail?"

"For crashing a reception? Nah."

"You're a very poor influence," she told him, needing to make the point that this was really, *really* not done.

His devilish laugh was very little comfort to a woman who liked things in neat packages, with very pretty bows, yet she found herself following, holding his hand, and perhaps her palm was sweating, but Ian didn't seem to mind.

The room was decorated in pink and white, filled with balloons and gleaming silver ribbons. All in all, a neat little package with a very pretty bow. Ian headed straight for the bride, kissed her hand and told her that she shamed almost every woman there with the light of her smile. The bride, a radiant redhead with clashy coral lipstick, blushed and giggled, and when the groom appeared, she looked at Ian, who held out a hand. "Ian Cumberland. Second cousin on her mother's side. But you know, tonight, I think you're the lucky man. Congratulations." He lifted two passing glasses, and pressed them into the hands of the couple.

"A toast, to new beginnings, and to the magic created when two souls merge into one, the Fates playing mischief and forging true love."

Rose struggled to keep a straight face, but ended up stealing a cocktail napkin, bearing the words, Larry and Allison, forever. When Ian wasn't looking, she tucked the napkin in her purse. A keepsake, because she suspected that tonight was a memory she would keep for a long, long time—assuming she didn't get thrown in jail.

The lights dimmed, the spotlights dancing on the floor, the music fell to a slow, soothing song and the room filled with the magic of what could be. Ian took her hand, tucked her into his arms and under the balloons and streaming silver ribbons they slowly circled the floor to a melody that few people were lucky enough to hear. When Ian held her so close, when her missing heart began to stir, it wasn't smoke and mirrors. This wasn't an illusion to her, or the Fates playing mischief.

With Ian, everything was startlingly real.

THE DREAM CONTINUED. Through the night, on the ride to her apartment. Magic floated everywhere he touched. When he looked at her with eyes that saw only the best, she got caught up in the spell of what could be. He kissed her, once, a thousand times, until she couldn't think, couldn't plan, all she could do was feel.

Everywhere his mouth touched her. Her face, her neck, the curve of her breasts, the line of her arm. It was the wine, it was the music, she thought, but she knew that it was him. Laying siege, plotting to possess her. At first she struggled, but then he stopped the siege, holding her close, stroking her hair—comfort. Such gentle comfort.

"Shh," he whispered, his lips on her ear, his mouth slow, insidious, making her forget, taking her under once again. He lingered at her breasts until she was lost. Her body struggled to regain control, but each time he stopped, whispered against her neck, his hands never still, always creating pleasure. Lower he moved, and she could feel her body freeze, feel her muscles tighten. Yet each time he was there with tenderness, comfort, peace and such glorious pleasure.

Weakly her legs parted, craving more, and he was between her thighs, kissing her, his mouth hot and wicked, possessing her, controlling her... Loving her.

Rose could feel the orgasm riding inside her, building, and she needed to explode. But she wouldn't do it, not with him, not like this. She wanted to go alone, she must go alone. But then, when she was sure she had him locked out of her mind, his hand took hers and twined their fingers together, linked. Merged. Joined.

Fate.

When Rose fell, when her body shattered like glass, she wasn't alone. Not this time. His name was on her lips, in her mind and coming to rest in a heart she hadn't known she had.

ROSE WOKE, THE DARK HOVERING around her, and she could hear her mother's angry screech, the hard slap on her thigh, and automatically she froze.

Wouldn't move. Can't move.

The scream rose in her mind, silent, echoing over and over. Her heart was pounding. No crying. Little ladies never cried.

No, she thought, she would be smart.

The hand moved, and she waited for the next slap, steeled for the pain.

"Rose?"

Carefully she listened; the voice was gentle, soothing, floating through the night.

"It's Ian, Rose." She heard him shift away, far away, and she opened her eyes, adjusting to the dim of the night.

He looked so worried, so gloriously perfect, soft hair, softer eyes, and Rose came fully awake.

"I can go," he told her, uncertain, waiting for her.

Always waiting for her.

Rose began to breathe, and inched closer. She took his hand, twined their fingers together, linked, joined, fated.

"I'll be fine," she told him, lying next to him, almost touching, but not quite. Not yet.

It wasn't long before she fell asleep again, and this time when she woke, when she heard the quiet sound of his breathing and her heart froze again, he squeezed her hand once—tender, not hard—and Rose went back to sleep. And this time, she smiled.

THE NEXT MORNING, IAN LEFT early. Not as early as he had planned, Rose thought, smiling to herself as she remembered her well-plotted diversionary tactics. Honestly, relationships were easier than she had realized. She'd worried about losing herself, losing control, but sex was a remarkable equalizer. Men had money and power, and women, well… Mentally she patted herself on the back. Well, women had some tricks of their own.

Rose picked up bagels on the way to the penthouse, mortally insulting Michael, the chef, but Michael would recover. It was a marvelous, blustery day, the sky a clear blue, the trees bare, but spring was out there, waiting in the wings. And spring would come.

When she got to the penthouse, she hung up her coat, walked into the kitchen and grinned, a cheeky grin that Rose would never have attempted before.

"I brought bagels," she announced, plopping the sack on the granite counter.

"Why?" Michael asked, not quite getting the new-improved Rose.

"I thought we could use a change. Shake things up a bit. Don't you think the routine gets stale?"

"No. You like routines, Rose."

"Not today. Today, I'm taking lunch."

"Sylvia's looking for you," he said, with a last disdainful glance at the bag.

Rose waved a cavalier hand and floated to the living room, her mouth coated with True Love Shimmer—smudge-free—and a permanent smile.

"Rose! Rose!"

"In here, Sylvia," she trilled, plucking petals to the steady rhythm of he loves me, he loves me not.

When she spied Rose, Sylvia skidded to a halt. "What is this? My God, do you see that smile? It's the cat that swallowed the canary, swallowed Godzilla, and truly, I don't know what else the cat has been swallowing." She grabbed Rose by the arms, studied her face. "Happiness. Yes, I think they call that happiness."

"Maybe," answered Rose primly.

"Wait, I came here for something. The nuclear brightness of your teeth, the radioactive glow in your eye, they fried my memory. What was it?"

"Plans for the auction, selection for the book club, new dress design from Stella M or massage therapy at three?"

"There's my girl. The auction. We have the dogs?"

Rose could feel the light from her tiara dim. "Are you sure? The Empire wants to charge an extra twenty-grand deposit, plus any additional cleaning and—" Rose rolled her eyes "—fumigation that might be necessary."

"Bastards and crooks. Every one of them. Squeezing the public until they bleed." Sylvia pinched her arm. "Oops. No bleeding. Go for it, doll. How many bachelors do we have in play, ready to be buffed and polished until they shine?"

"Ten."

"We couldn't get twelve."

"Ten creates elitism. A dozen is common. It's the better choice."

"I suppose you're right. You on with the printers?"

"Check."

"Sponsors?"

"Check, check."

The phone rang, and Rose answered. "Simonov residence."

"Yeah, this is Dwayne from Flowers by Dwayne. I need to confirm an address. Sorry about the trouble, but we got this new kid, and honestly, you should see the way he scribbles his numbers. I've seen prescriptions that shame him. Anyways, we've got an order for orchids from an...Irene Simonini."

"Anton Simonov," Rose corrected.

"Whatever. Anyways, it's headed for 401 West Seventy-Eighth Street. At least I think that's Seventy-Eighth Street, but 401 ain't on the map, so I'm thinking maybe that's a nine, could be a seven."

Rose glanced up, noticed Sylvia watching. "Let me check the computer," she answered efficiently. As if she needed to check; she knew this address. The computer record was there—901 West Seventy-Eighth Street, Apartment 45G. Blair Rapaport.

Rose smiled at Sylvia, held the phone away for a minute. "An invitation got clogged in the mail. Give me a sec."

"Dwayne, okay, here's the right address. It's 401 East Seventy-Eighth Street."

"That's not a nine? And the *West* seems real clear."

"Nope. Sometimes these things get reversed. Mistakes happen."

"I should fire the kid."

"Don't do that—give him a break. You never know how you can change a life with a little kindness." Or how you could change a life with a mafia hit. One bullet. Was murder really so wrong? Rose looked at Sylvia and nodded stupidly.

"Yeah, guess you're right. Anyways. Have a nice day."

After she hung up, Sylvia shrugged. "It's such a trial to do anything these days."

"I know," agreed Rose, fingering the letter opener. She could tell Sylvia. She could confront the count. She could drench Blair with peroxide, of course—the world would never know the difference. She looked at Sylvia again, opened her mouth, and promptly shut it. *Coward.*

"So, what's my lunch schedule for the day?"

"You're meeting Shelby Fitzsimmons at Diddier Dumas, one o'clock."

Sylvia pulled a face. "It's the pitch for a carbon-offset program. You be there, take notes. Make me seem official and environmentally friendly, because God knows, I'll never convince her."

"Can't make it."

"Does my hearing fail me?"

"Nope. I have a date."

"Remy?" asked Sylvia, her smile approving.

Rose shook her head. "Ian."

Sylvia's smile turned, but the twinkle in the eyes gave her away. "Is your love life going to be interfering with your absolute slavish dedication to this position?"

"Probably."

"Well, hallelujah and pass the mustard. You go, chicky. Take a long lunch. A long, long lunch, but reschedule with Shelby first."

"You're the best," Rose said, and she meant it. Why the count was hell-bent on destroying his marriage to Sylvia, she'd never know, but she was the hired help. She couldn't make a difference. She'd only muck things up more.

The countess fanned herself. "You're a wonderful shot to the old ego." Then her gaze lit on Rose's practical wool suit. "And wear something a little flashier. Tweed is not date material. A little cleavage. There's that black lace bustier in the closet. Put that under the tweed."

"I don't know, Sylvia," Rose started, but Sylvia was dragging her in the direction of the warehouse she called a closet, and then threw a bit of black lace at her.

"Trust me, doll. He won't know what hit him."

14

IAN WAS BUSTING HIS BUTT on the phones, but the world was not feeling the love. The elevator had been broken when he came in. After that he'd spent the morning grasping at straws for Hilda Prigsley. Following three curt "not at this time" responses and one heartless guffaw that was poorly disguised as coughing, Ian wasn't having his best day ever. However, at precisely twelve-seventeen that all changed for the better.

He felt her sneak up from behind, putting cool hands over his eyes. He knew the smell of honeysuckle and he knew those hands. Intimately. "Guess who?"

"Lola?"

Laughing, she planted a tantalizing kiss on his neck. "Jessica Alba."

"Don't tell Lola," he whispered.

After that, her tongue landed in his ear, and oops, she happened to land in his lap. Heroically, he restrained himself from a very inappropriate public display of affection. "Lola deserves everything she gets for ignoring her man."

"Rough day?" she asked, smoothing a hand through his hair while he pretended not to stare down the plump valley of her breasts. Black lace wasn't her usual style. In virginal white, a man could dream, but in sheer black, hell… He stowed his hands to safety and met her eyes.

"How'd you know it was a rough day? The menacing scowl, the brooding gaze?"

"The mussed hair."

Ian scowled, fingering his hair back in place. "Not enough product."

"Don't you dare spoil these artfully tousled locks with chemicals."

"Artfully tousled? Really?" For that, he gave her another kiss. And then one turned into two, and his hand was itching to dive under the silk and explore, but there was a roomful of the seething unemployed waiting for his attention, and deep in his soul, Ian wasn't that cruel.

"What's the problem?" she said, noting his heartrending sigh.

"Well, right now the problem is more of a physical inconvenience than an actual work-related problem."

She studied the glass panels that displayed the crowded lobby, and he knew exactly what was on her very clever mind. "There are ways…" he mentioned casually, not that he would be so crude as to actually suggest it, but if she did, well, hell that was a different matter entirely.

She did consider it, he could see the sensual possibilities churning in her eyes, but in the end her sigh was nearly as heartrending as his. "It's not the location, more the idea that all those people are here seeking gainful employment, and to find selfish pleasure while they're waiting? It feels wrong."

"It's not *exactly* wrong," he told her courageously, his gaze drawn to the mind-popping low edge of the silk.

"Ian," she said, and pulled her jacket together, ripping temptation from his grasp.

"Fine. It's wrong."

"I'll make it up to you tonight," she purred.

His heart leaped; his cock approved. "And with those magic words, all is forgiven. Did you come here just to arouse me, seduce me to the edge of sexual frustration and then leave?"

"I came for lunch." She pulled out a paper sack. "Hot dogs."

Rose looked so happy and thrilled with her choice, that he didn't have the heart to educate her as he watched her take a bite. He nearly moaned. Eventually a blush burned her cheeks, so Ian figured she knew, most likely because she was still sitting in his lap.

Prudently, she moved to the other side of the desk. "Sorry. I actually came to say hello."

"And it was the nicest hello I've had this morning. How's your day?"

For a few minutes she told him about the plans the countess had, the words tripping faster as she talked, and he could see how much she loved what she did. It was good that she had found her niche. His eyes found the rock on his desk. At one time, he'd thought her job was frilly, all societal froufrou, but he'd been wrong.

Funny, everyone took Rose as a lightweight, but she knew what she wanted and went after it with a drive that could put the marines to shame, leaving a lollipop- and rainbows-ravaged landscape in her wake.

"What about you?"

"Miserable," he complained, and then promptly shut up.

Rose, being the people-pleaser she was, noticed. "Tell me."

And so he proceeded to expound on the full extent of his miseries. Rose looked at him with great sympathy, taking his hand, and eventually Ian found himself milking the moment for everything it was worth.

It felt great to pile all his doubts and worries onto someone else. He was truly loving this job, but some days—like this one—the weight was killer, letting everyone dump on him and smiling as if everything was going to be okay. The old days at the bank, the pressures, the rarified air, it all seemed stale now when he compared it to the personalities that needed him here.

At the bank, he'd dealt with computer screens, faceless numbers and legal waivers that absolved him of all responsibility in case, God forbid, disaster struck.

And then it had.

Here, with less than a foot of space between him and his client, he worried all the rocks, all the cheery T-shirts, all the optimism in the world wouldn't be enough.

Like Hilda Prigsley, he thought, and explained the situation in detail to Rose.

When Rose watched him, believed in him, counted on him, all that weight—it felt good. It felt right.

"Why don't you go back to the bank? Go where the air is fresh and guilt-free?"

"I've talked to my old boss. It's a possibility. Maybe."

"That'd be fantastic," she told him enthusiastically. Too enthusiastically.

Ian frowned. "It's not even that close to a possibility."

"I can pull strings. I know people. Actually, I know people who know people."

"Not yet. I'm…happy."

"But for how long, Ian?" It worried him, that panic inside her when she contemplated anything less than a seven-zero bank account. He could stall for a while; he was adjusting to his altered circumstances. But what about Rose?

"I'm happy at least until tonight, unless you're cavorting with Doctor Dolittle." *Who had a seven-zero bank account. Hell, probably eight.*

"My calendar is open," she said and then a gleam came back into her eyes. "How old is she?" she asked, startling him.

"Who?"

"Hilda. Hilda Prigsley."

"She's sixty," explained Ian slowly, curious.

"Would she be willing to learn anything else?" she asked, and he saw where her mind was running.

He rocked back in his chair, wishing it were that easy. "Trust me, I've tried. I could get her computer training, but she doesn't think she can learn new skills."

"Can I talk to her?" she asked, then immediately shook her head. "No. Forget that."

Seeing her interest, Ian was intrigued by the spark in her eyes. "You have an idea?" he asked casually, not prodding, not forcing, not demanding, trying to kindle it before she killed it herself.

"Possibly."

Okay, maybe demanding was going to be necessary. He could ask, probably a couple of times to drag her idea out of her, and there was the off chance that it was something that he hadn't thought of, and then he could try…*to trample all over her plan.*

Her plan, not his. Not going to do that, he thought, digging through the files on his desk before triumphantly pulling out Hilda's file. Rose merely watched him, warily, not saying a word.

Ha. Ian cracked his knuckles, punched the speaker button on his phone and dialed.

Two minutes later, he had Hilda's okay to talk to another counselor. The very talented Rose Hildebrande, who the firm used on occasion for their most special cases. Ian scribbled Prigsley's phone number down on a piece of paper and handed it to Rose.

Rose stared at the paper, and then looked at him. "I can do this? You don't mind. If you…"

Ian cut her off before she handed the file back to him. "I've tried, Rose. I don't know what else to do, and honestly, the woman's getting tired of me. Oh, she doesn't say anything, but you can tell. I'd appreciate your help," he encouraged, willing her to try.

Her teeth dug into her lips before she realized what she was doing and stopped. "I'll do it." Then she checked her watch and stood up, dusting crumbs from her skirt. "I should go. I have some things to do for the countess. We could meet at your place about eight. I'm thinking we'll eat in."

Then, with a wicked glimmer in her eyes, she leaned over his desk, black lace gaping anew, exposing a treasure of creamy white flesh that begged to be plundered. Mindlessly, Ian swallowed, sitting on his hands, lest they plunder away. "You're heartless, heartless, I say."

"I know," she said, planting a saucy kiss on his mouth and left.

And how the hell was a man supposed to work after that?

TWO SNOWY NIGHTS LATER, Rose found herself sitting on the uncomfortable steel of the bleachers at the RAC. She kept wanting to squirm, find a comfortable spot, but she was too well trained, and Ian was watching her. Not like her parents, but worried. Ian cared like a person should. He must have sensed her nerves—he always did—and he twined their fingers together.

"What if they don't like me?" she asked, tucking her hair behind her ear, managing a furtive wiggle at the same time.

"You're very likable."

"I'm not as likable as you think."

"You won't be the problem."

Somehow that made her feel better. "Why not?"

"I neglected to mention this earlier, but they're high maintenance. Both of them." His gaze kept scanning the aisle, and Rose wished she could distract him.

"I'm sensing a trend," she told him in her bitchiest, most judgmental voice, but the sweat was starting to trickle down her neck.

"I don't want there to be a trend. What does that say about me? Do I seek out people who are high maintenance? Am I high maintenance, and by the way, the correct answer is no."

He turned to her, and his eyes were remarkably calm for such a big faker of anxiety. Very smooth, she thought, noting that it worked. Her nerves were already starting to calm, and she slid closer to him, snuggling under his arm. "You're very sexy when you're nervous." *And when you're trying to protect me,* she thought, but she kept that to herself because it felt so nice.

"That was a good answer. It dodged the bullet and made me hot all in one sentence. Why do I continually underestimate you?"

She gave him her best, most innocent Mary Jane look. "Me?"

Not falling for it, he kissed her, and she forgot about trying to appear innocent, her hand curling toward his thigh, just under the coat….

"Geez, Ian. Can you show a little respect here? Minors are present."

Rose broke off and got her first glimpse of Beckett and Phoebe. Phoebe was short, with slightly frizzed chestnut hair, clear gray eyes that shone behind her glasses and a distressing flair for frumpy clothes. Beckett was a foot taller than Phoebe, his clothes were equally awful, but the arrogant granite in his face reeked of money.

Under Phoebe's critical stare, Rose fought the urge to squirm once again. Failed. Ian caught her hand and held tight.

Quickly he performed the introductions, and Rose plastered her best, most implacable smile on her face. She'd been through worse. She'd survived. But she knew Ian was watching her, knew he worried, and she didn't want to disappoint him.

"You're Rose?" Beckett asked, and Rose nodded once.

Beckett nodded once, and then some silent milestone had been passed. Beckett and Ian plugged into the game, and Rose was left to bond with Phoebe.

Oh, God.

"Why are you here?" asked Phoebe, soft enough that Ian couldn't hear.

And thus, twenty questions had begun, but Rose had no idea what the correct answers would be. Social chitchat, pithy bons mots and heartfelt eloquence on the state of world hunger, sure, that she could recite in her sleep. But this black-ops mission on the state of Rose's heart, or lack thereof, was almost as bad as what she'd endured as a kid. No. Not really.

Rose steeled her spine, lifted her chin and threw back her shoulders, determined to do this right.

"Ian asked me," Rose replied, which wasn't the right answer, but she suspected that flawless makeup and the ability to explain the Continental style of fork etiquette weren't going to cut it with Phoebe. When all that failed, Rose's fallback position was vapid bubblehead.

"You're going to be nice to him now?" Phoebe asked, not falling for vapid bubblehead, and Rose blinked, feeling a pit spread in her stomach. Apparently Phoebe knew things. Phoebe knew what Rose had done to Ian, and she wasn't so quick to forgive. Unfortunately, or perhaps fortunately, females weren't nearly so gullible as men.

The first reply on her tongue, those fail-safe responses to be pulled in case of emergencies, weren't going to work. Rose was not going to blow this. She was not going to let her rigid personality ruin the very first, very best relationship of her life. Carefully she struggled to find the right words. "I don't deserve him, but he always sees the best in things, including me. There are a lot of things that aren't going to be easy for him, because where most people want two steps forward, I'll go forty steps around and then sideways until a sane person would give up. He doesn't give up, and I don't want to give up, either."

"What about the other dude?"

"What other dude?"

"Dr. McDreamy?"

"Remy?"

"Exactly how many Dr. McDreamys do you know?"

"One," lied Rose. Phoebe wouldn't understand.

"And have you broken it off with him?"

Rose wasn't sure if that was any of Phoebe's business, because she hadn't even told Ian, but the look in Phoebe's eyes said that death was possible, so Rose decided to tell her the truth.

Talking to Remy hadn't been easy. It had felt like a breach of all of her dreams. She'd taken out her military strategy books and could find absolutely nothing that covered the proper way to lose a war. Eventually, she had met him for drinks—at the Waverly. And when she'd walked away, she knew she'd done the right thing.

"I told him yesterday."

Phoebe stared, but Rose didn't blink and she didn't look away, not once. Eventually, Phoebe nodded, and Rose resumed normal breathing function again.

Another milestone passed.

"I like the sweater," offered Phoebe, "but I think our society is way too preoccupied with this concept of the superficial— looks, money. I don't think that's important? How 'bout you?"

Rose felt the strong urge to crawl under the seat, but Ian glanced her way, checking to see if she was okay. She shot him a reassuring smile, and was brought back to when she nine—the disastrous piano concert where she'd taken second and her mother had never forgotten. Thoughtfully, Rose stared at the ceiling, a considering expression on her face.

"Looks, money, intelligence, talent. All these things are gifts, raw materials that we can choose to better humanity. There are a lot of people who waste these talents, who use them for their own gain, and that's wrong. But no, I don't think that looks or money are a curse. I think, with the right attitude, an awareness of the needs of the world around us, they can be a force for good."

"That's some great bullshit."

Rose blushed. "Little Princess School of Charm. Rule Number Three Hundred Seventeen: You are a caretaker of the earth and the sisterhood that is womankind."

"Sucked for you, didn't it?"

"Yeah," agreed Rose. Her mother had counted on lace, ribbons and flowing tawny hair to be enough. That, Rose had in abundance. The inner beauty thing—that her mother had tried to beat into her. Gee, and why hadn't that worked? Rose managed a tight smile.

"Beckett's loaded. It makes him miserable."

"It doesn't have to be a burden. For a lot of people, money's security."

"Yeah, Ian used to think that, too. He's happier now."

Rose glanced over, watched the men cheering, laughing. Sure, for the moment, he seemed happy, but eventually he'd get beaten down, just like her. It always happened. "He wants his old job back."

Phoebe pushed at her glasses and frowned. "Nah. He's saying that because that's what he thinks he thinks. He's found his home. He's good at it."

"It wears him down," answered Rose quietly.

"Don't like that? Want him back the old way, loaded and stress-free?"

"Banking is highly stressful," defended Rose. "In a few months, he'll be back where he belongs."

Phoebe coughed. "If he's not, are you going to stick around, or does he get a cutesy kiss-off letter with a heart over the *I?*"

"I made a mistake. I learned from it. I don't…" Rose stopped, bit her tongue.

"What?"

"It's not what you think. I've been around a lot of poverty and I've seen what it does. It sounds so all-fired romantic to you, big ole families sitting around the kitchen table playing board games."

Ian turned, "Everything okay?"

Phoebe laughed. "Oh, yeah."

Ian looked at Rose. "Yeah?"

"Sure. No big here," she said, and for a little while, she tried to follow the game. Phoebe and Beckett argued about his clothes, about her nachos, about the game, about the everything, and Rose watched, studying the easy fighting, the impulsive behaviors, the mild insults that everyone seemed to accept.

In the third quarter, Phoebe spilled a drop of cheese on her linen shirt, and Rose kept checking, kept looking, her eyes drawn to the spot. Phoebe didn't seem to care, and Rose told herself it wasn't her place.

Eventually Phoebe noticed the mark, taking a napkin and grinding it into the thin material.

Not smart, not smart at all. Quickly Rose pulled the stain-stick from her bag, efficiently shooing Phoebe's hands away, and then worked the material in gentle strokes, not grinding. "You'll kill your shirt," Rose explained, as processed orange turned back to white.

Phoebe pulled at the shirt, admiring Rose's results. "You do that well."

"Always prepare for the disasters."

"A survivalist at heart?"

"Yes."

"I've never seen a survivalist that does such a great job with makeup. It's really natural. Not all fakey-fake."

"If you went with a darker tone for your blush, something in a coral, I think it'd go great with your hair."

"Are you giving me makeup tips?"

"No." Determined, Rose sat on her hands. "Yes. Yes, I'm giving you makeup tips." She leaned over and handed Phoebe a compact and blush. "Try it. It'll be very flattering. The lights in here are fluorescent. The worst for skin tone, but in candlelight, it'll be awesome."

Beckett turned, and his jaw dropped. "You're putting on makeup? At a basketball game?"

"Is there a law?"

"No." He peered closer. "It looks good."

Phoebe twisted toward Rose and smiled, apparently noticing the lost expression on her face. "You don't know basketball at all, do you?"

"Not a clue."

"Okay, see, the guys there, the ones in red, that's Rutgers. You want to cheer for them."

"Got it."

"And when the other team steals, you shout out, 'you suck.'"

A few minutes later, when the team in white stole the ball, Rose stood up, "Go!"

Phoebe nodded sadly, noting the male heads turning around Rose. Beckett saw her face, laughed. "It's going to be tough breaking her in."

"But she's really excellent when it comes to spot removal," Phoebe teased.

Rose was beautiful, polished, elegant and had a magical touch with makeup, but sometimes those gorgeous blue eyes were sad, looking at the world as if she'd been locked out. Ian had never been drawn to gorgeous and polished before. He usually laughed it off, but not this time. Phoebe could see the way he watched Rose.

Phoebe leaned over and whispered to Beckett. "I think he's in deep trouble."

"It's the abyss. It's a scary-ass thing, but you can't avoid it."

Phoebe covered his hand gently. "I don't know why that touches my heart, but it does."

FOUR DAYS LATER, ROSE WAS scrutinizing her apartment, adjusting the flowers, checking for dust under the refrigerator and straightening the paintings on the wall four times. No matter how often she righted them, they always looked a little off.

Tonight was her first night with Hilda, her first night as job counselor extraordinaire. Ian had warned her that Hilda was stubborn, but Ian had no idea what stubborn truly meant. Rose could do this.

At the sound of the buzzer, Rose took a deep breath and straightened her pink silk jacket. For Ian, she would do this.

Thirty minutes later, she was ready to scream. Oh, Hilda Prigsley was a darling. Charming, jovial and completely convinced that she could never learn anything. Rose had started out trying to explain that truly a computer was no big deal, and if Rose could learn it, then anyone could. Hilda laughed, gray curls bobbing, and explained that she was too old.

When further coaxing and then bribery failed, it was time to bring in the heavy artillery.

"Let's do this. I'm going to sit here, and you don't have to lift a finger. Just watch. Maybe you'll lose some of the fear."

"It's not my fear that's causing the problem, dearie. I'm an old dog, and new tricks aren't my cup of tea." Then she gave out a hoot of laughter.

Patiently, Rose pulled out the laptop, sat it on the coffee table and opened the lid. "Okay, so here we go. The first thing is to power it on. There's a little button or a switch or a lever or some contraption that you push and then the lights will start to flicker. They showed me how to do this just yesterday, and it was so easy. So…" She fumbled around the computer case. "Where was that switch?" For five minutes Rose poked every key and every button—except the most important one. "I know it's here."

Hilda sat, arms crossed, her eyes politely blank.

Rose smiled apologetically. "Sorry. Sometimes it takes me a bit to get going. After five, the brain shuts down."

Hilda coughed discreetly, not saying a word.

"It's a really big button…I think."

After another ten minutes, Hilda's foot began to tap, and Rose ran a hand through her hair, fighting the urge to run to the mirror and fix it. No, she would endure, she would thrive and in the end, Ian would be desperately proud. "I'm so embarrassed, but this is a new machine, and I'm not used to it. Would you mind taking a stab? Sometimes another set of eyes…" Rose pulled her very best, uncertain face.

"I don't see how I can be any assistance," argued Hilda.

Rose looked at her, hurt and dismay oozing from her very being. "I don't know what I'm doing. I don't know why I thought I should. I should just go back to perfume spritzing and leave this for someone more capable. When I was little, my parents didn't believe in technology—they thought idle hands would produce the devil's work. We spent a lot of time churning butter, making up our own entertainment because television was the worst sin of all. Two years ago I finally broke down and bought a TV. It's like a brave new world. But computers? They're the last bastion of technology. The Evil

Empire. I know my mother would be turning over in her grave if she could see how I've shamed her. But I'm determined to do it. I won't be beaten down." Her hair fell into her face, and she placed a delicate finger on her forehead. Incapable Woman Broken By Life.

Hilda was unmoved for a solid two minutes, but after Rose added a pious heavenward glance, the woman came and sat next to her. "Now, dearie, don't slight yourself. We'll tackle this bloody machine, and if two women can't conquer the beastie thing, then, Bob's my uncle."

Rose sniffed. "Are you sure? I'm such a failure."

"And don't you be so hard on yourself," she encouraged, with a motherly pat on the hand. "So we're looking for a button?"

"I think so. A large one."

At first, Hilda hit the enter key, and Rose fixed her hands in her lap. Hilda laughed, and then poked shift. Rose stayed granite-still. Eventually, she hit the power button and Rose had to internalize the whoop of joy.

"Aha! The lights are flashing! I think you've done it."

Hilda pushed at the bridge of her wire frames. "Do you, now?" She leaned in close, watching as the bootup sequence started and the words rolled across the screen. "I think we did. My goodness."

It took another two hours of abject failure and Rose whacking herself on the head—sometimes painfully—before Hilda showed Rose how to properly hold her fingers on the keyboard and then discovered the differences between insert and delete. Rose twirled her hair around a finger, looking breathlessly enthralled with each new revelation.

Eventually it was nearing midnight, and Hilda was fighting back a yawn. Rose took pity on the woman.

"It's getting late, and I'm keeping you up. You're such a sweet lady, helping me here. You must be exhausted."

Hilda waved a hand. "Shush. Not a peep from you. It was all great fun."

"Can you come over tomorrow?" asked Rose, shooting a dark glare at the laptop.

"Oh, Rose, I'm not sure," Hilda answered, pursing her mouth

like a fish. Rose knew that look, that defeatist spirit, but not anymore. They were conquering insecurities left and right.

"It's more the moral support, Hilda. When you're here, I'm sure I can do anything. It gives me courage." In case that didn't cut it, Rose placed an earnest hand over her heart.

"You're sure? An old woman like me?"

"I think you're fabulous," answered Rose, and that was true. The woman had a heart that was twice as big as most, and obviously couldn't stand to see someone in need.

Hilda giggled, and pulled her handbag over her arm. "I suppose I could. I have a cribbage game, but I'll put that off."

"You're a darling." Impulsively, Rose gave her a hug, surprised by the motherly feel of the embrace.

"Tomorrow at seven?"

"Make it six-thirty," said Rose. "I have to learn how to work the printer. It could take days."

Hilda tapped at her arm. "And you will."

Rose blushed charmingly. "We will. Two little troopers managing the dark forces together."

"We'll do it for Ian," Hilda announced with cheery pluck, and Rose now understood why he worked so hard to find her a place. Hilda only needed that one little shove in the right direction, and Ian had recognized that in her. He was good at that, recognizing those who needed the push.

Rose smiled to herself. Everyone needed a little push. Even Ian.

THE NEXT TWO WEEKS, ROSE spent her days at the penthouse and her evenings with Hilda, but her lunch hour belonged to Ian. Every time she saw Ian, her mouth opened, wanting to gush about Hilda's progress. She was well disciplined, though, and when Ian asked about Hilda, she'd shrug with disappointment, and say they were still working on it.

Sometimes they spent the hour at his office, sometimes they grabbed a sandwich and rode the ferry, and sometimes, oh, lucky day, they went to his apartment. Those stolen moments were magic, and he'd ask why he couldn't see her that night, and Rose would hide an elusive grin.

On their last night in computer hell, Hilda was emptying out her purse and out popped a biography on the English royal family.

"Is it good?" asked Rose, making polite conversation, curious because the prosaic Hilda with sensible shoes didn't seem the starstruck type.

"They certainly got some of the facts right, but they tried to build the whole business into some penny dreadful. Wasn't quite the truth, although I suppose it makes for good reading, and a brisk business at the shops."

"You're an expert?"

"Four years at Windsor. Not that it was Buckingham Palace, but it was a far sight better than the bowels of Highgrove."

Rose opened her mouth, quickly closed it. "You worked for the royal family?"

"The queen's aunt," Hilda answered with a brisk bob of her head. "I was a young thing, full of all sorts of dreams and it was my first job out of university."

"Why didn't you tell Ian?"

"It was a long time ago, and if I mention it, people expect me to spill all the tawdry doings, and I'm not a gossip. Not by any stretch of the imagination. It was why I lasted so long. Hilda Prigsley knows when to keep her lips zipped."

Rose looked at the woman in a new light. "Hilda, I think we've all underestimated you."

The woman gave her a saucy smile. "They always do."

It was midmorning at the penthouse, when Rose found the perfect moment to talk to Sylvia. Ian was a firm believer in fate. But Rose knew the hard truth of the world, that you had to make your own fate, your own opportunities, and this morning, bless the monarchy, Rose was going to make Ian's day, and by extension, Rose's day, as well.

Sylvia had finished a coffer-filling meeting with the Simonov Foundation, and was reading over the financials—never her favorite chore—when Rose pounced. "Sylvia, I have a friend who's looking for something similar to my role. Do you know anyone who needs a personal assistant?"

The countess glanced up from her schedule, thinking. "Not many. Kylie McMullen chased off another one last week, but between you and me, I wouldn't sick my worst enemy on that woman. She's got a tongue like a pit viper. Why they couldn't inject BOTOX into her mouth and freeze it permanently, I haven't the foggiest. You wouldn't want a friend working there, unless you're planning some sort of personal revenge, and Rose, darling, you don't have a vindictive bone in your body."

Rose twirled her pen between her fingers, all sophisticated wisdom. Not an easy look for her, but today, she managed it. "No, this woman needs someone…*special.* She's got a…past and I wouldn't want to throw her just anywhere."

"What sort of special?" asked Sylvia, sliding the financials aside. Rose took the papers, filed them on the desk.

"It's very hush-hush, so I can't really say. She's British and there are a lot of things that she's not allowed to say about her prior employer." Rose paused, waited, let the countess draw her own conclusions.

Sylvia's eyes grew saucer-wide. "She worked for Madonna?"

Rose kept her smile small, dangling the carrot oh-so carefully. She peeked around the room as if prying ears might be nearby. "Bigger," she whispered.

"Bigger?" Sylvia braced a hand on the piano. "How bigger?"

"I can't say anything, and she can't, either, but…" Rose began humming "God Save the Queen," and Sylvia fell back against the cushions, clutching her heart.

"I have to have her."

"Sylvia…"

"It would be the coup of the year. Are you kidding?"

"Well, yes, you could do that, but Sylvia, you are a countess, and royalty and titles, well, they become common if you have too much in one household. People would talk, say you're being flaunty. You need to pay it forward. You have to be generous with your absolute fabulousness."

"Rose," pleaded Sylvia.

"Sylvia," warned Rose.

"Why do you have to be such a little do-gooder? Can't a

woman have some vices? A selfish twinge of superiority in order to flaunt her lifestyle about the other, less worthy members of her acquaintance?"

"You'd be friends with Bitsy Mortimer if that was true. Every time you see her, she invites you to her club."

"Stuffy little aristocrats with their argyle socks and outdated membership policies."

Rose folded her arms across her chest because as much as Sylvia wanted to be the ruling elite of the New York social diaries, she didn't have the suck-up-edness.

Eventually, Sylvia heaved a sigh. "Rosie, you're a smart doll, keeping me on the straight and narrow."

"You have to be careful. Plus, she can't talk about it."

"Surely there are a few little tidbits she could share—just with me?"

"Not even with you."

"Well, then. If she can't talk about it, it's not nearly as fun. And I'd get frustrated. The stress level would be atrocious."

"Exactly."

Sylvia picked up her address book, thumbing through names. "Give me ten minutes, and we'll have ourselves a Manhattan-style bidding war. Any perks that she needs? A condo in Miami, flextime, her own personal assistant?"

Rose pulled out her phone, prepared to let Hilda in on the good news. "Let me make a call and we'll find out."

IT WASN'T THE MOST FULFILLING day of Ian's life. Every call was a dead end; every interview not a good fit. And then he had to tell the client that he was sorry, not to give up hope. Something was just around the corner.

It was after six; he was packing up for the day and had planned to kidnap Rose, no matter how busy the auction was keeping her. Today, he needed to hold her, needed to bury himself inside her, needed to make her smile. When he did that, when her eyes lit up, it gave him that same top-of-the-world feeling that he craved. He was about to pick up the phone and call when Mrs. Prigsley appeared in his doorway.

"Good evening, Mr. Ian. And how are you this fine day? I brought you an extra tin today," she told him, presenting him with a tin of biscuits, all wrapped with a sensible yellow ribbon.

Ian frowned, confused. "Did we have an appointment?" He sat down, pulled off his coat. "I must have forgotten. Where are we?"

Hilda remained standing, bouncing up and down on her heels. "As for 'we,' I wouldn't speak to that, but as for 'me,' I'm off to work."

Amazed, Ian gave the woman a once-over, noticed the extra glow in the face. "You found a job?"

"I did indeed. All because of your counselor extraordinaire. Although between you, me and the wardrobe, she's not all that good with machines. Poor dearie. It was the blind leading the blind for a bit, but I found myself a book and we muddled through, and studied some, and just this afternoon, I received a job offer from a Mrs. Elizabeth Carlyle. A PA," she added proudly.

"PA?"

"Personal assistant. I've quite a lot of lingo to brush up on, but I'm getting the 411." She leaned in confidentially. "That's information, you know."

Ian grinned, feeling better than he had all day. How had Rose done it? "You'll do great."

"I think so. You're sweet on her, Mr. Ian?"

"That's the understatement of the year," he told her, because sweet didn't begin to describe the swelling in his heart, the clarity in his vision. His life hadn't ended postlayoff, and his life hadn't been lived prelayoff. A man wasn't defined by a title or a paycheck, but instead how well he loved.

Ian loved.

"Just don't let her near the computers," Hilda advised.

And Ian made a properly concerned face. "No. I won't."

15

HE SHOWED UP IN THE BRONX with roses. He considered daisies, orchids, daffodils, lilies, but then realized that there was no more perfect flower. Soft petals, elegant symmetry, and enough thorns to make her deadly.

She looked at the flowers, looked at his face and beamed. "You found out."

"I suppose you're very proud of yourself."

"I am. You think you're the only one that can rescue the world?"

"I imagined all sorts of bad things about you—froufrou evenings with Dr. Buckeroo Bonzai," he told her, taking a definitive step into her apartment. "Long carriage rides in the park, flights to Paris."

"You have a wild imagination," she told him, taking the flowers, laying them aside, her eyes locked with his.

He shut the door, and merely smiled. "You have no idea."

"Dr. Bonzai, he's dead to me." She curled her hands in his hair, lowered his head, but Ian wasn't going to be diverted.

"Dead? How dead?" He tipped up her head and studied her, noting the sparkle in her eye. Happiness. Love. That's what they called it.

"Against you, he never had a chance." She raised her mouth to his, and Ian had the strength of character to feel sorry for the man—but not too long. Rose had that effect. Made him forget about everything but her.

Of their own volition, his fingers lowered the zip on her dress. He hadn't intended this. He'd intended dinner. Ian reminded himself to be careful with her, but her hands slid under his shirt, soft against his heart, and she didn't seem so fragile anymore.

The wispy blue dress fell to the floor, revealing black silk underneath.

"I think you're trying to seduce me, Mrs. Robinson."

"I am," she whispered. His fingers shook as he undid her bra, exposing the pale gold skin, the delicate pink nipples. He took one in his mouth. Her hands tangled in his hair, and Ian decided that dinner was overrated.

He loved her like this. Adrift in pleasure, with her quiet moans that nearly did him in. She was never loud, and he lived for those little sounds that she worked so hard to suppress. It was a challenge to him to make her forget the barriers, to make her let go.

His thumbs slipped underneath the black silk at her hips, then followed the long line of her legs. When she stood before him, he held his breath, because there was no woman as beautiful as this.

Her warm blue gaze met his, liquid, spilling over with things he'd longed to see. Carefully he picked her up in his arms, carrying her to bed. Her arms didn't wait to reach for him, but Ian had other plans in mind. Quickly he stripped, lowering himself to her, his eyes stayed locked with hers, making sure the panic stayed far away. Tonight, he wanted it to be Rose and Ian. No ghosts. No fears.

His mouth tasted the satin of her neck, the elegant line of her shoulder. She closed her eyes, a small smile on her lips.

Lower he went, satisfying himself with one breast, then the other. Lower still to the curve of her hips, but there Ian hesitated, raising his head. Her eyes were open, not so panicked, but not so sure, either.

The radiator hummed, covering the heavy thud of his heart. One beat. Then two. Her teeth sank into her lower lip and she nodded, her body arching in invitation.

Ian didn't waste another beat.

With his hands, he spread her thighs, finding her pink and wet. One finger slid inside her, and he watched her face, her expression sharp with desire. He'd waited for this—ultimate trust.

With each push of his hand, her hips curled upward, urging him on. Her fists curled into the soft down of the duvet, twisting with the same slow rhythm.

For long moments he played and tested, never going too far or too fast, keeping the ghosts far at bay. The sight of her, open, wanting, trusting, was a picture he would never forget.

Slowly he lowered his head, one touch of his tongue to her clit, and her body jerked. His hand splayed over her stomach, gentling her, easing her, and he paused until he felt her relax. This time, he stroked, back and forth, his tongue, his finger, and he felt the tension ease, felt the slow drain of her, heard the quick gasps of pleasure at each touch of his mouth.

Bolder now, he sucked, tasting her honey, hearing the quick gasps grow longer, huskier. Her hips were moving with him now, and he knew she was close.

Ultimate trust.

Her fingers clasped his head, pressing him there, keeping him there.

Ultimate trust.

His hands moved beneath her, lifting her high, and this time, his mouth wasn't gentle, drawing her in, drinking her in.

Her back arched, stiff and tight, and then…

Finally.

Rose fell.

THE NEXT SATURDAY NIGHT, Ian Cumberland was cordially invited to the home of Count Anton and Sylvia Simonov for an evening of fun and festivity, but mainly so that Sylvia could decide if he was worthy.

Rose was a basket case.

That afternoon, she had made a list of suggested topics for them to discuss, prepped him on the appropriate answers and went over his suit choice five times.

Ian was not amused.

"Honey, this is not a huge thing."

"It's huge."

"It's dinner."

"It's my boss, it's the count. It's your shot, Ian," she said, and then immediately shut her mouth.

Of course, he noticed. "What do you mean?"

"Mingle, comingle, mix, this is your world."

"Not really."

"It used to be your world."

"No, Rose," he said firmly. "Is that why you want me there?"

Rose decided it wasn't the time for this discussion. Not yet. "No. I want you to meet Sylvia. I want her to love you. I want you to meet the count because he can do great favors for you."

"I thought you didn't like the count. I thought he was—and these were your words, I wouldn't have been so nice—a cheating son of a gun. I don't want great favors from a cheating son of a gun."

"I don't know that he's cheating. I don't think he's cheating. I think he's thinking about cheating. Blair's just…"

"You're worrying way too much."

"I don't worry. I plan. I organize. I have a strategy."

"Will I doom our entire sexual relationship if I don't have a strategy?"

"Be serious."

"I was serious," he said, then he took her in his arms. "Rose, I'll be fine. You'll be fine. We'll be fine."

"We'll be fine?"

"Perfect."

"You'll wear the gray suit with the blue-striped tie?"

"Of course," he said, wisely choosing not to argue.

DINNER WAS FABULOUS, IAN WAS fabulous and Rose was starting to breathe normally.

"I like him," Sylvia whispered. "He's bonkers for you, not that that's any surprise."

Rose fanned her face, suddenly finding herself short of oxygen. "You think?"

"I *know,* honey. But he's not Remy."

At that, Rose winced. "He's worth ten of Remy."

"Not in actual U.S. dollars," the countess reminded her.

"He's very ambitious, and given the right opportunity…" Rose trailed off.

"You want me to say something to Anton?" asked Sylvia.

Rose frowned. "No. Not yet. Give it time."

"He doesn't seem like the impress-his-betters type."

"He doesn't need to. You should see him at the office. He's always thinking, always making connections, hooking up somebody with somebody else. Sometimes we'll be out on a walk, and he gets this look, and he pulls out the phone. And boom. Somebody new is gainfully employed. Ian gets ahead the old-fashioned way. He earns it." She liked to watch him work, liked to see that flash in his face, liked to know that the world was a better place because Ian Cumberland was there.

"Earning it? Quaint, yet slow."

Without the proper incentives that was true, and Sylvia, attuned to the machinations of the female's drive for security, saw the determination in Rose's face. "Be careful, sweetie," she cautioned. "I'm not so sure that he wants to drive in the fast lane. Sometimes things aren't laid out exactly like we wish they were. What do you do if you have to make a choice?"

Rose watched Ian, lifting his glass, chatting with the count. Okay, maybe the two men weren't the best of friends, and Ian was keeping a distance, but there weren't swords at dawn. She just needed to work a little harder. With Ian, there were no nightmares, there were no shadows, life was perfect. And she would do everything in her power to keep it that way.

"I want to be with him, Sylvia. I'm going to hand him the opportunity of a lifetime, just like you gave me. There won't be a choice. In the end, the human condition is predictable in its need for security. Nobody wants to struggle, nobody wants that pain, the yelling, the constant pressure to do more. There won't be a choice for me. It only takes a strategy."

THE PLANS FOR THE BACHELOR auction were proceeding perfectly. She'd verified the menu, triple-checked the reservation list, picked out the music and met with her team of bachelors, reassuring each one that the proceedings were to be conducted with the utmost respect and dignity for their reputation and, also, physical safety.

As for her nights, they belonged to Ian, and the nightmares stayed at bay—at least most of the time. Sometimes he watched her, and she knew he wanted to know, but shrugged it off as nothing, and she stayed quiet. No one was better at keeping quiet than Rose.

Except for maybe Ian. He stopped saying anything about his old job, he stopped checking in with his old boss, and when she asked him—all very carefully, all very discreetly—he shrugged it off casually and stayed quiet.

Empowered by Hilda's success, Rose knew it was time for Cinderella to take the bull by the horns and plant the glass slipper under Prince Charming's nose. It would take careful timing, charm and a devious mind, all of which she possessed in abundance.

She bided her time, writing down her lines and practicing them until she had perfected the delivery with the right amount of sincerity, spontaneity and uncertainty. And one brilliant February afternoon, she cornered the count in his office.

"Mail for you. A ski junket, something official from the State and a letter from home. Sorry, I couldn't translate."

He took the mail, glanced through it and then looked at her when he noticed that she hadn't left. Rose wasn't usually one to hover, and she didn't do it well.

"Yes?"

"Anton, you're on the board at that bank, aren't you?"

"Several."

"So—" she blanked her face, staring in the distance "—you know the head guy, right?"

"I had lunch with the head of Citi this afternoon," he said, which she knew because she'd logged the invitation in his calendar. "Why the sudden interest in finance?"

"Nothing," said Rose, then turned as if to go.

"Rose? Do you need something?"

She hesitated at the door, opened her mouth, closed her mouth, exactly three times.

"Go ahead, tell me what you're after," he urged. Deep inside—impending midlife crisis notwithstanding—Anton was a man who was as softhearted as his wife.

"It's not for me," answered Rose.

"Someone needs a loan?"

Rose looked horrified. "Oh, no. It's Ian. He's doing well. Or…he's managing well, but before… He had this great position as an investment banker. When we first met, he'd go on about how much he enjoyed all the excitement and risk and the reward. And he was good at it, but then—you know, the economy went south and he was laid off. And now he's got this second-rate job, and sometimes I can see how much he'd love to get back in the game, but he's too proud to say anything, and I thought…you have all these great connections."

"It's a very hard time," he told her, stroking his chin thoughtfully.

Not the moment to press. "You're so right. I can't imagine what I was thinking. Of course, you're not a miracle worker. I'm used to seeing you and Sylvia…it's as if anything is possible. I forget," she told him, adding a self-conscious shrug.

"And you think I could wave my magic wand and poof, he's back at the bank?"

"It sounds silly, doesn't it?" Rose ducked her head, chagrin in her voice.

Anton laughed, that hearty, confident laugh of a man who's used to granting favors for the serfs. "For an ordinary man, perhaps. For a Simonov, nothing is beyond reach. Let me make a few calls to Stan. Perhaps I could let him beat me at golf. He doesn't do it very often."

Rose's mouth gaped open charmingly, full of the appropriate wonder and amazement. "You can do that? Really?"

"Sometimes I surprise myself, as well."

"Thank you, so much. I was worried. I didn't want to assume, but you and the countess…you're the best," she told him. The phone rang and he waved her off.

As she walked away, she began to hum to herself, something that sounded suspiciously like bad Ethel Merman.

Ian would never know.

IT TOOK NEARLY A MONTH for the job offer to come through. Three weeks when Rose was on pins and needles, hoping and praying. Every night she spent at Ian's, rearranging his shelves, organizing his closet and conquering a spot on his curtains that was particularly stubborn. Finally—finally!—after all her impatient waiting, Ian called her at work. "Guess what?"

"What?" she asked, closing her eyes, crossing her fingers and thinking every positive thought she was capable of.

"I didn't want to tell you because it might be nothing, but I got an offer from Citi."

Rose hit the mute button and squealed. When suitably calm, she unmuted and cleared her throat. "Doing what?"

"Investment banking in the overseas division. European investors looking for the security of the dollar."

Rose gasped. "Really? Ian, that's fabulous! You must be thrilled," she said encouragingly, because honestly some of the thrill wasn't there in his voice.

"I am," he said. She still wasn't getting all the thrill, however, this was too big an event not to celebrate.

"When do you start?"

"I have to put in notice at the agency first. I think two weeks is fine, but if they need me for longer—I don't know that I'd turn them down." At that, she definitely heard it. Sad.

Rose stopped the happy dance and sat in her straight-backed chair, feet firmly on the floor, posture rigid. "Why aren't you excited about this?"

"I am. I'm thrilled. I mean, wow. It's completely out of the blue. I had talked to my old boss a few months ago, but... I didn't expect anything."

"It's fate," she told him firmly.

"I guess. Anyway, it'll be nice to not have to worry about keeping the heat down at night, although I have to say that as long as you're sharing the covers, I don't mind energy conservation so much."

"If you like, we'll set the thermostat at fifty."

"See, that's my girl."

"You're going to love it. I know it."

"We'll have to celebrate."

"Pizza at Fontini's."

"Really?"

"I'm feeling the urge to harass Fabrezio."

Ian laughed, and she felt the warmth again. She'd made him happy. She'd done that. Rose Hildebrand.

Little Miss Sweet Pea? Not a chance.

A FEW HOURS LATER, IAN WAS sitting at the bar with Beckett, staring into his beer, excited, nervous, but the old spark wasn't there. He looked in the long mirror over the bar, tried for the devil-may-care grin. Sadly, the devil was refusing to care.

"Missing the mano-a-mano ambience? Need some locker-room talk, some politically incorrect jokes, or want to bitch about the women?" Beckett scowled. "I can't bitch anymore. It seems disloyal. You can bitch if you need to, but I know—stop the presses, here—I'm going to keep my mouth shut."

Ian blew out a breath. "I accepted a job offer today."

"Dude, you're back. And can I say it's about time, because I was tired of the 'disgruntled, life-kicked-you-in-ass, we have to tiptoe about your sensitivities' attitude." Then he broke into a grin and lifted his glass. "Just kidding. Congratulations to a stellar new year. May last year's debacle rest in peace."

Ian clinked glasses, drank, but then returned to cracking peanuts between his fingers. "What if I've lost my touch? What if I've lost the edge? I think I'm getting soft, Beckett. I want to sleep late on Saturday. And the *Wall Street Journal?* It's a very depressing paper. I never realized that before."

Beckett studied him, nodded. "It's to be expected. You're not sure if you can live up to overinflated expectations, dreading that the hype is more than what you're capable of."

"That wasn't exactly it."

"It's all rolled up together. Don't sweat it. Jump in, headfirst and prepare to live."

"That would be so much more effective if it hadn't taken you ten years to sleep with Phoebe."

"I had to be sure."

Ian laughed, because Beckett was probably right. This was jitters, nothing more. "You're going to pick up the tab?"

"Dude, you're in high finance again and you're going to stiff me with the bill?"

Okay, some things didn't change. Ian leaned back, contemplated the new world order, and smiled. He looked in the mirror once again. Almost. With a little bit of practice, he'd be fine.

16

THE MANHATTAN OFFICE FOR Employment Displacement was booming, the reception area lined with applicants three-deep. As he made his way through the crowd, Ian avoided their eyes. After nearly a year at the agency, it was the first time he'd ever done that. Undaunted, he manned up and told himself that this wasn't his problem anymore. He was going back to the big time, going to soar with the eagles. However, when he got to his office, the eagle on the motivational picture looked…ticked off.

Ian reminded himself that eagles always looked ticked off. It was their natural state. He shouldn't be taking it personally. Still, two hours later, he got up and moved the picture behind the printer where he couldn't see those two beady eyes glaring at him as if he was betraying some eagle-esque code of honor.

His letter of resignation was typed up and sitting on the desk, awaiting only his signature before he turned it in to his boss.

The files needed to be ordered, notes needed to be drafted, there were calls that he should make in order to transition his caseload to someone else, although they would transition it to Arnie who didn't have enough of the real dogged perseverance to do anybody any good. Sadly, that same never-say-die-I-don't-care-if-I'm-an-asshole quality that made him good in finance, was also a plus in job placement. Who knew?

He was half-way through his first set of notes when Hilda came into his office wearing a rather fetching forest-green dress and bearing the usual tin of cookies. Dragging behind her was a hesitant stick of a man with a tweed cap on his head.

"Mr. Cumberland, this is Mr. Fergus Moore and he's seeking

employment, preferably in the tailoring industry. I said that you and Ms. Hildebrande were top-notch at finding a position, yet he was skeptical. Tell him, Mr. Cumberland."

Ian pushed the cookies back in her direction.

"Hilda, I can't take on the case."

"Of course you can. Compared to my own pitiable situation, Fergus is a foregone vocational conclusion."

"I'm sure he is, but I won't be here."

Her eyes grew huge. "They sacked you? I'll go speak on your behalf. Right now. It's an injustice, it is."

"No, I'm putting in my notice. Two weeks."

"You're quitting, Mr. Cumberland?"

Her shocked dismay hurt more than he expected. "I got my job back on Wall Street. It's a fantastic opportunity."

"Where you'll be mingling with the dregs of the earth?" she said with a huff.

"They're not that bad."

"But your calling is here." She nodded toward the crowd on the other side of the glass partition. "They need you."

"No one is indispensable, not even me. Whoever handles their case will do great." Assuming it wasn't Arnie—or Melinda, who hated people. Why, everybody else was… Almost okay.

"You've disappointed me, Mr. Cumberland. I pleaded and begged with Mr. Moore for a good ten days, promising him ten months' worth of shepherd's pie if he'd only come to talk to you and see the great promise in your face. Tell him, Fergus."

The man held his hat in his hands and bobbed his head. "That she did."

Hilda stared him down, using that same beady, eagle-eyed glare. Once again, Ian failed to live up to expectations. "Well, I suppose this finishes it. Good luck with your life, Mr. Cumberland. And Ms. Hildebrande, would she be able to help Fergus?"

"I doubt it, Hilda."

"I see," she answered, as if everything could be summarized in two words. Actually, it could.

No and *Shit*.

After they left, Ian studied the faces in the reception room, picked up his lucky rock and tossed it up and down, letting the smooth stone weigh in his hand, a Magic 8-Ball telling him all the right answers. Where did he belong? Here? On Wall Street?

As long as it was with Rose, did he really care?

Yes. Yes, he did.

She'd be disappointed if he didn't take the job. What woman wouldn't? And Rose's standards were higher than most. But if he stayed here, they would never starve, they wouldn't lack for shelter, or heat. It wasn't as if he was condemning her to a life below the poverty line.

He was needed.

He liked it here. He belonged here.

He was staying.

Feeling better, he ripped up the letter and threw it away. Relieved, he took a long breath, planting the rock back on his desk where it belonged.

Hopefully, Rose would understand.

IAN SEARCHED FOR THE RIGHT time to say something to Rose, but every time she looked at him with those blue eyes that were now full of hope and excitement, he couldn't do it. There were so many pieces to Rose that he didn't understand, and he kept waiting for her to trust him, but she didn't, and he wasn't sure she ever would. It wasn't the world's best relationship. In many ways it flew in the face of everything he wanted in a relationship, but since he had important things that he didn't want to tell her, either, he couldn't blame her for keeping the bad things at bay.

However, Ian wasn't Rose. In the end, he knew that motivational posters didn't do crap, shit happened, and that sometimes people couldn't abandon their high ambitions no matter how badly you wanted to hope. He couldn't run away from this any longer.

Tonight, he'd carefully planned what he needed to say, figured out the perfect phrases to make her understand that he liked working where he was. He liked what he did; there were people who depended on him, and he couldn't go back. Not now, not ever.

But it didn't matter how often he practiced the trite affirmations in his head; there was a sinking in his gut, in his heart, because he knew this wasn't going to go down well.

They were sitting on the couch, and she was laughing at the late night shows, touching him as if he were the mightiest man on the planet. When she lifted her face, shining with happiness, he opened his mouth and then kissed her as if he never would again.

"Ian?" she asked, but he didn't say a word.

Carefully he undressed her, memorizing the feel of his hand on her skin, the scent of honeysuckle teasing his mind. In this, she trusted him. Somewhere, they'd passed the point of battles and tactics, and when he thrust inside her, he could see the love flaring in her eyes.

She never said the words, and neither did he. Ian was fast learning that words were useless things when compared to what the heart knew.

He took her hand, their bodies joined, eyes locked, and slowly they moved together, tenderness, passion, love.

Afterward, he held her, a little tighter than normal, a little more possessive than what he usually dared, and she trailed a soft finger on his face.

"You seem different," she said, and he brought her hand to his lips, kissing it softly. When he first met her, when he first kissed her, it was her beauty that had stolen his breath. But her beauty was the least of what was Rose. She had a tentative courage that her scars couldn't mask. A cynical heart that hadn't quite forgotten how to believe. And a generosity that was destined to hurt her. People looked at Rose, and assumed. Ian had made that mistake, as well. But because of her, Ian had learned to look beneath the surface for what was real.

Now he was different. He was different because of her.

THE NIGHT OF THE AUCTION, Rose wore a sea-foam green silk—simple, elegant, not too much glitz. Being glitzy while asking for contributions never gave a favorable impression. Her makeup was flawless, the hotel staff was buzzing like bees, but the pit in her stomach kept growing. The countess was watching, Ian was watching, the most eligible bachelors were watching, and everyone expected her to perform perfectly.

At one time, she'd have pulled off a flawless show without a wince. She'd endured a pipe against the back with nary a scream, she'd been thrown into that goddamned closet for days, and yet she smiled as if she didn't have a care. A little girl learned not to care. She learned not to dream.

Ian caught up with her behind the staging area, rubbed her hands. "You're sweating."

"I know. It's a terrible habit." She searched for a napkin to get rid of the offending evidence.

"Rose. You'll be fine." His eyes approved of her, warmed her, thrilled her. She took a deep breath, but then from the other side of the room came the furious barking of a dog.

The napkin in her hand flew to the ground.

"You shouldn't have brought in the dogs," Ian told her, retrieving the fallen cloth, and he wished he could retrieve her fallen sanity just as easily.

"It was Sylvia's idea. I can do this, Ian. It's silly to be afraid of dogs."

"Have you been bitten before?"

It was the first time he'd specifically asked about her fears, and instinctively a lie sprang to her lips, but instead she opted for some bit of the truth.

"No. I had this great dress. My parents had spent a fortune on it. This huge dog, a monster, he jumped up. He was just being friendly, but the dress… The dirty paws ruined it and my mother wasn't happy."

Ian pulled her close, stroked her neck—a lot of comfort for a ruined dress, and she wondered how much he guessed. Still, she'd changed. Grown.

"I have to go," she told him.

"I'll be in the back," he said, giving her a kiss for luck, and then he disappeared, leaving Rose to pull this off. Alone.

Behind the main ballroom was a staging area, filled with tailors, hair designers and ten of New York's most eligible bachelors, dashing in their black tuxes, donating their social services for the benefit of the butt-ugly canines on the other side.

Sometimes people surprised her.

She eyed the dogs on the leashes nervously. Slowly, she approached the beasts as if she weren't terrified, though not foolish enough to get within dress-destruction range. Once bitten, twice shy.

The shelter had brought out the lively ones, the ones that jumped and yelped and wanted to get into people's faces, thinking people would be happy and wouldn't scream.

"You're doing a great thing," said a voice from behind her.

It was Remy, darling, dashing, richer-than-Trump Remy, who had asked absolutely nothing of her. Ever.

"So are you. You don't even seem nervous. The ladies are going to break the bank to have a night with you."

He even blushed charmingly. Sadly, it was true. The man had no flaws. "I've gotten over the fear. You're a fabulous cheerleader. And look at those faces. How can I turn my back on that?"

"Remy…"

He stopped her in midsentence.

"He's the one, isn't he?"

Rose nodded apologetically.

He took her face in his hand, tilted it up and smiled. "I've never seen a woman try so hard to make something out of nothing."

"It wasn't nothing," she insisted, not wanting to insult him, not wanting to annoy him, not wanting to make him mad.

He raised his brows, but she stood her ground. "It wasn't. You're a good man."

"And you're a good friend," he said, marvelously calm.

"Thank you for not being angry."

"You showed up in my life at the right time. Mother wants me to find someone appropriate. You were appropriate."

"You have someone 'inappropriate'?" she guessed.

"She's a waitress."

"Tell your mother to take a hike," said Rose, the woman who'd never told anyone to take a hike.

"I think I will."

"What's her name?"

"Steph."

"It's a nice name. Go get her, Remy. Don't wait too long."

"And what about you, Rose? Who is he? I don't think there's a man who couldn't love you."

"His name is Ian, and he's honorable, and loving, and strong and he makes me believe there's hope in the world."

"So…"

"It's complicated."

"That complicated?"

The poodle barked, and Rose's hand shot out to whatever would support her. In this case, Remy. "It's only a dog."

And that was Rose's world. Full of secrets that weren't meant to be told. It wasn't a world she wanted to share. In the past, she'd thought she could, that she could act her way into happiness, but not anymore.

"It's not always easy, Remy."

He shrugged in understanding. "No. I guess not."

THE BALLROOM WASN'T THE MOST perfect venue for black-tie accompanied by a melee of dogs, but Sylvia pulled it off. The auctioneer, imported direct from Christie's, was a short, pudgy man with a dour smile and a wicked gavel-rap that made Rose flinch at regular intervals.

But the auction finished without a hitch. Ten handsome bachelors, ten squealing winners, two dozen dogs straining at the leash and one smug, slutty Blair Rapaport.

It was right before dessert when Blair approached.

"I got the flowers from Anton. I wanted you to know."

"Your adventures in botany aren't my concern," Rose told her, striving to be polite. She snagged a glass of cabernet, needing something in her hands. Preferably a weapon.

"He asked to meet me tonight. I'm going to win."

Rose stepped up, face-to-face. "I'll tell him about the bet. I'll tell the countess. Honestly, you can't imagine her when she's mad. There's dragon fire in her eyes, and she'll rip you a new one before you can say ouch."

Blair only laughed. "I love pissing you off, Rose. You have

these fuming heaves like you've been pricked in the ass with a pineapple. But you would never do a goddamned thing."

A dog barked, and Rose jumped. Blair laughed, and for Rose that was it. Her arm spazzed, and oops, she threw the cabernet right onto Blair's previously pristine dress.

"You bitch!" Blair shrieked, while Rose graciously handed her a napkin.

"The stain's going to be killer to get out. And your mascara is running. If you used waterproof, it wouldn't be a problem. And look at the count—oh, my—he looks horrified."

He didn't, but Blair checked just the same, and Rose quietly rocked on her heels.

"You think this is done."

"For now," answered Rose, her heart pounding, but she hid it, just as she always did.

Two seconds later, Rose realized how much trouble she'd stirred. Blair stalked toward the trainers, grabbed the leashes and in a great show of bad taste—threw them to the floor. Two dozen dogs charged through the dining room, women shrieking, bachelors scrambling, while Rose watched in horror.

She took a step back, away from the chaos, away from the noise.

A German shepherd loped toward her, a happy smile on his doggie face, and Rose felt the double-time thud from her heart, the sweat on her palms, her neck, but she planted her heels firmly on the ground. *Not going to run, not going to run.*

The dog rose on his great doggie paws, his black eyes shining happily, and in slow motion she saw him lunge. At her.

Thankfully, Rose fainted.

_17_

IAN FANNED HER FACE, trying to get blood circulating, trying to get her to wake up. Eventually, yes, thank God, the lashes flickered and the pale blue eyes worked to focus.

"You okay?" he asked, rubbing her hands together.

"The dogs. The room. The people. Oh, God. Blair." She sat up on the couch, stared in confusion.

"You're in the manager's office, Rose. They're gone."

"How?"

He wisely skimmed over the more chaotic parts and focused on the end results. "The countess took over. Flawlessly, by the way. You should have seen her, the concierge had some doggie treats and she herded them onstage and stood there, two dozen dogs sitting at her heels like some Joan of Arc among the hounds. Honestly, it was awesome."

She whopped herself on the head, once, twice, until he grabbed her hand again, making her stop. "I wanted to do this, Ian. I wanted to do this right. I wanted to do it great. I thought I could get over the Giant Monolith of Roseness. She said I'd never do a goddamned thing. She was right."

Ian held her close, feeling her tremble, feeling the shivers. "Until you threw the wine on her?" he reminded her, because she needed to hear that, needed to know that she had done something. Something kick-ass.

"You saw?"

"A lot of people saw. My table broke out in applause."

"Really?"

He gave her an encouraging smile. "Rose, it's never as bad as you believe. She deserved it."

"I should tell the count I'm onto him. I should tell Sylvia. I should…"

"You'll figure it out. For tonight, I think the count's virtue is safe."

He helped her to her feet just as Sylvia burst into the room, the door slamming behind her. "Rose! You're good?"

"I'm good."

"Thank God, I thought you had died. You looked so white, your eyes were like saucers. And you know this is going to hit Page Six. Throwing wine at Blair. Every man in the place was waiting for hair to rip and clothes to fall off. Honestly, I couldn't have done it better. What did she say to you?"

Rose glanced toward Ian, seeking guidance, but truth be told, he wasn't the best one to be dishing out advice on how to break news.

So he waited.

She opened her mouth, and then the count appeared in the doorway.

"She's not very nice," Rose answered primly. "She said some very rude things about you. I didn't approve." Then Rose gave the count a dark glare. "I don't approve."

"Pshaw." Sylvia waved a hand. "Do you think I let that little twat bother me? Let it go, Rose. You'll be better tomorrow. Ian, take her home, will you?"

Ian nodded and the couple watched them leave. Ian relieved, and Rose, well, Rose seemed disappointed, and she didn't deserve to be disappointed. Not tonight. She'd done great things tonight.

"I should have told her. I wanted to say something, but I couldn't."

Quickly Ian made up his mind. "Stay here a minute, would you? You look like you could use some water."

He ran down the hallway, caught the count as they were nearing the door.

"Sir? A second?" Ian shot an apologetic glance at the countess. "Sorry. Boring financial stuff."

As soon as they were alone, he started in, winging it all the way.

"It was quite the auction tonight."

"With Sylvia, it is always an adventure."

"She's amazing. Rose is really fond of her. She's been a good friend, as well as a boss. That's pretty rare. You must be very proud of her."

"I am, yes. This is what you wanted to say?"

"Give me a sec—it's not so easy. Not that it's my business, but I see these great, long marriages, and—you know how I feel about Rose—it makes me think about how relationships take a lot of work."

"I've been married to Sylvia for twenty-five years. It's not as hard as it seems."

Ian whistled. "Wow. Twenty-five years. Don't you get…stifled? Bored?"

"Never," answered the count, who'd probably never been doubted in his entire life.

"That's really noble with all the…talent that falls into your lap."

The count's eyes narrowed, arrogant, infallible and not to be tweaked. "You have something to say?"

"You're a bet, sir."

"I beg your pardon?"

"Blair. It's a bet, nothing more. She told Rose. It's been bugging her—Rose, not Blair—because she wanted to tell you but she didn't think it was her place. It's not my place, either, but you should know, before you do something that's less than smart."

Pissing off a Russian count was probably something less than smart, as well, but sometimes less than smart had to be done.

Anton pulled at the collar of his coat, his eyes flashing to black. "It is none of your concern, nor is it your place. I expected more gratitude and less…disrespect for a man whom you're indebted to."

Slowly Ian lifted his head, the angry words sinking home. "I wasn't aware I owed you any favors."

"I was wondering about that. You didn't seem the sort. She came to me for you."

"Who?" he asked, not that he didn't know.

"Rose."

It hurt more than he would have expected. It would have been less painful if it were her lack of faith in him. Hell, she probably thought she was doing him a favor.

But in his heart, he knew exactly why Rose had done this. She didn't have a choice.

"I don't need your favors. I don't need a new job."

His smile was coldly polite. "Apparently Rose disagrees."

"I won't presume to speak for Rose."

"Yet you do so before? Suddenly, it's not easy, is it?"

No, it wasn't easy. Ian touched his forehead in salute. "Touché."

"As much as it shames me, I thank you for your concern, warning a foolish man before I ruin something that is very valuable to me. I love her. I will not tarnish that. My choices, they are much easier than yours. Go home, Ian. You have some decisions of your own to make."

ON THEIR WAY BACK TO his apartment, Ian kept a cheery smile on his face, while a storm raged in his gut. At what point was he supposed to step in and demand that she trust him? And how worthless was that? How long was he supposed to live with the mystery that was Rose Hildebrande? His heart told him to wait forever. His brain told him that once he let her know that he was turning down the job, his wait would be over. But not yet.

That night, he woke up to the sound of her shrouded scream and he reached to touch her, then stopped himself.

He knew the routine, knew the code. He didn't know why there was a code; he didn't know why there was a routine, but he knew that what haunted her in her dreams kept her trapped in it. And now, he was trapped there, too.

"Rose. It's Ian."

Her eyes opened and she shot up in bed. He saw the fear first, then recognition flared back into place.

He took her hand, and she curled into his arms. "Stupid dreams," she said, her laugh shaky, forced.

"It's all right now," he murmured, burying his face in her hair. Honeysuckle.

"I'm so glad you're here. It's easier. So much nicer."

"What happened, Rose? I don't want to ask. I keep hoping you'll give me a clue, some idea of what I should do, what I shouldn't do, but…"

At that, she lifted her head, her body stiff, her eyes now nervously awake.

"It's nothing," she lied, and she kissed him, as if she loved him, as if she needed him, as if she trusted him. Ian wanted to press her, but her hand closed over his cock, stroking, tempting, and he didn't want to think about nightmares, or jobs, or long-delayed resignation letters.

He only wanted this.

ROSE KNEW SOMETHING was wrong. At first, she'd been convinced it was her. That she'd put her foot in her mouth, complained too much, demanded too much, and so she'd cleaned his apartment—twice, but the uncomfortable belief remained. Something was wrong.

It was a stunning March Saturday afternoon when he discovered her with a can of scouring powder and pine cleanser, and he took them away.

"Let's go out to eat tonight," he said, and they ended up at the same restaurant where they'd started. It should have thrilled her, but the taut lines in his face made her nervous.

He'd arranged the same table by the kitchen, a bottle of champagne, and this time when the flowers were brought in, the two dozen white roses were delivered to her.

The pit in her stomach only grew.

Desperately she searched the depths of his eyes, looking for that spark of hope and optimism, needing it, but tonight it'd gone missing. It hadn't dawned on her how much she'd come to depend on that spark.

The steward opened the champagne and poured two glasses. Ian touched his to hers.

After the man left, Ian broke the silence. "When I saw you here that night, I'd never had a shock like that, never met someone that made me swallow my tongue. When you look at me with that faith shining in your eyes, everything falls away, Rose. You make a man feel like he can do anything, conquer anything. But I don't want anything, I don't need anything. Everything I need is here. It's you."

They were words she'd waited to hear from him for days,

months, longer than a lifetime. Her hands began to shake, and she didn't want to be here in this damned restaurant with a thousand staring eyes.

"No one's ever needed me before," she told him, which meant "I love you," but he probably wouldn't know that unless she said it. Carefully she laid the napkin over her hands, stilling the noise, stilling her nerves.

"I have to tell you something," Ian began, his voice serious.

She didn't like the regret in his gaze. Ian never regretted anything. Rose regretted her entire life—until she'd met him.

"I'm not going to take the job," he said, and she exhaled, beginning to breathe once again. That wasn't so bad.

"It's the wrong company, isn't it? That can be fixed. I can fix it."

"How?"

"It's a different world, Ian. If you're connected to the right people, anything can be fixed."

Slowly it dawned on her that he knew what she'd done. Strangely enough, she'd never considered this conversation before, but she sensed it would go badly.

Exactly like this.

"You talked to the count. He told me."

"Yes. I wanted to give you something."

"You should have asked."

"You would have said no," she told him, needing to point that out.

"Damn right, I would have said no," he answered, and his fingers tightened over a spoon, harmless, anger carefully controlled.

Rose winced. He noticed, and a shadow of sadness rolled over his face. Perfect. She'd put him back on Rose-alert. Lately she hadn't been so great at hiding her feelings, hiding her fears. "You want this. You told me you missed your old job."

"I thought I wanted this, Rose. But I don't. I like where I am. I don't want the high ozone anymore. The world changed. I changed, too."

"Okay," she answered in an agreeable voice, but her hair was in her eyes, and her back was hardening into its default ladylike position.

No.

Rose pushed her hair away, met his eyes, never wavering, never blinking. She didn't back down, not once.

Words came to her tongue, words she'd never spoken in her life. *I love you. I'll stay with you, whatever you choose. Whatever you do. Don't leave me. Please.*

They were easy words to say. So much easier than anything she'd ever said before. So much easier than what she'd ever been through. She'd survived hell, this was a walk in the park.

His eyes flickered. That same defensive vulnerability that had affected her before. The defiant bravado that shouted: "Go ahead. Get it over with so that I can move on with my life."

But he didn't think she could move on, and something small and fragile within her, died.

"I haven't changed," she told him, because she hadn't. She hadn't changed a damned thing.

"I think you have."

"Some. Not enough."

"Why, Rose? You're not greedy, you'd never have a maid, and you'd never let anyone else touch your laundry. That isn't who you are."

"No. But money can buy anything. It's power. Control. The dreams go away, because you have it all. When you live up there in the penthouse, no one can touch you. You're invulnerable to the rest of the world."

"Only if you're made of stone, Rose."

"It's not a bad thing," she defended, because stone was a material of myriad uses. She wouldn't be sane if she hadn't been stone. She wouldn't be alive if she hadn't been stone.

"So, do I take you home and you write on the mirror again?" he asked. And somehow in this conversation, somehow in this relationship, she'd not only lost all the hope in herself, but she killed it in him, as well. Another one of those myriad uses of stone. It protected, it destroyed.

"I love you," she told him, which was so much more composed than "You make me want to believe. I almost did."

However, Ian was too smart to be sidetracked or flattered by mere words. He waited, knowing what else was there, and she longed to tell him how badly she ached to be somebody new. But she'd molded herself into a statue to survive. And statues didn't change, didn't move. They stood timeless and immobile. For a second she let herself drift, let her shoulders sag, but in the end, her posture was ruler-straight; her chin could only angle at a perfect ninety degrees.

"Please take the job," she asked, her voice carefully polite.

"No."

"You're going to force me to pick?"

"Yes."

"I can't."

His eyes flashed, shuttered, the hurt hidden so completely. Then he downed his glass and the vulnerability there was gone. His gaze was hard and flat. Stone. "Do you want to order dessert?"

"No. I think I should go."

"I think that'd be best."

Carefully she stood, walking on eggshells. As she glided out, she didn't hear Ian. And he mustn't have moved. Not once.

18

THE RAC WASN'T THE SAME. The Knights were on a losing streak, Phoebe and Beckett were happy as clams, and Ian did his duty buying Beckett's beer and letting Phoebe steal his nachos.

She swiped a chip and he watched the cheese dribble on her shirt. Rose would have insisted on making it clean.

"You seem glum tonight, Ian. Why are you glum?" she asked.

"I'm not glum," he replied, eyes now glued firmly on the game.

"Phoebe, let him alone," Beckett warned her, Mr. Sensitivity in Training. Ian nearly smiled.

"He should know he has friends. We're the Three Musketeers, and even though Athos and Aramis are doing the deed, the basic dynamic doesn't change."

Ian looked at her. "Now I'm glum."

Beckett whopped Phoebe on the arm. "Told you."

Ian lifted his glass, drank, and the Knights delivered a three-point shot with a mighty swoosh and cheer. Ian smiled, beamed full of good cheer and nonglumness.

"See? Everything is looking up."

Beckett sighed. "I'll get you a beer. This time, it's on me."

FOR THREE WEEKS, ROSE lived in a fog. Sylvia asked about Ian, Rose shrugged her shoulders casually and told her things didn't work out. Sylvia wasn't fooled, but for the first time ever, she didn't pry.

Every day, Rose worked from early in the morning until the sun had long set at night, walking home from the subway station, wishing the Fates would have pushed a little harder, wishing that she was a little stronger.

It was a warm May night when she passed by the pet store and waited for the puppies to come out and cheer her up. The court jesters of the animal world, designed to make her laugh.

She stood in front of the glass and waited, and when nothing stirred, she rapped carefully. Once. Twice.

Eventually the hay shifted and the shadows began to stir. The puppies were gone, most likely taken to a loving and caring home, and it was only the big black hulk who was eyeing her carefully from his solitary position, safe in his cage.

She lifted a hand, placed it on the glass, but the smart dog stayed immobile.

"Hey," she said, watching his ears perk at the sound.

He barked, but Rose didn't jump. Her hand stayed on the glass, and the midnight eyes watched her with interest. Watched her with hope.

"I'm sorry," she whispered to him. "You shouldn't be alone."

Warily, he lifted his head, still not making a move in her direction.

"I don't want to be alone," she told the dog. "I could do this, couldn't I?"

The dog stared at her, dark unblinking eyes that cowered at monsters, that knew the silent tears in the night. The dog wouldn't push her. The Fates wouldn't push her. Even Ian wouldn't push her anymore.

There was no one left but Rose.

Little Princess School of charm hadn't covered how to abandon every survival rule she'd known. They hadn't taught her how to trust. She needed to trust him. She could trust him. Her heart knew it. Her very real, very alive, very still-beating heart.

Warily, she lifted her chin to a perfect ninety degrees, and gave a sad smile to the animal. "It took so much out of me. My dreams. My courage. But there's something left, something good." Her smile grew a little stronger, a little surer. "I hope."

WHEN IT CAME TO PLOTTING a strategy there was no one better than Rose. She had disappointed Ian, she had disappointed herself, but no more. He needed to believe in fate again, in the meddling gods that pushed them together, and when she focused on what he needed, it made the hard parts easier. She did trust him. She knew that. All she lacked was the courage to take that one small—okay, it was a huge one—step.

She'd seen all of Ian. The strong, the noble, the angry and the vengeful—and after all of that she knew she loved him. She wasn't afraid. She'd never been afraid. Not of Ian.

And that thought cheered her, kept her focused on the plan.

She decided that she was going to play on the "hand of God" angle. In her mind it was all worked out. She's coming to talk to him, they step into the elevator, she begins to speak, she starts to apologize, he isn't happy, but then ooops—the elevator stalls, stuck, and he has to listen to her. A captive audience. And she convinces him. She puts back the glowing optimism in his eyes, the belief that they were not just meant—but *fated* to be together.

In the end, she didn't care what job he did. Yes, she was terrified, but for the first time in her life, she wasn't going to let the shadows rule her life.

Rose took a deep breath. This was for Ian.

She made a call to Manny, the maintenance supervisor in the building. A bribe didn't work, but then she explained what she required and why, and bless his darling romantic heart, they were set.

From here on out, it was up to Rose, and nobody could deliver like Rose.

She wore blue jeans and a trim-fitting T-shirt that clung nicely, but casually. Her makeup was light, almost nothing. She needed a look that said that the old Rose Hildebrande was over, and she could be anything she wanted, including casual.

The speech was done. There were parts left unwritten because she still couldn't say those words, she didn't want to talk about her past. It shamed her that she never fought back. But she had to hope—today, she had to believe that when she saw Ian, when she stared into his eyes, that she could.

New hopes, new opportunities, a new start.

At exactly nine-oh-seven she was in the building, waiting for

Ian, watching the clock, praying he wouldn't be late, because today of all days, she didn't want fate to interfere.

He appeared, exactly on schedule, and Rose sighed at the sight of him, relief, happiness and the unshakable faith that everything was going to be all right. "Ian!"

He turned, his face wary. "Why are you here?"

She glanced at the clock. Thirty seconds. "We need to talk. I'm sorry."

As if he had all the time in the world, he folded his hands over his chest. "Go ahead."

Another glance at the clock, nine-ten, and panic bubbled inside her. "Your office," she ordered, pushing him toward the elevator. The doors slammed shut. Exactly on schedule. Perfect.

Once they were in the car, Rose brushed her palms on her jeans, realized what she was doing and stopped. "How are you?"

"I've been better," he told her, looking at her wearily, anticipating that she would hurt him once again.

"You were right," she announced, precisely as the elevator ground to a halt.

19

IAN STARED AT THE BANK of buttons, then back at Rose, not ready to believe that fate struck twice. No, the elevator conked out all the time. Not going to read anything into this at all.

"Are we stuck?" she asked, and he wished he couldn't see that flickering vulnerability in her eyes. He didn't want to hope this time. He didn't want to assume. He didn't want to believe in things that weren't going to come true.

"No. We're not stuck. Sometimes it hangs. Or they're doing maintenance. It'll start in a sec."

Impatiently he punched a button. Then a whole bank of buttons, watching them all light up, but the elevator didn't move.

Rose didn't seem alarmed. In fact, she appeared happy, satisfied, content. Obviously life without Ian was treating her well.

He hit the alarm button. Silence. Did anybody care about safety anymore? Apparently not.

"I think we're stuck," she told him, a blinding glimpse of the obvious, if one was inclined to latch on to the obvious. Ian wasn't there yet.

"I can call," he answered, pulling out his phone.

She jumped toward him, ripped the phone out of his hand. *"No!"* Then she recovered. "Sorry," she answered, returning the phone. "But when life stalls you in an elevator, you have to listen, Ian. You can't argue, you can't fight it. You have to accept it." She was lecturing him, with his own words. He remembered. God knows, it was probably slathered on a motivational poster somewhere.

Feigning a casualness that frankly any idiot could see through, he stuffed the phone in his pocket, reckless hope building inside him once again.

"That's a big change for you."

"I'm learning to embrace the chaos. Look," she answered, spreading her arms wide. "Trapped in an elevator, and I'm not nervous, not panicked, not even a tinge of hyperventilating."

"Nicely done," he told her, and at her tiny smile, he felt the familiar warmth inside him, that tug at his heart that would always forgive her. How could he not.

He loved her.

"I'm sorry about the job plan. I thought you'd be happy, but I should have known better. I should have anticipated it, because I understand you. But I didn't see it, because I couldn't face the things that were inside me." Carefully, she brushed the hair from her eyes, meeting his gaze, staying there. "I don't want to be poor. It terrifies me."

"Why?" He'd never pushed her, never prodded, but it was time.

"I didn't write this part down. Give me a second." She held up a finger, her breathing began to speed up, and he longed to hold her, to reassure her that it was okay. But it wasn't. They needed to do this. She needed to do this, and he was going to have to wait.

Eventually she began to talk. "You knew we were poor?"

He nodded. "You told me that part."

"I lied about some of it," she admitted, her face uncertain. "My parents, my mother, she was never going to win awards for childhood development. I was such a stupid girlie-girl. I loved the lace dresses, the shiny shoes, the smell of flowers in the air. God, somebody mentioned a rainbow, and I was off to chase it." As she talked, her tone turned hard and cold. Bitter. A lot of bitter for a girl who wanted nothing more than to smell flowers and chase rainbows.

Ian took a step toward her, but she raised a hand. "Don't. If you're too close, I can't do this, and I have to finish. They—my mother—she got this idea about beauty pageants because I was such a perfect little doll, but I was never good enough. Clarinet playing didn't cut it, the other girls smiled a little better, their answers were a little cuter, a little less rehearsed. Mama said I was making excuses for my own failures."

She stopped, sliding down against the elevator wall, and this time, Ian sat beside her, because for too long Rose had stood alone. As a kid, as an adult. He wasn't going to let that happen. Not anymore.

"You don't have to say anything, Rose."

She ignored him, her hands fisted together. He untwisted her hands, cradled one in his own, but she didn't notice, her face white, her skin cold. She didn't look at him. He didn't know where she was, but it wasn't here. It was a long way away, it was wherever she went to when the nightmares came.

"After that it was charm school. She thought that would teach me, and they bet everything that I could be taught. Every day we'd drive down to Charleston in Daddy's old pickup, and Mama would tell me how much they depended on this. How much they depended on me. I watched Daddy hit her, and she said it was because there wasn't enough. She said that if I won, we'd have enough. And I tried. I gave it everything, just to win a crown. It was fake, with glue so cheap you could see it, but when you're eight, nine, it doesn't matter…" She trailed off and her hand tightened, hard and harder still. Her mouth worked, tried once, but nothing emerged.

"What did she do, Rose?" he asked, keeping his anger hidden. Later, he'd let it go, but for now he'd be as calm, as still, as stony as she was.

"She was very careful. She had a plumbers' pipe. It was thin so it wouldn't leave a mark. She hit me when I didn't do good, and it didn't matter how much I won, or how perfect I walked, or how cute my answers were. She kept on hitting me. Over and over." She took her free hand and slapped her thigh. Over and over, and those pale blue eyes were so old, so worn. Gently, Ian covered the hand, stilled it.

Her pulse thudded, and she looked at him, blank for a moment. Then she came back to the present. Back to him.

"She's gone. They're gone. You're here." He cursed the words, stupid words that were meaningless. Ian wanted to help her, to make her believe that everything would be okay, but words jammed in his throat. He wanted to take away the scars, take away the pain, but he was fifteen years too late.

"You don't look surprised."

"No." He'd known. The people who cut the hardest were the people who had bled the most.

Awkwardly she turned her face into his shoulder, needing comfort, but not sure how to ask for it. Ian stroked her hair, her back, tracing lines of bruises that he'd never see. For a second, one infinite second, his hand fisted, but he kept that hand away. Far away. She wouldn't see that from him. Not ever.

Her body slowly relaxed, the tension at ease for now, and she started to speak again. "I thought money made me invulnerable. It was this giant cocoon that kept you separated from all the bad and all the unpleasant in the world. My mother said they wanted to have financial security. She told me how lucky they were to have such a talented little girl that was going to make my father's dreams come true."

"She was making excuses, Rose."

"I know."

"What now?"

She lifted her head, met his eyes, and she saw pain and strength…and love.

"I want to please you, Ian. I want to make you happy. At first, I did it because it was all I knew how to do. And now… It's because I love you. I need to be with you. No matter what you do, or how wealthy you are or aren't, or how secure things are or aren't. You're my rock."

Ian wasn't sure he was well equipped to be anyone's rock. That sort of responsibility weighed heavier than job placement, than billion-dollar transactions, than anything he'd ever tried before, and he found the legal waivers slipping from his mouth.

"Do you want me to take the job, Rose? I'll do it." If it made her happy, how could he tell her no?

She shook her head once. "No. I'll do this. I have to do this."

"You might change your mind. I'm not the most rocklike man on the planet."

"Do you think I can do this?" she asked, in a voice that still couldn't quite hope.

He nodded, because he didn't doubt her for a minute. "Yes."

"I think I can, too. Whatever you have inside you, whatever that irresistible something is that's in the air you breathe, it's contagious, Ian. I watch your face, and I believe I can do that, too. It's why you're so good at what you do. It's why Hilda is right. It's why you have to be where you are. People get better around you. The world gets better around you. It's why I met you that night. It's why I dropped my phone. It's why I don't want to be without you. Somebody, somewhere wanted me to get better."

"You're sure?"

"Please, Ian. I need this. I need you."

He kissed her then, soft, gentle, full of promise, full of love. And somewhere in the skies, in the place where the Fates plotted and planned, Frank Capra was there with a wink and a smile.

IT WAS TWO HOURS LATER before they were "rescued." Rose didn't mind that Manny was late. Sitting there with Ian, it was the best sort of dream. When the doors opened to the lobby, Rose noticed the uniform, noted the badge. "Thank you, Norman."

"Where's Manny?" asked Ian. "He's usually a lot faster than this."

"Not today. The lucky bastard picked a winning lottery ticket and took off last night for Paris."

Rose gaped at the elevator man who looked at her blankly. "Is that a problem?"

"Manny isn't here?"

"Nope."

"The elevator it just…broke? Like that."

"Happens all the time," explained Ian.

Her knees buckled a little, but she recovered. "It just…broke? Nobody flipped a switch, or turned it off or cut a cable?"

"She needs to eat," said Ian, pulling her toward the outside world, a fine May day where everything would be all right.

Norman called after them. "She's not going to sue, is she?"

Ian nudged Rose, noting the pale skin, the astonished blue eyes, but it was a good look for her. Awe. "I think we're going to have to invite Norman to the wedding."

Rose only nodded once. "Whatever you say."

Epilogue

ANXIOUSLY, ROSE STARED around the apartment, checking for telltale dust marks, adjusting the bowls so that they were arranged in a pleasing circular arrangement. This shouldn't be a big deal, but her stomach kept tumbling in great heaves, and she'd checked her makeup four times.

Ian had told her to relax, had told her that she'd be okay, but still… Her eyes checked the clock. They should be back any minute.

The writing secretary was in the corner, white mums spilling from the vase, and the kitchen was not only well stocked, but organized, as well. Two months ago, she'd moved in, and between Ian and her therapist, things were progressing nicely. Today was her first big step, and her palms were sweating like a high-strung pig.

Frustrated, she wiped her hands on her white cardigan. Then she heard the shuffling out in the hall, followed by Ian's soothing voice.

After one last check, she planted herself in the middle of the room, a queasy smile on her face.

The door opened and Ian emerged, towing the giant black monster on a leash.

Immediately he noticed the queasy smile. "You're sure? We're not committed to this."

Firmly Rose nodded, her knees starting to wobble. "Positive. Let him go."

The leash dropped to the floor, and the dog walked slowly, cautiously, a great hulking mass headed straight in her direction. Huge black paws stood in front of her, waiting, but she stood strong—until her breathing started to fail.

"Deep breaths," Ian reminded her. "One. Two."

"I can...breathe." She stared deep into the dog's wary midnight eyes, and felt a crack inside her. Concrete cracking under the sun.

Tentatively she lifted a hand, patted the huge head. For the dog, that was all the invitation he needed. Two bear-size paws landed on her chest and Rose was falling, falling...

The dog was all over her, licking and barking—and completely killing her outfit. There was mud on the floor, the rug would have to be cleaned and awkwardly Rose kept patting him between the ears.

Ian's hands were locked across his chest. "I'm standing here. I'm waiting. Not moving until you tell me to move, but you're white as a sheet, and if you throw up, I don't care what you told me not to do."

Rose met his eyes, and managed a wobbly smile. "He's nice, isn't he?"

"He likes you."

The giant tongue took a sloppy sweep of her face, barked twice and charged straight for the secretary. The flowers crashed to the floor, water spilling on wood, papers flying. Chaos.

"No!" she yelled, just as Ian dived for the leash. At the sharp alarm in her voice, the beast cowered on his belly, eyes expecting the worst.

"I can take him back," Ian whispered.

Unsteadily Rose got to her feet, taking one nervous step after another, until she made her way to the giant animal. Tentatively she reached out and stroked the trembling head. "No," she said firmly. "I think we need to keep him."

"What are you going to call him? Chaos? Hellhound? Terminator?" he asked, as if all was right with the world. It was the thing she loved most. Because with Ian, it always was.

The dog flicked a giant tongue over the palm of her hand, as rough as sandpaper, as strong as stone. "No. I have the perfect name."

Gingerly, she settled on the floor, deluged by dog. Underneath, the panic still lurked, but now there was something new, something warm, something safe. It had taken her nearly twenty-eight years, but she'd finally found home.

Rose looked up at Ian, and his eyes were full of hope and the future. And fate. Never forget the fate thing.

"Kismet," she proudly stated. "We're going to call him Kismet."

* * * * *

"AREN'T YOU GOING TO SAY 'Fly me' or at least 'Welcome Aboard'?"

Amanda Bauer didn't. The softly muttered word that actually came out of her mouth was a lot less welcoming. And had fewer letters. Four, to be exact.

The man shook his head and tsked. "Not exactly the friendly skies. Haven't caught the spirit yet this morning?"

"Make one more airline-slogan crack and you'll be walking to Chicago," she said.

He nodded once, then pushed his sunglasses onto the top of his tousled hair. The move revealed blue eyes that matched the sky above. And yeah. They were twinkling. Damn it.

"Understood. Just, uh, promise me you'll say 'Coffee, tea or me' at least once, okay? Please?"

Amanda tried to glare, but that twinkle sucked the annoyance right out of her. She could only draw in a slow breath as he climbed into the plane. As she watched her passenger disappear into the small jet, she had to wonder about the trip she was about to take.

Coffee and tea they had, and he was welcome to them. But her? Well, she'd never even considered making a move on a customer before. Talk about unprofessional.

And yet…

Something inside her suddenly wanted to take a chance, to be a little outrageous.

How long since she had done indecent things—or decent ones, for that matter—with a sexy man? Not since before they'd thrown all their energies into expanding Clear-Blue Air, at the very least. She hadn't had time for a lunch date, much less the kind of lust-fest she'd enjoyed in her younger years. The kind that lasted for entire weekends and involved not leaving a bed except to grab the kind of sensuous food that could be smeared onto—and eaten off—someone else's hot, naked, sweat-tinged body.

She closed her eyes, her hand clenching tight on the railing. Her heart fluttered in her chest and she tried to make herself move. But she couldn't—not climbing up, but not backing away, either. Not physically, and not in her head.

Was she really considering this? God, she hadn't even looked at the stranger's left hand to make sure he was available. She had no idea if he was actually attracted to her or just an irrepressible flirt. Yet something inside was telling her to take a shot with this man.

It was crazy. Something she'd never considered. Yet right now, at this moment, she was definitely considering it. If he was available…could she do it? Seduce a stranger. Have an anonymous fling, like something out of a blue movie on late-night cable?

She didn't know. All she knew was that the flight to Chicago was a short one so she had to decide quickly. And as she put her foot on the bottom step and began to climb up, Amanda suddenly had to wonder if she was about to embark on the ride of her life.

Do you have a forbidden fantasy?

Amanda Bauer does. She's always craved a life
of adventure…sexual adventure, that is. And
when she meets Reese Campbell, she knows he's
just the man to play with. And play they do. Every
few months they get together for days of wild sex,
no strings attached—or so they think….

Sneak away with:

Play with Me

by LESLIE KELLY

*Available February 2010
wherever Harlequin books are sold.*

---

red-hot reads

www.eHarlequin.com

HB79525

REQUEST YOUR FREE BOOKS!

2 FREE NOVELS
PLUS 2
FREE GIFTS!

HARLEQUIN®

Blaze™

Red-hot reads!